dixi books

J. L. Harland

Two authors with one voice makes: J. L. Harland.

Janet Laugharne and Jacqueline Harrett enjoy the creative process of working together and producing stories that have a unique, blended voice. *What Lies Between Them* is their debut novel and they are currently editing a sequel. J. L. Harland short stories have been published in anthologies and online and a novella is out on submission. Their website, jlharland.co.uk, has a blog on writing where further information about their work can be found. Individually, Janet Laugharne's poetry has won or been placed in competitions and appeared in Black Bough, Atrium Poetry, Sarasvati and The Dawntreader (forthcoming). Jacqueline Harrett's crime novel, *The Nesting Place*, featuring D.I. Mandy Wilde, is recently published with Diamond Books.

What Lies Between Them is a moving novel about resilience and compassion, and what it takes to follow your dreams. It's a story of love, friendship and family, asking questions about power, particularly for women - how much can be sacrificed before we lose our sense of self? How much are we defined by the events of the past and can we outrun our own history to find the future we desire? A compelling novel for our times.'
> Katherine Stansfield, poet and novelist, author of *Cornish Mysteries Trilogy* and co author of *D.K.Fields's Tales of Fenest Trilogy* with Dave Towsey.

'Emotional, sensitive and thoroughly satisfying.'
> Judith Barrow, author of *The Heart Stone, The Memory, A Hundred Tiny Threads, The Haworth Trilogy*.

'A slice-of-academic-life novel that underscores the role of the personal in the political cut-and-thrust of today's university milieu. How is she [Elin] going to face a reiteration of the tug between family responsibility and personal achievement?'
> Angela Graham, author of *A City Burning*.

WHAT LIES BETWEEN THEM

J. L. Harland

dixi
books

Dixi Books

What Lies Between Them - J.L. Harland

Editor: Gina Edwards
Proofreading: Andrea Bailey
Designer: Pablo Ulyanov
Cover Design: Nagma Tabassum
I. Edition: February 2022

Library of Congress Cataloging-in Publication Data
J.L. Harland
ISBN: 978-1-913680-35-0
1. Fiction 2. Contemporary Women's Fiction 3. Academia 4. Career

© Dixi Books Publishing
293 Green Lanes, Palmers Green, London, England, N13 4XS

info@dixibooks.com
www.dixibooks.com

Acknowledgements

We would like to thank Ayse Ozden at Dixi Books for giving us the opportunity of publishing *What Lies Between Them*. Thanks to our editor, Gina Edwards, for all her hard work as we moved through the stages of editing to the finished product. We have learnt a lot. Thanks to artists, Nagma Tabassum and Rosa Llano Ferro, who worked on the beautiful cover for the book; to the team at Dixi, including our lovely community of fellow authors.

We would also like to thank author and editor, Sally Spedding, whose practical advice and ongoing moral support over the years has made a huge difference to us, especially at the inevitable low times in the process of writing and editing a book and bringing it to market. Sally, you are the most generous of souls. Two authors whose encouragement has been hugely appreciated are Kath Stansfield and Louise Walsh. Heartfelt thanks. Among many others who have helped, too many to name, we appreciate the constructive remarks from our writer friends at U3A's Writers Enjoying Words and our inspiring Criminal Fairies writing group. We are grateful to our helpful readers and those who offered critique and comments – Megan, Fliss, Bridget, Alys, Ann, Bec, Keiron, Adela, Pete, Honor, Caroline, Morag, Jen; and special thanks to Paula, whose insight into Welsh/Italian culture was invaluable.

Writing courses at Cardiff University have enabled us to share our work and develop skills through constructive criticism from tutors and fellow writers. We love attending, and have gained so much from, author events, book fairs and festivals. Our journey to publication has taken us on many steep learning curves, including knowledge about social media, website and blogging. A huge thank you to our webmaster, Doug, who designed and maintains our website at jlharland.co.uk.

Jan would like to thank her family for their love and support. Wonderful to know they are there encouraging her on. Thank you to dear friends, the *Fforest Fawr* ladies, Angharad, Kath and Judith.

Jacqui also would like to thank her family and friends who have encouraged and sustained her through this rocky voyage. Thank you for listening, even when you were bored to tears.

Finally, in a cowriting partnership, we would like to express our gratitude for the wonderful, serendipitous way we discovered we could write together; the trust and support we have for each other in our joint and separate projects; and, above all, the sheer buzz and fun of sparking all those ideas off each other.

To women everywhere...

Chapter One

Elin

Mid-December

The university car park was deserted, as Elin Fiorelli pulled into her usual spot beside the library. It was good to be driving again after three months away. In late September, when she'd left Cardiff, it had been a hot day, an Indian summer mixed with Autumn leaves, crimson, gold, amber and brown carpeting the earth. Today, there was a light covering of snow on the ground, crunching underfoot, still crisp and frozen. Seven a.m. and dark as a raven's wing. She shivered as she inhaled the icy air, her breath leaving ghost-like traces as she hurried to the entrance of the main building, where Brynderwen University slumbered in the December stillness.

The night porter nodded his balding head to her as she passed. A Christmas tree twinkled behind him, its multi-coloured lights a welcome reminder of the festive season. She stepped around the young girl, head down with purple-tipped hair bobbing as she mopped the floor in the corridor. The familiar smell of the lemon-scented disinfectant filled the air making her feel as though she'd never been away. A comforting feeling. Her high-heeled boots clicked on the laminate floor and echoed in the near empty building. As Elin climbed the stairs, she could hear her breathing in the silence.

When she arrived on the top floor, Elin found her office airless and musty, abandoned, as though the room hadn't been used for quite a while. She opened a window and a blast of fresh, cold air whipped around, rustling a pile of papers that encroached on her half of the space; discarded by a visiting professor. As she took her set of research notebooks out of her bag and placed them on the desk in a neat pile, a cloud of dust puffed towards her, making her sneeze. She shrugged off her coat, flopped down in her desk chair and paused, staring at the blank computer screen. Once logged on, she knew the flood of emails would delay her from delving into the research notes.

A knock on the door startled her, as Sue Deacon's smiling face peeped round. 'Elin, great to have you back from the wilds of Finland.' Sue's blue eyes were full of warmth as she greeted her friend.

'Good to be back.'

'I didn't expect to see you today. When did your flight arrive?'

'Four a.m. You know what it's like.' Elin sighed. 'Exhausted, but brain doing overtime. I managed to sleep for a couple of hours and that was it. So, here I am.' She grinned, holding her hands aloft.

'Oh God, I know that feeling. You want to sleep but your head's buzzing.' Sue nodded in agreement, adding, 'You look really well, though, glowing.'

'I look a mess. In desperate need of a trip to the hairdresser and to get my nails done.' Elin pulled at her unruly dark brown curls, almost the same shade as her hazel eyes. Three months without a haircut had left her pixie style overgrown.

Sue came in and sat on one of the office chairs, after clearing a pile of the professor's papers. Elin noticed she looked smart in a new black trouser suit and scarlet blouse; her hair was a shade blonder and she seemed to be wearing more make-up than usual. A whiff of sultry perfume wafted around her. Was there a new man on the scene?

'Anyway, I needed to come in and make a start on writing up the research. I wanted to add some extra observations, while it's all still fresh in my mind.' Elin glanced up at the clock on the wall. 'And what are you doing in so early? There was no one around when I got here. I thought most people would be off on leave. No rest for the wicked, eh?'

'Big Departmental meeting this afternoon, you know,' Sue said, leaning forward a little and frowning as she thought. 'I need to check through the monthly finance report before the rest of the office staff get here. So, then, Elin, tell me... how was your research partner, Herr Wolfgang Richter?' Sue winked.

Elin knew what she was implying. Before the trip they had discussed the probabilities, possibilities and temptations of time spent isolated with a rather fit young male.

Wolfgang and Elin were research partners on a project called TechSWell, looking at the links between technology and well-being, funded, in part, by Fonetym, a multi-national technology company. The three months away had been spent in a study house in rural Finland without access to any technology and little contact with the outside world. The house itself, set on the edge of a pine forest, was basic, but the landscape of snow-capped mountains, sparkling waterfalls and varied wildlife more than compensated. Elin had visited Sweden and Iceland before to present papers at research conferences. This was a whole other Nordic experience.

At twenty-eight, Wolf was several years younger than Elin, and Sue had teased that he might want more than a professional relationship.

Elin laughed as she recalled her research partner. Her memories of that first night were fresh in her mind. 'Ah, Wolfgang. Tall, gorgeous and a prude. The first night I went to the sauna and when I jumped into the outside pool afterwards, he was just on his way for a walk. I thought he was going to pass out. He went pink and turned away.' Elin giggled at the memory. 'Wolfgang doesn't do nude. That evening at dinner he asked me if I intended to use the sauna and pool every day.'

Elin pulled her slight frame into a more upright position and assumed a severe expression. She was a great mimic. 'I think, Dr Fiorelli, that perhaps a rota we should have for the sauna, yes? I should not wish to you... em, er... by sharing your... em... private.'

Hand over her mouth, Sue's shoulders shook with laughter as she pictured the scene.

'He meant privacy, of course, and it's naughty of me to make fun of him. He didn't finish what he wanted to say as I was giggling so much. So embarrassed, poor boy. Anyway, I explained that I'd been to Finland before, and it was quite the norm to be in the nude in the sauna. He was *not* impressed.'

'So, you didn't become more than research colleagues? No sex in the sauna?' Sue tucked a smooth strand of blonde hair behind one ear and grinned.

'No way.' Elin shook her head, grimacing as she recalled the scene. 'He told me all about his mother's great cooking and how he missed his girlfriend. Such a techno geek. Once he realised I wasn't after his body, he relaxed.' Elin grinned and added. 'I felt liberated after the first few days without all the tech stuff, but poor lad, he had trouble hacking it.'

Sue nodded, eyes wide. 'I can't imagine being without my phone, or computer, or even television for a week, never mind three months. I understand poor Wolfgang's point of view. What did you do all that time, Elin? Apart from flaunting yourself in the sauna, that is.'

'And discuss the meaning of life with Wolfgang, of course.' Elin laughed and tilted her head to one side, remembering. 'What did I do? Read a lot, walked a lot, learnt how to catch and cook fish. Believe me, I know a dozen ways to prepare them now. We ate so much it's a wonder I haven't developed gills.' Elin's voice wobbled with laughter.

She stroked her notebooks, relishing the texture and smell of the leather covers, as she explained. 'We had to keep these diaries for the research, so that took a bit of time. Writing in longhand is a different experience than hammering on the keyboard. And I made lots of notes for the book on well-being that I'm writing.' Her eyes sparkled and her voice thrilled with excitement. 'Honestly, Sue, it was like a wonderful retreat as far as I was concerned. Poor Wolfgang leapt on his phone the moment it was given back to him. I've left mine switched off. I know my mother will be waiting to nag me, so I'm in no hurry. I rather think Wolfgang's findings on well-being and technology will differ considerably from mine.'

The knowledge that her findings would be controversial and stir up debate, not only in the university, but in the research community was exhilarating. This was the final step to her professorship. Elin bubbled with anticipation as she smiled at Sue. 'It's all up in the air at the moment. We'll see. So, get me up to speed before I pop in to see Huw to tell him I'm back. I want to give him the potted version of the research. What's been happening while I've been in exile? Any gossip?'

For a moment Sue had a startled look, eyes wide and her hand clasped over her mouth. 'Oh, God. I'd forgotten you hadn't had the news.' She hesitated; her tone strained. 'Huw had a heart attack–'

'What? He isn't...?' 'The coldness of the room made her shiver again. All Elin's senses seemed to be on alert, as she braced herself for more bad news.

'No, no. He's alive, but he's had a triple bypass operation. He's probably going to be off for the whole year.'

Elin released a pent-up breath of relief. The Dean of Humanities, Huw Bevan, had always been supportive to her, not like some of the other management bods. God, at death's door, and she hadn't known. One of the negatives of being isolated in the research field for months. Must include that in the findings. Poor Huw.

'So, who's acting Dean? Not Geraint, I hope. Organisation isn't his strong point. He's a bit too fond of being one of the lads. He'd think you could sort everything by taking everyone down the pub after a match. A lovely man, but not a great manager.' Elin frowned. What a difficult time for the Department and for Sue in her role as finance officer. Shocking how suddenly things could change.

At the mention of Geraint, Sue shook her head. 'No, they headhunted for someone to cover for a year. Thing is, when Huw went off ill, it was only the week the auditors were in. It was hell. A full-on nightmare. You know how Huw was so free and easy with money? The Department's in a bit of a state financially now.' Sue chewed a thumbnail. 'I tried to warn him, you know, but he kept on spending. To be honest his heart attack got him out of a tricky situation. Mind boggling how much we have to save. A bloody nightmare, you know.'

Despite her groomed appearance, when Elin looked more closely at her friend, she could see that Sue had lost weight. The black rings under her eyes, hidden in part by make-up, told their own story. Was Sue's job on the line because of the financial mess? Anyone could be given the push or persuaded that they should go elsewhere. It wasn't a pleasant thought. Elin's voice held a hint of her concern. 'So, they brought in someone who can do that? Turn things round quickly?'

'Yeah.' Sue continued to worry at her thumb. 'The new guy has a reputation for efficiency. Was working in the United States, but his wife is Welsh, and they were thinking of coming back to the UK in any case. If he can sort this, they have a bigger job in mind for him, you know, down the line. The role of Dean would be up for grabs anyway if Huw doesn't come back.'

Her head buzzing with questions, Elin just stared at Sue. She'd forgotten how fast Sue spoke sometimes when she got excited or nervous. Huw out of action. So unexpected. And how was that going to affect Elin's application for the professorship? Would the new Dean support it? Surely with the TechSWell project under her belt, Huw had hinted as much, but this new bloke... 'Hmmm. So, who is this Wonderman? Is he old? Young? What do you know about him? You've been working with him for a couple of months?'

Sue blushed and her eyes had a shine to them. 'Oh, Elin. You wait. He's drop-dead gorgeous, you know. Forties. Dark-haired with a touch of grey at the temples. Sort of James Bond type. He has all the women academics, as well as the office staff, eating out of his hand. He's very distinguished and has loads of charisma. Confident, know what I mean?'

Elin guessed that Sue's more groomed appearance was not co-incidental, judging by the gush of words. 'Americans often seem to ooze confidence. So, someone from outside.' Elin raised an eye-brow. 'I see. Interesting.'

'Oh, he's not American, just been working there. He's English. Worked in Bristol, then Edinburgh, set up a consultancy with his second wife. Huge. Big dosh.' Sue paused for a moment. 'Went belly up with her and then he started over again in the United States. He's got a great reputation, you know, and we're lucky to have him.'

This new guy seemed to be too good to be true. Elin listened but had her doubts.

In her usual garrulous fashion, Sue was still rattling on with enthusiasm. 'I think he's been recruited because of his reputation for troubleshooting. Plus, he's got heaps of contacts in the UK and abroad. Maybe you know him? You did your doctorate in Bristol, didn't you? His name's Michael Hardwick.'

Elin's stomach churned, light-headed, as her breath seemed to be stuck somewhere in her chest. It couldn't be true. She fought hard to keep her voice steady when she replied, 'Oh, I know him alright, although I've managed to avoid him for the last fifteen years.' She closed her eyes for a second. 'Huw gone and Michael Hardwick in his place? I can't believe it. Sue, he's totally unscrupulous. He'll do anything to get his own way. My God, what have I come back to?'

'No,' Eyes opened wide in disbelief, Sue said, 'that's not the impression I've had. I can't believe he's that bad.' She pulled her hand with its bitten nails away from her mouth and thrust it in her trousers pocket. 'What did he do to you to make you dislike him so much? Steal an idea? You academics are so weird. Anyway, he floats my boat.'

With a glance at the clock, its ticking clear in the moment's silence, Elin replied. 'Appearances can be deceptive. I'll tell you about Michael Hardwick sometime, tho' shouldn't you be getting ready for that meeting?'

At last, Sue noticed the time, 'Oh, God, got to go – now. Papers should be ready for me from the copy shop. See you later.'

Sue rushed out, leaving a trace of her perfume in the air. A groan escaped from Elin as she sank back into her chair, shoulders slumped, weariness taking over as she contemplated how much everything had changed in the three months she'd been away. Outside the sparrows were chattering and a blackbird joined the morning chorus heralding the new day. She had planned never to see Michael Hardwick again and here he was, invading her world once more.

Chapter Two

Elin

Switching her computer on, Elin turned her attention to emails. The first one was a message from the new Dean, sent to all staff, about the afternoon's Departmental meeting. It had a link to his bio and she couldn't resist that, compelled to open it and look at his photo. As she paused and scrutinised the image, she noticed he looked heavier around the jawline and his brown hair, still kept quite long, was grey at the temples. Older but no wiser as, reading on, she discovered he had married for a third time, with two young sons now. The last Elin had heard of him in any detail was when he and Natasha, the second wife, had been an academic power duo, setting up a spin-off education business, commuting between London and their rural idyll in the Highlands, and being paid shedloads of money for their expertise. But he still had it: those intense dark eyes and that charismatic smile. No wonder Sue was smitten.

It was quiet in her office, with just a muted hum of the photocopier from the room next door. Elin thought back to when she had first met Michael Hardwick. She'd been rushing from a drama rehearsal, arriving late for her first PhD tutorial and they'd collided in the corridor outside his office, papers with her careful notes flying all over the place. That had been the start of her research career – and the affair.

Blinking, Elin pulled herself out of her reverie. Her insides churned, felt worse than on the flight home when the plane had hit some rough weather. Emotions she'd suppressed for years were coming to the surface and she felt clammy and woozy, almost as if she was going to be ill. She dreaded the thought of the staff meeting as she ran her fingers through her curly hair with a groan. Why hadn't she just stayed at home for the day? She felt a wreck. Bloody Michael Hardwick.

Despite the cramped space, Elin paced back and forth with unseeing eyes between the window and her desk, deep in her thoughts. Dawn was breaking, a pencil line of light on the horizon but she didn't register its beauty, lost in a different place, a different time. Michael's alluring aftershave, the tingle of her skin when he touched her... Why had he come to Brynderwen of all places? Part of her uneasiness was tiredness, partly it was due to the prospect of seeing Michael again. He'd always said Welsh universities were too petty and parochial for his taste, giving that winning smile of his as he dismissed them.

After some time walking up and down, muttering to herself, Elin decided she'd focus on the research. Professor Lars Nordin, the TechSWell team leader, would expect the preliminary findings by the beginning of January, so best to get started. And work always helped. Even in her worst moments, it proved the salve to her wounds. When Elin's beloved Papa had died two years ago, she'd taken time off to arrange his funeral but afterwards, much to her mother's dismay, returned to her usual routine.

'I don't know why you have to go back to work so soon,' her mother had complained, 'not when I need you here.'

'There's nothing more I can help you with for now, Mum. I'm sorry. The longer I'm off work, the more my students will suffer. It's what I do. It's who I am. I can't sit around here all day. Papa always said that life has to go on, no matter what.'

'But not at a hundred miles an hour. Honestly, Elin, I don't know why you're so driven. You set yourself these ridiculous goals. Why you can't just get married and have babies like any normal woman is beyond me.'

It was a constant refrain, and Elin had gritted her teeth to avoid saying the words whirling around in her mind that she knew would lead to another argument. She reminded herself that her mother was fragile, still grieving after the death of the man who'd adored her and protected her from everything. As far as Elin was aware, from family stories, one of the few times he'd refused his wife anything was when their baby daughter arrived. Catherine had wanted to name her after a wealthy aunt, but Angelo Fiorelli had insisted she was Welsh, with a forename reflecting the land where she lived. Angelo loved to recount the story of how she became Elin.

'Wales has been good to me and my family,' he'd announced. 'We show our pride in our country. I am Italian, yes, but also Welsh. Our daughter will be Welsh too. Elin is perfect for *una bella bambina.*'

Elin twisted the ring on her finger. The ring Papa gave her. She still missed him, his unconditional love and pride in her work, but there was no point in thinking about that now. Concentrate on the research. That's what she needed to do. There'd be questions for her at the meeting, inevitable after an absence of three months. It was important to sound in control, her usual professional persona, even though feeling far from it. Her working-class background, despite her academic success, was a shadow in the back of her mind, always reminding her of her humble roots and how she needed to prove herself.

'Focus. Focus,' she muttered to herself, opening the research diary on the top of the pile and running her fingers along the indentations made by the writing. Her italic-style handwriting filled twelve of the notebooks they had been given to record research findings, to express their day-to-day emotional responses on being isolated. A welcome slowing down for Elin and a chance to dive deep into her research passion: studying well-being in practice. Living in nature without the stressors and distractions of technology, it had been fascinating to observe and record how she adjusted to life without constant and instant access to people and places around the globe. So much to analyse in the diaries of the day-to-day and week-by-week changes.

In September the study house had been bordered by trees the colour of jewels, the air filled with woodsmoke and water as clear as a mirror. They had foraged for mushrooms, yellow chanterelles and porcini, rich brown, just like Papa loved. Berries also were in abundance, and they were able to fish in the lake. It was satisfying to eat food so fresh and natural, although Elin had a pang of guilt every time she saw the fish on the grill.

The isolation created space for a new rhythm to the day. It had also given her opportunity to think through ideas for her book on well-being and write some sections in long-hand ready to check later when she would have access again to online library and reference sources. How poor Wolfgang had struggled. There would be interesting comparisons when the team exchanged the data in Brussels in the spring. She and Wolfgang had sent a couple of emails back and forth after they had returned to their respective universities, discussing plans for a joint academic paper, as well as their individual research reports for Brussels. She felt a surge of excitement thinking ahead to the conference as she started reading the first diary.

It had seemed strange, at first, to be writing by hand, but Elin soon relished the aesthetic quality of the ink's interaction with the paper. She patted her notebooks now, buzzing with ideas and adrenaline. The links between social interaction and well-being were something she had always found fascinating. And the book. The idea had been simmering in the back of her mind for years. The research retreat had enabled it to flourish. The draft book proposal was ready.

With a determined motion, she set to work, making notes and highlighting points as she read. She'd draw on these to write up the report and had plans to publish at least two articles as well as the joint paper with Wolfgang. 'Work, work, work...' Elin chanted the mantra as she settled to read and reflect on her diary observations, smiling to herself as the words evoked happy and thought-provoking memories, like the day she'd spotted a golden eagle skimming the lake. Pure magic. One occasion when a camera would have been welcome.

When Sue put her head around the door mid-morning, Elin looked up, startled by the interruption.

'Coffee break?'

Elin ran a hand over her forehead and pushed a stray curl out of her eye. 'Thanks, but not now. I'm just getting stuck in again and don't want to disturb the flow. Maybe a drink after work to catch up on the gossip? It'll have to be a quick one though. I should go and see my mother. Which reminds me.' She bent down and retrieved the phone from her bag, placing it on the desk. She hesitated, touching it with her finger, but not turning it on. 'Maybe when I finish this.'

'No worries,' Sue said. 'I wish I had your determination and dedication, you know. Plenty of time to chat later. I'll bring a drink up and there may even be mince pies.' She was on the point of leaving then stopped and added, 'By the way, your Mum seemed okay, if a bit tired, when I spoke to her on the phone last week. I've been meaning to pop in, but it's been frantic here... I'll let you get on.'

When Sue returned with the coffee five minutes later, Elin barely noticed her, raising her eyes for a brief second, so engrossed was she in reliving the observations from her research trip. She decided the first thing to prepare was a presentation for the next Departmental research meeting in January. It would be a lively debate. Barbed comments from some and searching questions from everyone. Best to have everything well prepared.

The world faded as Elin recalled skies the colour of lapis lazuli, air fresh, dry and so cold it made the hairs in her nostrils ping, and a landscape shrouded in drifts of crystalline snow, like something from Narnia. Lost in Finland, she relived cosy evenings with logs crackling, snuggling up in woollen blankets and savouring hot chocolate whilst engaging in debate with Wolfgang. Elin was so absorbed that it was almost lunchtime before she emerged from her deep concentration, like a sleepwalker confused by their surroundings. Only an hour before the staff meeting. When she next glanced up at the clock another thirty minutes had flown by.

Elin checked herself in the mirror on the wall by the door, wishing she didn't have to attend the meeting. Her cheeks were flushed and her curly hair refused to be tamed. Her mixed English and Italian heritage had given her a clear pale skin which was in contrast to her dark hair and eyes. She switched on her mobile to make an appointment for a trim. That's what she needed. To feel in control again.

'Tony. Hi, Elin here. Do you think you could squeeze me in?

I'm desperate. I look like a hedge. Next Tuesday would be great. Thanks. Oh?' A little frown crossed Elin's face as she listened. 'Maybe Mum forgot which day she had booked or perhaps it clashed with her committee meeting.' If Mum hadn't turned up for her appointment, she'd probably swapped hairdressers again. Either that or poor Tony had offended her in some way.

Elin ended the call and smiled. Tick. A step to regaining her groomed professional appearance. She could get her nails done at the same time.

Ten minutes to the meeting. She closed her eyes, trying to regain some calm. The jet lag was beginning to catch up with her. Then her mobile rang, a shrill awakening.

Mum.

Elin sighed and prepared for a tirade of emotional blackmail.

'Elin. What *have* you been doing?' Catherine Fiorelli's tone was sharp, unforgiving, and as ever, demanding. 'I expected you to ring me as soon as you got home. You were due back last night. Sue told me. I've been trying to get through, but your phone has been off.'

Damn. Elin's shoulders slumped and then she braced herself. 'Yes, I know, Mum. The flight was delayed, so I didn't actually get home until about four this morning. I came into work early. I was going to call you this afternoon after the Departmental meeting. How are you?'

'Not very well at all. It's these dizzy spells. I don't know what's wrong. I'm just not myself.'

Elin was glad her mother couldn't see her roll her eyes. Since Papa had died, Mum had become more and more dependent on her. Elin could deal with all the practical matters, such as the bills, but the emotional demands were draining. It was one of the reasons she'd wanted to be involved in the research project. Three months away from all her mother's claims on her time had been bliss.

'Have you seen a doctor, Mum?' Elin tapped her foot up and down. She could do without this hassle just before the meeting.

'What do they know? I can't be bothered. You have to make an appointment at least three weeks in advance and then they have you in and out in minutes. Besides, they all look about twelve and treat you as if you've one foot in the grave because you're over sixty.' Catherine's voice took on more energy as she spoke about this, indignation overriding self-pity.

Despite her annoyance with her mother's complaints, Elin's lips twitched. Another of Mum's imaginary illnesses. Had Sue been treated to these grumbles when she called? Probably not. Mum seemed to keep her complaints for her daughter.

'How long have you been having these dizzy spells?' Elin asked, trying to be patient, her foot still going. 'Have you an ear infection?'

'Oh, I don't know. I'm so tired as well. I've no energy and I look like the Bride of Dracula. I haven't felt well enough to go and have my hair done.'

That made Elin sit up and listen. So that's why Mum hadn't made it to Tony's salon. She had her hair washed and blow dried at least once a week; more often if she had a special occasion. Why hadn't Sue said anything? But she might not have noticed. Now that Elin was more alert, she heard how her mother's voice sounded a little frail and hoarse, at times. Something was amiss.

'Look, Mum, I'll call in this afternoon. I've a couple of things to do here first and then I can make my excuses for the meeting. I've been away for months. They won't miss me. Why don't you lie down and have a rest and–'

'Yes, dear, I think I will...'

'–I'll pop into Marks at Culverhouse Cross and get us something nice to eat.' Elin checked the time. 'Be with you in about an hour or so.'

'I do feel terribly tired. See you later.'

Elin frowned as she dropped her mobile into her handbag. Was Mum being a drama queen? She didn't sound herself. Plus, she'd agreed to lie down during the day. That was unheard of. And missing her hair appointment. Maybe it was more than a touch of hypochondria. Maybe, just maybe, she was unwell. In any case, it was a good excuse to get out of the meeting. Elin straightened her shoulders as she made a mental list of things to do before she came face-to-face with Michael Hardwick again. She sent a brief text to Sue.

Mum poorly. Going there now. Doesn't sound herself. Have to miss meeting. Catch up soon. E.

Her next task was to compose a short email to the Dean's personal assistant, Jodie.

Due to unforeseen circumstances, I'm unable to attend this afternoon's meeting. Please convey my sincere apologies to the Dean. Dr Elin Fiorelli.

Fifteen years since their last meeting. As Elin closed her office door and headed to her car, she pondered on what Michael remembered about her. But perhaps he didn't think about her at all.

Chapter Three

Michael

Michael Hardwick slammed the outer door of the Dean's suite as he entered at speed. The hinges sighed in protest.

What a shitstorm. He was ready to kick something, or someone. He strode over to the water filter, poured himself a cup and stomped into his office without a word to Jodie, who raised her grey eyes, registering surprise. Michael slammed the inner door as well, pushing it hard with the flat of his hand. A better thwack from the wood. Shit hitting fan, big time.

He yanked at the door again, put his head around, 'I don't want to be disturbed for the next half an hour.' Delivered between clenched teeth it was almost a growl.

Once back inside, he strode up and down, gulping the icy water. It was a spacious room, fitting for the role of Dean, with his work-station at one end and a wall lined with solid looking oak shelving matching the long conference table and chairs. Painted in neutral shades, the other walls were hung with certificates and photographs of Huw Bevan shaking hands with the VC and other dignitaries. As if he needed reminding that he was only filling a gap. The scent of bergamot and lemon drifted past from the diffuser; bought to create a relaxing ambience, but to hell with that today. Michael paused to look out at the front car park, irritated to notice a large pothole had appeared after the winter storms, near the visitors' parking bays. Must get Jodie to ring Estates. He slurped the last of his water, savouring the coldness as it trickled down his throat. Another ping from the computer. Another thing landing on his desk. Likely the figures. Bloody hell. Being para-chuted in to troubleshoot was one thing, no wonder Huw Bevan had health problems. Enough to give anyone a heart attack.

He picked up the phone and barked a command to Jodie in the outer office. 'Get me Sue Deacon. Now.'

Jodie's voice sounded nervous. 'I think she's still in a business managers' meeting. It's not due to finish for another hour and–'

'Well, find out and as soon as it finishes tell her to come here. It's urgent.'

Michael banged the phone down and turned to his computer. He sat for a moment and then with a groan opened Excel. He had a headache over one eye and a muscle at his jaw twitched but he couldn't avoid it any longer. He concentrated on the spreadsheet on the screen in front of him, the latest figures and associated in-come targets for the Department, sent over after the meeting with the university accountant. As far as he could see, things were very, very bleak. A soft knock on the door alerted him to his visitor.

'I had a message you wanted to see me?' Sue blinked at him, pink-cheeked, flustered as if she'd run up the stairs. 'My meet-ing this morning was postponed so I've come straight up. You've had the latest figures? I was going to come and speak to you, you know.' Sue's blue eyes met his and then went straight to his com-puter. 'I take it you've had the accountant's report. Not good,' she said, 'Worse than we first thought.' She stood by the door, straightening the sheaf of papers she was carrying and scanning his face for reaction.

'More like a bloody disaster. It's not going to be a very happy Christmas, or more to the point, New Year, for the Department and staff.' Michael nodded towards the screen. 'Tell me more about what's been happening. I've just come from a full-on meet-ing with the university accountant and Pro VC. Told me their view of the situation, in no uncertain way, but I want to know what's going on from you. Your view, here on the chalk face, so to speak.'

Michael smiled, and although his smile did not reach his eyes, Sue's shoulders relaxed and her worried look disappeared. She was quite attractive, in a brassy sort of way. Michael waved a hand for her to sit at the conference table and pulled up a chair opposite.

'Well, you know, I've only been in post a year. You can see from the figures that we're looking at big scale financial problems. It's a crisis that's for sure.' She paused as if not sure if she should say more. 'It's not just happened. Things were all over the shop when I arrived.'

'Yes, staggering.' Michael shook his head. 'I've run several Departments before, in charge of large budgets, and a deficit of this magnitude is appalling.' He grimaced in disgust. 'How the hell did it happen? Why were there no checks and balances? I don't understand why this was allowed to occur in the first place.'

Sue squirmed in her seat as Michael adjusted the gold cufflinks on his crisp white shirt. He exhaled, trying to remain calm and controlled, voice measured. 'This is quite a situation. I enjoy a challenge, although I may not have taken this one on if I'd been made aware of the size of the problem. How could the Department of Education and Social Sciences have got into this mess?'

He waited as she blinked rapidly and avoided his gaze. He knew it sounded like an accusation, but he had to get to the bottom if it, no pussyfooting around. She needed to explain what had happened. Looking at figures was one thing, finding the root cause could get results.

Sue raised one hand to her mouth, as if to chew her already untidy nails, thought better of it and tried to meet his eyes, staring at his shirt instead. 'I think it's the staff. Staff salaries are always the biggest cost, you know, and some courses haven't recruited well over the last two years.' She waited for Michael's go ahead to continue. 'I've been getting to grips with how you do business in Higher Education, getting my head around it all. It's kinda weird in many ways.'

She frowned as she elaborated on the theme. 'It's so different from the private sector, you know. I mean, don't get me wrong, I'm really enjoying it, but it has taken me most of this year to begin to understand how things work – or don't work rather – in Higher Education. And, oh God, don't get me started on academic prima donnas who treat you like dirt and don't answer your emails unless it suits them.'

As Sue tried to explain her puzzlement about the workings of university administration to Michael, he considered his options, catching the gist of her complaints and thinking she could be a useful ally. She was the staff member who had the best insight into this mess, at any rate, and he could use that expertise to help him get out of it.

'Well, all that's true enough. The thing is we need to find out how, and why this has happened, and more importantly, what we've got to do to fix it. I'm expecting your knowledge and expertise to provide part of the solution. We'll have to work together to address these problems.' It was quite charming how Sue blushed when he praised her. 'I'm reporting to the university finance committee in February about my immediate plans in response to the Department's deficit, together with my proposals for a strategic vision to take us forward. It goes without saying that whatever we come up with should be confidential, tightly costed, and carefully monitored. You understand?'

'Yes, Michael.' Sue's guileless blue eyes looked across at him. 'Between ourselves, it'll be great to work with someone with a vision for the Department, you know. Things have definitely gone pear-shaped. And money wasted too.'

'Well, we'll put a stop to that, won't we?' Michael's eyes crinkled as he lent towards her. 'You say there's been money wasted. Where? Suggestions for immediate savings?'

Sue hesitated for a moment before she responded. 'Huw supported some staff with a research budget he didn't have. Okay, I know that research is important–'

'Yes, it is.'

'– it wasn't always small amounts he doled out and he refused to compromise on that. Shedloads of dosh, you know.' She examined her hands for a moment. 'That sounds disloyal and he's a lovely man,' she paused again, 'though not financially savvy, if you know what I mean. When you look through minutes of last year's research committee, you'll see I raised the finance issue several times. But it was no good.'

'Hmmm, okay. Any research money coming in? Staff *should* be made aware that they're expected to bring in revenue as well as spend it.' He could feel the muscle tick in his jaw.

A moment passed as Sue mused over the question. 'There's only one big project on here now, funded by Fonetym.'

'Ah, really?' That was interesting. Fonetym were big technology players with equally big spending power and they wanted to invest in universities. 'Could be part of the solution.'

'Maybe. I'm not sure where we are on that,' Sue said. 'I'd need to check the latest figures.'

'Do that.' Michael turned and gazed out of the window. It looked as if another winter storm was approaching with heavy charcoal clouds filling the sky and a rising wind buffeting the window. This job was turning out to be another stressful bugger. Not such a sleepy backwater. Still, step at a time and Sue's knowledge would help.

'So, we'll need to ensure the spending on research is pared right down for now. We don't have any leeway at all, no wriggle room.' Michael leant forward, putting his clasped hands on the table between them, its polished surface smooth against his skin. 'Look, Sue, I know we can work well together on this. I want you to write up a confidential forecast on the financial health of the Department, costing it with two or three scenarios, including job reductions and re-allocations.'

He lowered his voice. 'For the moment this forecast will be strictly for our eyes only and I must emphasise that you are *not* to discuss it with anyone. Have it ready for me by the start of the new term in January, please, and we'll take it from there.' Michael stood up to signal the end of the conversation.

Sue rose as well and nodded. 'I understand. I won't breathe a word. Thanks for giving me this opportunity, Michael. I won't let you down.' She put her papers away, smoothed the front of her jacket and picked up her bag. 'I'm sure we can find a solution, but, as you say, difficult decisions. Glad that's for you, not me.' A faint frown appeared as she seemed to realise just how huge the challenge ahead was.

'Keep me updated on developments,' Michael said, adding, before opening the door for her, 'and I must reiterate this is highly confidential. If staff got wind of it, confidence in my position would be damaged.'

Sue glanced up at him as she passed and he caught a provocative hint of Shalimar, his second wife's signature perfume. She appeared both nervous and excited at the prospect of working on this proposal, eyes glowing and a slight increase in her breathing. Michael had become aware during the meeting she found him attractive, but he was sure she could also see the potential for her career, if she helped find solutions to the financial jeopardy the Department was in. Things were going to change around here, after the previous Dean's mismanagement.

He congratulated himself on getting a useful player onside as he turned back to reading a set of documents for the next meeting. He was impressed by Sue Deacon. Recognised her type, ambitious and clever, with a vulnerable side, almost naive. Clawed her way from her East End of London background to a senior position in the Department. She couldn't be more than mid-thirties and she'd have loyalties, but nothing too entrenched. A perfect ally in his attempt to control the situation. That was soothing. He'd need every help possible to get through all this crap. Worry had made him short-tempered at breakfast. Not good. Must remember to pick up flowers on the way home.

The next item on the schedule was the staff meeting. When he put the date in, he'd had no idea the Department was founded on such shifting sands, envisaging an end of term celebration to build morale. Not going to happen now. In fact, he couldn't see any other way out except job rationalisations or even losses. Under no circumstances could he be Mr Nice Guy. He groaned, rubbing his forehead. The road ahead was looking more than bumpy. Dealing with human resources, job descriptions and the unions. God, the unions...

He shuddered, remembering the last time he was in a similar fix. That American university some ten years ago. It had contributed to his duodenal ulcer, without a shadow of a doubt, and played its part in the breakup with Natasha.

Still, he'd learnt the hard way how to be the perfect husband. Just time for a quick call home before the staff meeting. He'd tell Anwen when he'd be home, apologise for his grumpy mood and hope to be forgiven.

'Hello, Daddy.' Iolo, his youngest. 'Mam's busy. She's cooking. Can we play the dinosaur game again when you get back?' There was the muffled sound of a woman's voice, a lilt of Welsh, in the background. 'Mam says she's made some lovely food for when you come home, 'cos she says you've got a busy day today.'

'That's nice. Tell her I've got to go now. I'll be home in time to read someone a bedtime story and we'll do the dinosaur game tomorrow.'

Michael relaxed, settling back into his chair, calmness bringing a lightness to his chest as he replaced the phone in its cradle. They sounded busy and happy. He needed that solace. Then he buttoned his jacket, rolled his shoulders and rotated his neck to relieve the tension. Time to face the staff.

Jodie was filing papers into the cabinets in the corner of the room. She stiffened, no doubt unsure of his mood after the display of bad temper earlier.

'Any apologies for the staff meeting?' he asked in good humour, back to his usual urbane self, and picking up the sheaf of papers she'd prepared for the meeting.

She lifted a sheet from the printer and handed it to him. 'There's only a few apologies. Quite surprising. It's usually like the Marie Celeste here at this time of the year.'

Michael blinked at her analogy. He, too, felt like the captain of a doomed ship, as he glanced down the list, without paying much attention. Just one name caught his eye: Elin Fiorelli.

Chapter Four

Elin

The drive to Sully, where her mother lived, soothed Elin. A light drizzle peppered the windscreen and the wipers swishing from side to side formed a soothing rhythmic beat. The route through the outskirts of Cardiff with its numerous traffic lights wasn't too congested; and she knew the sight of the Bristol Channel and caress of the sea breeze would lift her spirits when she arrived. The love of the sea was something she'd shared with Papa. The red brick detached house with its art deco features in Seaview Close, an affluent suburb of Sully, was the symbol of his journey from a humble café gofer to owning a chain of fast-food outlets.

As she thought about him, she imagined she could hear Papa's voice, when he stood outside one of his shops, announcing proudly to the world, 'You gonna eat Fiorelli's besta fasta pasta. No one beatsa Fiorelli pizza!'

Poor Papa. It seemed such a sad trick of fate that, after his life of hard work and enterprise, his retirement had been cut so short with heart disease. Elin's eyes misted over. Even two years after the event, it was still fresh in her mind. She sighed aloud as she drove and tried to cheer herself up by humming to the Beatles on the radio. The soundtrack of her life. Papa loved those songs from his youth, singing aloud in a deep baritone and dancing around the kitchen.

The mid-afternoon traffic was light around Culverhouse Cross shopping centre and the drizzle had eased, so she stopped and went to Marks and Spencer. The hustle and bustle of people shopping seemed more frantic than usual until she remembered it was December and Christmas was approaching fast. Grateful that she had completed much of her present buying before her trip to Finland, Elin went to the food hall where she bought some soup and other hearty food suitable for the bleak winter days. A pang of hunger reminded her she hadn't eaten much for hours.

The sky threatened more rain as Elin drove into Seaview Close. Coupled with the iron-grey clouds the watery sun had dipped below the treetops making the late afternoon feel more like mid evening. When she turned into the drive, she was surprised that the house was shrouded in darkness. The curtains were open, but she couldn't see any lights on inside. That wasn't right. The winter months were gloomy, depressing, and Mum compensated by illuminating every room with various lamps and ceiling lights. Papa had joked about it, laughing at his wife's extravagance. 'I'd be better off paying for the Festa di Santa Dominica than the electricity for this house.' A family joke, shared with love.

When Elin opened the front door, she saw no sign of light anywhere. The scent of pine disinfectant greeted her before she turned on the hall switch and looked round at the familiar surroundings. It was a spacious house with polished wood block floors, stained glass inserts in windows, traditional and solid. An oriental rug in reds and golds was soft underfoot as Elin surveyed the clutter free hallway and its reflection of her mother's impeccable taste. The heat was cloying, the air still, as if the house was listening. It was too big for one person, Mum rattling around on her own but lacking the impetus to move to anything smaller after Papa's death, clinging to her memories.

'Mum. Mum. Are you in?'

Elin made her way through to the lounge with its expansive bay window and timber surrounded fireplace. By the light filtering through from the hall Elin could make out her mother was lying on the sofa, covered by a mohair blanket. For a second her heart skipped a beat. She switched on the table lamp, a soft glow, and was relieved to see her mother's chest move. Mum never slept in the day. Elin touched her mother on the arm, a gentle nudge, her fingers brushing the softness of her mother's sweater.

'Mum... Are you alright?'

Mum opened her blue eyes and stared, unseeing for a moment before shaking her head and looking around her. Her hair was knotted at the back, and her cheek creased where she'd been pressed against a cushion. She blinked a few times and yawned before passing an arm in front of her face. Elin caught a whiff of *Je Reviens*, her mother's favourite perfume, with its floral notes.

'Oh goodness. I must have fallen asleep. How dreadful.'

'I'm just relieved you're alright. I'll make us a drink, shall I? I bought some tomato and basil soup – your favourite – and bread and stuff. Would you like a fresh scone with a cup of tea?'

'Thank you, Elin. That sounds very nice. I should go and put the kettle on.' Catherine roused herself to a sitting position, still blinking a little.

'Don't worry, Mum.' Elin touched her mother on the arm. 'Give yourself time. Sleeping in the afternoon,' Elin added, teasing. 'Whatever next?'

Catherine sniffed and grimaced at her daughter. 'I'm glad *you* find it amusing. I don't. I did *not* intend to nap in the afternoon. I'm not in my dotage yet. It's this terrible tiredness. I can't seem to raise much energy these days.'

Elin studied her mother with more care. She was unusually pale with shadows under her eyes, despite a covering of make-up, and she winced as she rearranged herself on the sofa, her movements slow and deliberate.

'Are you sleeping at night?' Elin asked.

'Not very well. I seem to wake about three or four in the morning and then I can't get back to sleep. I don't know why. Being on my own, maybe. Sometimes,' she lowered her voice, 'I think there's someone else in the house.'

That was a surprise. Mum was usually calm and matter-of-fact. 'Well, it's no wonder you're tired if you're not sleeping. Maybe you *need* to rest during the day. Or, have you thought about sleeping tablets? The doctor might be able to give you something to help.'

Elin hesitated for a moment. Dare she? 'Perhaps you're just a bit depressed?'

Mum sat up straighter and glared at Elin. 'Stuff and nonsense! I'm not depressed. I'm dizzy and tired, that's all. And before you start nagging, I did see the doctor about three weeks ago. He told me to go out walking by the sea every day. That I needed to get out and about. Fresh air and exercise.' Her voice rose with indignation. 'Stuff and nonsense. What does he know about me and my needs? He didn't even look old enough to be a qualified doctor. Probably some student posing as one.'

Elin suppressed a giggle. She felt sorry for that doctor, whoever he was. No doubt he had endured a few waspish comments. Still, it was a relief that Mum *had* seen someone, despite her earlier protestations. Could this illness be another attempt at emotional blackmail? Just like complaining the house was too big and that she was lonely.

'Well, I'm glad you've seen someone about it, Mum. Perhaps you're just a little bit run down. Have you been eating properly? You look as though you've lost a bit of weight.'

'Of course, I've been eating. Stop bossing me, Elin. What do you care? If you were really concerned about me, you wouldn't have gone off gallivanting to the wilds of Sweden for months.'

'Finland.'

'Pardon?'

'I've been in Finland. Working. Research. Not gallivanting.'

Though perhaps she should cross her fingers. In many ways the research trip had felt like a holiday – time to indulge herself by reading, walking and thinking without interruption. Now, after listening to her mother's tirade, she was almost sure the mysterious malady was another case of self-pity and the usual demand for attention. Mum was so different from Aunt Anne. She'd be dying to hear about her niece's adventures, about the fishing and the story of the prudish Wolfgang in the sauna.

To avoid any more nagging, Elin went to the kitchen and buttered scones while she waited for the kettle to boil. For the next hour or so they chatted amicably enough, and Catherine seemed to be a little brighter. At seven o'clock Elin heated the soup and warmed some rolls.

'Shall we eat in the breakfast room, Mum? It seems a little silly to eat in the dining room when it's just the two of us.'

Catherine nodded her consent and got to her feet to follow Elin. She wobbled a bit when she stood up, then steadied herself. Elin watched, concerned. Mum was never as stiff and doddery as this.

'Perhaps you should go to the doctor again if that dizziness returns. It could be an ear infection.'

Mum gave Elin one of her stares.

'Elin, you may be well qualified. However, you're not a medical doctor, so please don't try to diagnose anything. I'll be better after a good night's sleep. It's helped to have some company this afternoon.' Catherine's voice was quiet but there was an edge of self-pity too.

More guilt came over Elin in waves. It would be so easy to suggest staying the night. Mum would like that. But she wanted to get back into her own bed and sort out her unpacked suitcases. The silence between them was broken only by the sounds of spoons on crockery.

'I suppose you're going now. You've done your duty. Off you go.' Mum's face was taut, her eyes held accusation.

Elin sighed. 'Mum, don't be like that. I'd have come to see you tonight, in any case. I left early, as I said. Sent my apologies for a meeting this afternoon and came here to see you. I was worried.'

'That job means more to you than I do. You don't have to spend every waking hour working, abandoning me for... for a desk. Who cares what you do, really?' Catherine's voice became more strident. 'You're far too independent, Elin. You've always had that hard streak in you. Your father couldn't see it, but I do.'

Elin braced herself, exhaustion claiming her. She could feel tears on their way. Papa always told her how proud he was of her, and she still missed him so much. She'd had enough. 'I don't see anything wrong with wanting to be independent.' She tried to make her voice quiet and calm.

'You take it too far. You should have got married and had children. I wanted grandchildren, but you were too busy pursuing your important career,' Mum made quotation marks with her hands to indicate her disdain, 'to take time to find a husband. We bought this big house in the hope that when you got married, you'd bring the children here to stay in the holidays. But no. You wanted the job more than anything. No grandchildren to keep me company in my old age.' Mum's voice had risen, more strident, then turning almost to a sob.

Elin closed her eyes and counted to ten. She could feel her body tense and her heart thumped in her chest. 'Why aren't you proud of me, Mum? My research on well-being is important. It can make a contribution to people's lives. I'm on track to become a professor before I reach forty. I have a career; financial independence and I've achieved more than a lot of women of my age. Why can't you see that? And, for the last time,' Elin felt her voice wobble dangerously with frustration, 'I've accepted I won't have children. Why in heaven's name can't you?'

'Because I don't understand you. I just don't understand what you want out of life. You drive yourself so hard. Why?' It was almost a cry and Catherine's face had reddened as she delivered her tirade.

'Because that's the way I am. Papa would be proud. You should be.' Elin stood up and slung her bag over her shoulder. 'I'm going now. I don't need this. I'm tired, too, and I've a few busy days ahead of me before going away for Christmas.'

'That's right. Walk away from it all.' Mum's lips were a straight line of disapproval. She waved an arm in dismissal. 'I'm glad I'm going to my sister for Christmas. Anne will listen. She'll understand.'

Elin just raised an eyebrow. Aunt Anne might listen, but she very often disagreed with her older sister. Chalk and cheese.

Mum's voice had become more querulous as she continued. 'In any case I don't want to spend Christmas with a selfish daughter who doesn't have time for her mother – and doesn't appreciate anyone else's point of view.'

Elin looked over to her mother, their eyes meeting for a brief moment. 'I'll ring you when I get in.'

As she walked out, Elin resisted the temptation to slam the door, pulling it behind her with a click. Instead, she drove too fast and fumed the whole way back to Cardiff Bay. She was still in a foul mood when she reached her flat and gave a curt nod to the security man instead of her usual friendly smile. If only Mum knew... then perhaps she'd understand.

Chapter Five

Elin

Elin gazed out at the clouds scudding across Cardiff Bay, playing hide-and-seek with the full moon. Below, the choppy, grey waters, murky and gloomy, reflected occasional glimpses of silver light. In contrast, if her glance turned towards the Senedd and the various restaurants around that area, the water was coloured with the reflections of the lights from the buildings, emerald, sapphire and ruby, festive and cheering. In her cosy flat on the third floor, she found it exhilarating to take in the big skyscape. That was one of the reasons she'd chosen to live in the Bay. It gave her a sense of space and freedom as she tried to relax and get her mother's fretful tones out of her head. She was frustrated and felt dragged down. Mum had wasted no time in laying on the guilt trip. Typical.

Making a beeline for the fridge, Elin took out a bottle of Chardonnay and poured herself a large glass, enjoying the delicate aromas of apple, lemon and peach. She didn't need this heavy emotional stuff on her first day back. 'Here's to you, Mum, and to you not getting under my skin,' she said aloud, taking a sip of the golden liquid, crisp and dry in her mouth.

Her voice echoed in the quiet of her flat. Oh, it was so good to be home again. She pushed the fridge door with more force than needed, but it felt satisfying to release some of the pent-up emotion. Glass in hand she headed over to the sofa, where she threw herself down into the fluffy cushions and pulled her feet up to rest under her. What a day. Mum in one of her moods. Not even a welcoming hug. Huw ill, and Michael Hardwick, in Brynderwen. God, who would have believed that would ever happen? As her thoughts turned to Michael, she remembered their time together. And what followed...

Secrets. Elin thought about the secrets and the heartache she had buried inside her for years. The Christmas tree lights twinkled in the flats around, reminding her of that Christmas, fifteen years ago, when a phone call from him had been the start of their affair. She had never known such highs as that year. It had seemed so simple then. Michael wanted her and she, Elin Fiorelli, wanted him; more than any man she'd desired before. But it wasn't simple. At all. Michael was her PhD supervisor. And he was married with a young child.

The phone rang and cut across her thoughts. Elin put her wine down on the glass coffee table and picked up.

'Hi, Elin. How's it going?' Jenny Spencer's voice with its deep, honeyed tones was unmistakable. It was almost as though she had been reading Elin's mind.

'Talk about sixth sense,' Elin said, with a smile. 'I was just thinking about our student days when we were in that grotty flat in Bristol.'

'Very different from your spanking new pad in Cardiff Bay.' Jenny laughed. She'd come down during a half-term school holiday a few years ago to help Elin move and had given her approval. And, of course, they'd had lots of girly weekends in the flat since. 'That flat was the pits, wasn't it? I thought it was about time that we firmed up on our holiday arrangements – and I've some news for you. You're still able to get away? Things okay with your Mum?'

Elin's stomach knotted with guilt, even though the trip had been planned months ago, before Finland. Both busy career women now, they made sure to factor in time together.

'You bet I'm on. Nothing would stop me getting some sunshine.' The winter night with its bleakness and howling wind was something to escape from. 'I can't wait for touchdown at Fuerteventura on Christmas Eve and spending quality time with my bestie. In any case,' her voice changed to a flatter note, 'it's business as usual with Mum and me.'

'What's she done now?'

'Not best pleased that I'm away at Christmas, naturally. She told me off. "You've only just got back from abroad. You should be spending time with me, not going away again on holiday."' Elin mimicked her mother's middle class English accent perfectly. 'She's fine really, I think. Big fuss over nothing. She's going to stay with Aunt Anne in Kent in any case. Anne will sort her out.'

Jenny laughed. 'You and your mother love each other to bits but wind each other up a treat.'

'Talk about laying it on thick.' Elin sighed with exasperation. 'She's complaining about dizzy spells and going on and on about feeling awful. Anyway, forget that for now, there's some other news I've got to tell you. You'll never guess what I found out when I went into work from my Finland trip.'

'Don't tell me. They've made you a professor in your absence because of all the wonderful research you've done for them?' There was a smile in Jenny's voice.

'I wish. Not yet and...' Elin paused. 'You remember our Dean?'

'Huw something?' Jenny said, 'Nice guy, you said.'

'Well, when I got back, I found out he'd had a heart attack and–'

'Oh no. Is he–?'

'No, thank God, he's okay, but... It's not that, well, not exactly.' Elin bent to pick up her glass and took a sip of wine. 'It's worse. They've parachuted someone in to take over Huw's job, and wait for it, this is the thing...' She shook her head. Still couldn't believe it herself. 'The new Dean is Michael Hardwick.'

'Bloody hell. I thought he was heading up some swanky consultancy firm and going backwards and forwards across the globe and to God knows where else. What's the swine doing in Brynderwen?' The dislike in Jenny's voice was evident.

'I know how you feel after what happened. He's well regarded, though, a great communicator. He has an excellent reputation as a consultant and project manager–'

'–A womaniser, a total–'

'I know precisely what he is, but Huw had lost his grip on the finances, Sue Deacon told me. Michael's been brought in to clean things up. She thinks he's the biz. Really rates him. Maybe he's changed.'

'Bollocks,' Jenny answered, snorting her disgust down the phone. 'Maybe I'm Mother Theresa. I'll never forgive him for what he did to you. He's a total bastard.'

Jenny paused and Elin could almost detect her thinking. Michael's behaviour fifteen years ago had been selfish, ruthless, heartless and resulted in the most difficult period of Elin's life. How would she have coped without Jenny's support? Elin could hear the puzzlement in Jenny's voice.

'But seriously, why would he come back to Britain and Wales?

'He's on his third wife. Young, Welsh and two small children. Probably the reason... but, God knows.' Elin's heart rate increased just thinking about Michael invading her world of work.

'I rest my case,' Jenny said. 'You see? Obviously still a player. You want to be careful, Elin.'

'No way is Michael Hardwick ever going to hurt me again.' Elin dug her nails into the cushion.

'I didn't mean falling in love. Don't let bitterness eat you up.'

Jenny knew her so well. Elin gave a shaky laugh. 'Point taken. I'll try. It's going to be tough though. So, tell me, what's your news and how's that gorgeous man of yours?'

There was a short silence at the other end.

'That's the other reason I rang. I've got some news too. Good news. Paul and I are... we're moving to Australia, beginning of April, we hope.'

'God, that's huge. Australia?' Elin hadn't seen that coming. She tried to inject enthusiasm into her voice, 'Wonderful news. I'm happy for you.' Her rock to lean on in times of trouble. Shared confidences and an enduring friendship that was unbreakable.

'Of course, you'll come and visit when we're properly settled.'

'You bet, you know me and the travel bug.'

When the call ended, a mix of emotions flooded Elin. She was happy for Jenny, but... Australia. The other side of the world. That was the last news she expected to hear. It looked like the Christmas holiday in Fuerteventura would be their final one together as two single women.

She gazed out over Cardiff Bay, at its most atmospheric and festive at Christmas time. A time for memories. Nostalgia. The year before, she and other senior members of staff had had a great meal in a restaurant nearby, and Huw had been in fine form. Now... now the world was a different place.

Elin wrapped her cardigan closer round her. A day that seemed as long as a week. She switched the television on and finished her glass of wine, brooding over the telephone call and struggling with the jetlag which seemed to have caught up with her. As the muted screen flickered, she tried to come to terms with two unwelcome pieces of news. She'd soon be forced to confront Michael Hardwick as her new boss. And she might also have just lost her best friend.

Chapter Six

Elin

New Year's Eve

'I'll be over tomorrow evening to bring in the New Year with you.' Elin was unpacking her suitcase with one hand while holding the phone to her ear with the other.

Mum sounded a bit brighter than when they'd parted at the railway station just before Christmas. Their disagreement hadn't been mentioned again and they'd patched over things by being polite and distant to each other. New Year's Eve, when Papa was alive, was always party time and Elin knew Mum would become anxious and depressed if left on her own.

Full of Spanish sunshine, laughter and relaxation, Elin drove to Sully the following afternoon, humming to herself. She pulled into the driveway, to a house ablaze with lights. The gold and red of the Christmas tree twinkled in the bay window, just like it used to do when Elin was a girl. It was a bit of a struggle to find the key to the front door with the bottle of bubbly and Mum's present in one hand and her bag flopping down over her shoulder. She opened the door and was greeted by the wonderful aroma of meat, garlic, onions and herbs. Anticipation made her mouth water as she headed straight to the kitchen to see Mum in charge of her domain, face flushed with the heat, several cookery books open and timers set. Hot air, blowing from the oven as Mum put in a tray of vegetables, was a welcoming contrast to the frost that was already beginning to form on the ground outside.

She gave Mum a hug, sniffing the air. 'That smells fantastic.

What have you made?'

'Boeuf Bourguignon with pavlova to follow. Your favourites. It's not the sort of thing you'd ever make for yourself.' She winked at Elin. They both knew there was no competition when it came to cooking.

'And you're wearing the jumper I bought you for Christmas. I've got something to go with that.' It was a last-minute gift bought at the airport but best not admit that. She pushed the paper package across the worktop towards Mum. Elin held her breath as Mum unwrapped it – a rich blue, silk pashmina.

Mum patted the soft material, bringing it up to her cheek. 'Beautiful. Perfect with my jumper. Such good taste, even if you can't cook.'

'Yes, I inherited your taste in clothing, not Aunt Anne's. How was she? Did you have a good time? You sounded merry when I rang on Christmas morning.'

Elin put the champagne in the fridge. 'Bubbly from Jenny.'

Mum half-laughed, half-sighed. 'Anne's taste is, how can one put it, unique. We did have fun though. You know your aunt. Full of surprises. She took me into the West End for a show with a fabulous meal afterwards as her Christmas present. Now, let's open that bubbly. New Year's Eve needs to be celebrated. I've put out some nibbles.' Mum shimmied a little to The Beach Boys playing in the background. 'How was Jenny? She's such a nice girl. I expect she's looking forward to moving to Australia with her boyfriend.' She searched Elin's face. 'You'll miss her.'

Elin pierced an olive. 'Mmm. Anything I can do to help? Apart from opening that bottle?'

'All done.' Mum checked a timer, looked at the casserole and decided everything was as it should be.

They took their champagne into the dining room where Mum lit some white table candles, little trails of smoke twisting towards the ceiling. Elin took in the starched linen and polished silver cutlery; smoothing the crisp tablecloth and flicking a fingernail against the crystal glasses to make a clear ringing sound. Mum must have spent hours in preparation. A surge of gratitude filled Elin's heart as she thought about the unspoken love that had gone into all her mother's efforts. She was determined to make the evening as light-hearted as possible. No rows to spoil the harmony. The room, with its solid oak furniture, had a sadness about it, neglected despite the high sheen on the polished wood, and feeling cavernous with just the two of them. Papa had filled every space with his laughter and expansive exuberance.

Over the meal they discussed Mum's visit to Aunt Anne and Anne's latest escapades. Visits to her younger sister always resulted in tales of adventure.

'She's still driving like a rally driver and her latest flame is Brazilian. And would you believe it she's going to meet him in Rio de Janeiro.' Mum shrugged her shoulders, before lifting her wine glass, studying its golden depths and the bubbles rising to the top. 'I do like a glass of champagne.'

Elin could never work out whether Mum disapproved of Anne's unconventional actions or admired them. Anne the daredevil. Elin's lips twitched at the thought of her crazy aunt.

'I don't think it would suit me. Too much sun and a long plane journey. Far too tiring.' Mum gave a little shudder. 'But I would like to go to Scandinavia.'

'Really, Mum?' Elin regarded her mother's wistful face. Of course, the last time Mum had gone abroad had been the cruise when Papa was taken so ill. 'You never mentioned that before.'

Mum dealt out a generous portion of pavlova, the snowy top making a satisfying crack as she did so. 'No. I think it was your trip to Finland and those pictures you showed me. It did look like fairyland, quite ethereal and magical.'

'When there wasn't an elk trying to get into the kitchen.'

Laughter echoed around the room. 'And, of course, I wouldn't dream of going naked into a sauna in the open air or something risqué like that.' Mum said in a serious tone.

Elin giggled at the thought of Mum in a sauna and the memory of Wolfgang's face. Plus, the wine was making her feel giddy.

'I would like to see the Northern lights,' Mum added.

'I think you'd love that. We were so far north and so far away from the city lights that whenever there was a display it was spectacular.' Eyes aglow, Elin continued, 'The colours aren't as vivid as you see in photographs but it's the best lightshow on earth.'

'I thought it was all pinks and greens. In photographs it looks amazing.'

'They take those with different shutter speeds, I think. We saw a display one night that just looked like cloud at first then changed so it seemed as though someone was playing a giant keyboard in the sky.' Elin put a hand to her heart. 'Simply indescribable.' She lifted her glass, a recklessness taking over. 'Let's go at Easter.'

'Pardon?'

'I'll look into it, book a long weekend for us.' A risk, but somehow Elin thought the experience would be a bonding one. The Aurora Borealis was something wonderful to behold. To see Mum's face... She reached over to touch her arm. 'We can have a Nordic spa day as well as seeing the Northern lights.'

'That would be fabulous, dear.' Mum clapped her hands. 'It's so quiet nowadays here in this house. Do you remember...' She sighed. 'All those New Year's Eve parties we used to have.' Then she added in a resolute tone. 'A toast. To absent friends.'

Papa was there with them both, in spirit. Elin could almost see him beaming at his guests, hear the Italian songs being played, listen to the chatter of a roomful of his Italian Welsh friends and associates. Mum would be going round, pressing delicious food and drink on the guests – in her element – as they looked forward to the countdown to midnight. How she missed him. Mum's vitality and zest for life had gone with Papa.

There was a whoosh of rockets out in the street, and a couple of dogs barked somewhere in protest. The New Year had arrived.

Elin wrapped her mother in a hug. 'Happy New Year.'

'Happy New Year, dearest.'

They clinked glasses.

'Here's to a fantastic year. Finland and the Northern lights for us.'

Chapter Seven

Michael

January

D awn was just breaking on the first day of the spring term as Michael drove into the car park at the university. The sullen pewter sky suited his mood. The Christmas holiday had passed in a blur of family activity. The boys were over-excited; and he'd seen more than he wanted of his in-laws. The holiday should have been an opportunity for him to relax, but he'd worked every day. Even on Christmas night, when the children had gone to bed, he'd buried himself in his study, poring over the nightmare of the finance figures.

Today he'd come in early, to check over various documents. He hoped to God his calculations were wrong, but he knew in his heart they were there, or thereabouts. He was surprised to admit that despite his views on provincial universities, and the unforeseen challenges of the job, he was enjoying life in Cardiff and Brynderwen. His colleagues, of course, didn't regard their city, or university, as parochial. After years of international travel and his spell in the United States, it all seemed small town to him. Still, there were plenty of attractive parks, a great cultural centre, good schools and activities for the boys. Much better than he had anticipated. He could even see himself and Anwen settling on a permanent basis. Perhaps he was mellowing. God, what a thought. He manoeuvred fast into his reserved parking spot, where "Dean" was marked on the ground in thick white letters.

The greeting from the vice chancellor on his first week in office popped into his mind.

'Cardiff is the last stop. Once someone gets here, they don't want to leave. You'll see what I mean after a while, Michael.'

Now, after a few months, he saw the VC's point of view. The institution had a less grasping, more familial attitude to staff and students. In reality, as well as in its mission statement, people seemed to matter. It made his job more pleasant on a day-to-day basis, but – if the figures were right – the going was getting tough. For everyone.

Even the happy sound of sparrows twittering in the bushes nearby didn't lift his mood as he took his briefcase out of the boot of his car and thought of what lay ahead at work. The building was chilly after being closed over the Christmas period making it seem inhospitable, barren even. Michael knew, though, that within an hour, computers would be humming, mugs rattling and voices chattering as folk returned to work and 'normality' after the ten-day break.

He strode down the corridor to his office and saw Jodie wasn't at her desk. No surprise there. She was used to a different regime and clearly intended to stick to it. Set break times and no going the extra mile. She'd had it cushy for too long with old Huw. Still, she was discreet – and confidentiality would be all important in the months ahead. He didn't want any scaremongering and discontent. Not before it became necessary.

The documents he needed were stored in a locked cabinet. He extracted the files and read over them for a while, placing the ones he had discarded into a neat pile. He'd tried to find easier solutions, but it was impossible. Due to the mismanagement of the previous Dean – what a waste of space he was – there was no other way the place could be kept afloat.

The recruitment drive Michael had instigated as soon as he arrived had shown some results. Yet, the Department was still in sizeable deficit. Job losses, playing with people's livelihoods, was a dirty and dangerous game. Could be the only solution though. He'd get Sue Deacon onto the figures again. See what the options were.

She picked up on the third ring.

'I'm just looking over my calculations,' Michael said. 'The first report is due to the governing body in a week, and between ourselves, I'm extremely concerned with how things are looking.' He checked the door to his office was firmly shut.

Sue's voice sounded high and stressed as she rushed to answer. 'I know. It's not good, however you look at it. Um, I did try telling Huw we needed to put on the brakes, especially with the research side, I really did try, as I told you, but he wouldn't listen. Said it was necessary to keep staff happy and on board. I couldn't understand it myself.'

'Well, it hasn't worked.' Michael snapped. Her voice was getting on his nerves today, with its breathless, apologetic tone and nasal twang. 'There's going to be a few unhappy people around here after I tell them about the cuts.' He jabbed his finger at the staffing list. 'I need to work out all the costs and scenarios, such as if anyone is thinking about early retirement.'

There was a pause before Sue responded. Michael wasn't sure whether it was because she was being cautious or if someone had come into the room. He heard Jodie open the outer office door and rustle about. Although she wouldn't enter his office without knocking, she might still hear something if she came straight in with papers for signing.

'Mmmm.' Sue came back on the line. 'Was just checking. We do have staff on temporary contracts and the HPLs, the hourly paid lecturers. I don't think that would cover it, though. I'll run the figures for you.'

'Yes. Good. Get all that to me, will you? Complete staff list with salaries, years of service, contracts and the rest. Liaise with Human Resources. Confidentially. Okay? I needn't tell you I've lost sleep over this. Nobody wants to unsettle people, or get rid of staff, but if it's what's needed, then so be it. I expect you know my reputation. Hatchet man.'

He let out a gruff laugh and Sue was silent, avoiding any comment. His reputation for ruthlessness was a front, the part he least enjoyed, but it came in useful at times.

At that moment a noise in the outer office distracted him. He could hear a man's voice raised in anger and then Jodie replying, muted and higher in tone than usual. What on earth was going on out there so early on the first day after the holiday? And the rumpus was getting worse.

'Look, Sue. Got to go. Something odd going on in the outer office. Book an hour with me tomorrow. Okay?'

What the hell? Jodie was trying to reason with a dishevelled young man. At over six foot tall, he towered over her. His greasy hair hung around his neck in lank strands and his face stubble was scrubby, three days growth or more, not quite a beard. His dark eyes were bloodshot and his tracksuit bottoms and hoodie were creased, as though he'd slept in them. Michael's nostrils flared at the stale smell of cigarettes and body odour. His first thought was that a tramp had wandered into the building, and he was about to ring for security when the young man turned and glared at him.

'Well, the Dean himself has graced us wi' his presence. We *are* honoured. Ah came in tae ask about getting an extension but this wee... hen,' a wave of the hand towards Jodie, 'decided I needed tae make an appointment wi' my tutor.' His speech was slurred. ''parently, if I need to see the almighty Dean, then I make an appointment for next week. It's too fuckin' late anyway. I'm needin' it sorted *now*.'

The young man swayed a little on his feet and Michael could detect the further unpleasant smell of stale alcohol on his breath. Jodie moved away behind her desk, looking frightened and unsure what to do next. Michael pulled his shoulders back, standing to his full height.

'You're one of our students then?'

'O' course I'm one of your students. Why else would I be here?' He laughed, a sort of manic sound without mirth, rocking unsteadily on his heels. Seeing he had the Dean's full attention, he appeared to pull himself together and answered. 'Aye. Transferred from Glasgow. My bird's here. Hard time settling. Home for Christmas, family probs, you know? Just need someone tae cut me a bit o' slack. Sort my shit out.'

'Hmmm. Crashing into the Dean's office and frightening my PA isn't the best way to get what you want, is it?' Should he call security, or could he defuse this situation? Weighing up the situation Michael opted for the latter. 'It's not a matter for me to deal with, in any case. And I suggest you apologise to Jodie, immediately.'

Michael's voice was firm, he expected obedience, but the young man leered at Jodie.

'Oh, Jodie, is it? Your bit on the side, eh? So sorry for disturbing you, *Jodie*.'

Jodie's eyes widened at the unsavoury comment. Michael's jaw tightened and he clenched his fists. How he'd like to punch the cheeky bugger.

'Now, the next thing you need to do is to see your personal tutor.' Michael managed to keep an even tone to his voice. 'You should speak to him, or her, as the case may be, about a possible extension. Fill in a form for extenuating circumstances and support it with evidence. It is not, I repeat, *not* a matter for the Dean's office. What's your name?'

The student stood and grinned at him but said nothing, waiting for some reason. The lad had attitude in buckets. As he made no attempt to move, Michael took a step towards him and frowned. There was something vaguely familiar about him.

The student made a bow then and touched his forehead in mock deference. 'Nick Mackenzie, sir, at your service. You dinnae recognise me, dae ye? Too many years since you bothered enough to care.' He glared at Michael. 'Well, that's hardly surprising, is it... Daddy-o?'

Chapter Eight

Michael

'Nick?' Michael blinked and shook his head a little, as if in disbelief. Somewhere within the shambolic figure in front of him was the little boy he had felt guilty about, when he remembered. His firstborn. With a wave of his hand, he indicated the door to the inner office. 'You'd better come in.'

Michael glanced at Jodie, whose jaw had dropped open hearing the Dean call the disruptive student by name and then invite him into his office. She still gripped the side of her desk, looking ready to run out. As if sharing a confidence, Michael raised an eyebrow and smiled at Jodie, who continued to keep an anxious eye on the student. Damn. He'd have to invest some time talking to her. She must be wondering what the hell was going on. Under the circumstances it was hard to sound calm and reassuring. He felt his eyelid twitching again and the headache above one eye was getting worse.

'I'll handle this now. Thank you, Jodie. I'm not to be disturbed while I'm dealing with this... situation.'

A frown of puzzlement, or perhaps concern, still creased her forehead, as Nick slouched into the inner office. Bloody hell. Another problem. He hoped her discretion extended to unusual situations – like this one.

'Nice office you've got.' Nick smoothed the polished grain of the oak conference table in a gesture of appreciation, and glanced around, checking the bookshelves filled with files and academic books, the expansive desk with a new computer and the window with its view of the car park and beyond. 'Done alright for your-self.'

He seemed a bit calmer, but Michael was still wary, suspicious. 'You are Nick, aren't you?' Michael asked, his lips pursed with annoyance, pain from the headache and stress. Didn't he have enough on his plate without a troublesome long-lost son? He hadn't seen Nick since he was, what, about seven? Was this un-savoury young man really him? 'Where's your Student ID card?'

'Dinnae want to believe it, dae you?' Nick jutted his chin out, a challenging glare in his eyes. 'Big disappointment. Well, it's true.'

Now, in the inner office with no one to show off to, Nick seemed more willing to be cooperative. He delved into a pocket of his scruffy hoodie and brought out his student card, which he slid across the table.

Michael picked it up, read the information. Nicholas Mackenzie. That was a puzzle at first, then he realised Karen had done what she'd threatened – changed the boy's name to hers after the divorce.

'Do you really not recognise me, Daddy-o?' Nick sneered, his lip curling upwards and to one side. 'Ma said you were a slippery customer, and you didnae want to have anything to do with me. You and other women...'

'Now look here, that's enough.' Michael had to put a stop to the diatribe and take back the initiative. He rolled his shoulders and shook an elegant finger at Nick. 'You're lucky I'm not calling security after your aggressive behaviour to my PA. I'll thank you to keep a civil tongue in your head.'

'Oh yeah,' Nick went on, oblivious to Michael's threat. 'Ma told me about you and your womanising. "Always after a bit of skirt. Couldn't be trusted." That's what she said. When Ma had a skinful, she'd go off on one about you.' Nick was righteous in telling this tale, swaying a little as he spoke.

Michael squirmed at this accusation. 'Now, that's unfair. It wasn't like that. Your mother had post-natal depression–'

'Bullshit.' Nick scratched at his chin with its unkempt facial hair. 'Of course, Ma's cleaned up her act now she's remarried. Her new fella really looks after her tho' he's nay so keen on me. Made that fuckin' clear enough.'

Nick staggered and grabbed the back of a chair, moving it out so he could drop into it. His skin had gone pale, grey-tinged, his eyes red-rimmed and sore. Putting a hand to his forehead, he groaned, 'Can I have some water? I'm kinda dry. Bit of a heavy night last night. Dropped off the wagon.'

Michael hesitated, then he called through to Jodie to bring some water. Nick sat, hand over his eyes, and Michael sat opposite.

When Jodie knocked and entered, carrying the glasses and jug over to the table, she kept a wary eye on Nick. 'Do you need anything else, Professor Hardwick? I have a secretariat briefing meeting now.'

Michael noticed Nick look up and leer at Jodie's large breasts, encased in a tight red sweater, and his voice was harsher than he intended when he responded. 'No, that's fine, thanks. I shall naturally expect this incident to remain between ourselves, Jodie.'

His mouth was a grim line, teeth clenched, glaring at Nick, as Jodie retreated. Not long after that the outer office door clicked closed as she went off to her meeting. There was a momentary pause while Michael watched Nick gulp the water in one long draught.

With a sigh of relief, Nick leant over to pour himself another glass before looking up and pronouncing, 'Your secretary's hot. Is she your latest one, Daddy-o? Little bit of–'

'Shut up, Nick.' Michael found it a struggle to say his son's name. The man in front of him bore little resemblance to the young boy he remembered. 'I understand you're angry and maybe I haven't been the best father, but this is getting us nowhere. I've told you, if it's an extension you want you have to go through the proper channels.'

Nick shrugged and smirked, staring at Michael, but then his attention slid off towards the window as he began reminiscing. 'Dae you remember that Christmas? The one before you buggered off? You bought me that train set I'd wanted for ages.'

Nick's dark eyes returned to Michael, intense and mesmerising. The boy knew how to press the emotional blackmail buttons all right. God, how he needed some headache tablets.

'Yes. I remember. The house in Bristol. I thought Scotland with her family would–'

'Crap. When we went to Scotland, everything went tits up.

You didnae hang around long, did you?' Nick stretched his long legs out, warming to his theme. 'Always away, working or pumpin' some student. That's what Ma said.'

Michael wanted nothing more than to get Nick out of his office as soon as possible, and ideally, away from Brynderwen. Nick had always been subject to tantrums, he remembered, more manageable as a boy, but now... Christ, this was the last thing he expected, or needed. How was he supposed to deal with a fucked-up, long-lost son, on top of everything else? He ran a hand through his hair, trying to keep his frustration in check, glanced at his watch and realised he had missed an appointment. Damn. What the hell could he do to sort this bloody mess? 'So, what do you want me to do? What's the problem? More than a late assignment, I'm guessing.'

'Well, I'm homeless. Been sofa-surfing a lot this holiday.' Nick said this with a sniff.

'What do you mean? Don't you have student accommodation? And you've got a home in Scotland, haven't you?' Michael asked.

'Och aye, at uni it's okay.' Nick shrugged. 'Girlfriend lets me kip over her place. Home? That's a fuckin' joke. Told you, didn't I? Crap. Ma threw me out for doing the booze and a bit of weed. Acting all holier than thou over it.' Nick unfolded himself from the chair to his considerable height. In two strides he was by the desk and had picked up the photo of Anwen and the children.

'Don't touch that.' Michael's hands formed fists. He was close to pushing his chair back and striding over but stopped himself in time. Every muscle in his body felt taut.

Nick traced a finger over the photograph. His voice was subdued when he spoke. 'Playing happy families.'

'Right, Nick,' Michael said in a controlled tone. 'Your mother was good at emotional blackmail too. I think I get the picture.'

With surprising gentleness, Nick placed the photo down again, came back to the conference table and sat down. His shoulders had slumped, a forlorn expression on his face, his dark eyes deep with some indefinable emotion. 'Oh, you do, do you, Daddy-o. I dinnae think so. I dinnae think so, at all. Fact is, bottom line, you owe me.'

What was Nick after? Not a reconciliation, or he'd have made his presence known sooner. Michael exhaled and glanced over at the photo, which Nick had put down the wrong side of his computer. A small oblong of dust showed in the space where it had been. He'd be glad to turn his back on the problems of work and get home. But for now, he needed to get to the bottom of what Nick was asking for. 'So, if I understand you correctly, you're behind on a couple of assignments and want the university to consider your personal problems in a mitigating circumstances case?'

Nick wiped his nose with the back of his hand. 'That's about it, yeah, but it's got to be sorted, now. I dinnae want to screw up again. I need this. I fucked up last night. Been tryin' not to use.'

Michael didn't like the new wheedling, self-pitying tone in Nick's voice. It was distasteful. He could see, though, how close to the edge Nick was by the change in his breathing and the rapid blinking of his eyes to hold back tears. Decision time. Leaning forward Michael said, 'Okay. Okay. I'll sort it, but on condition you go to student counselling and get professional help.' He met Nick's eyes. 'And this conversation is confidential between us.'

'Thank you... Mike.'

Michael started as if he'd been prodded with something sharp. The name Karen used to call him. Better than the taunting Daddy-o at least. 'Alright. Fill in the forms and I'll pull a few strings. Then, to put it bluntly, keep out of my way.'

'Like you've done for years?' Nick sneered and then shrugged. His attitude changed from belligerence to comprehension in a flash. 'I get it. Fuck off and shut your gob. It's okay. I just want tae get my degree.' Nick seemed almost pathetic in his gratitude.

His behaviour was certainly erratic and unsettling. A prickle of unease crossed the back of Michael's neck. He would sort it. Everything would have to be above board. 'What's that on your arm?' he asked, spotting a dark shape.

Nick held out his forearm and Michael saw the shape of the black snake writhing around it. 'Just a tattoo, man. Everyone's got 'em now. Had it done one night after a heavy sess in London.' The turn in the conversation seemed to give Nick back the initiative and his swagger. He stood up, winked at Michael and headed for the door. 'Thanks again, Mike. Be seeing you... or not.'

After he'd gone, Michael took two painkillers with water and sat still for some time, thoughts whirling like a snowstorm in his head. He rubbed a hand over his chin. How genuine was Nick? He hadn't asked for money and seemed sincere in his desire to get his degree. This girlfriend might be a good influence. It was a mess that had come to light, however you looked at it, and Michael felt a wave of guilt at how he had so easily abandoned the boy when the marriage ended. Too late now to have regrets. The past was over, and he had enough worries in the present.

Michael hadn't intended to go to the Staff and Student Liaison meeting that day, had earmarked the time to work on the Department figures. The confrontation with his son had left him with a sense of gloom and foreboding. Getting out of the office might shake off some of that and showing his visibility as the Dean was good. Demonstrate to people he was keeping their interests at heart. He got up and strode over to check his calendar. He'd be late, but he should still be able to catch part of the meeting. Playing the game he was good at. He checked his watch and set off at a rapid pace down the corridor.

Chapter Nine

Elin

January

The first week back after the break had been quiet and somehow, Elin had avoided seeing Michael, although she'd noticed his car when she walked over to the library to return books, blown along by a blustery, raw, winter wind. It would have been difficult to miss the large, black BMW, shiny, with personal numberplates, in its reserved place. Time enough to face him once the term was in full swing and she was back to her hectic schedule of teaching and research. She'd submitted her professorship application to the Dean's office on the first day back, using the holiday for final polishing. She could do nothing more now than wait for it to be signed off and sent forward, with the Dean's support, to the Readership and Professorial Committee. How she wished Huw was still in post.

However, after a week in the sun in Fuerteventura, and a lovely New Year's Eve with Mum on her return, she felt re-energised, ready to face the world – and the research meeting that afternoon where she would be presenting on the TechSWell project. Difficult questions and barbed comments from a few awkward colleagues were to be expected, but she was confident she could cope. Her skin had a faint honey-coloured glow, and she knew she was well-groomed, her short hair curling around her ears and nails painted a deep pearly pink. A new cobalt blue trouser suit made her feel more confident. Her professional armour was in place, and she was prepared.

She'd discussed the research meeting with Jenny as they lay

by the pool sipping fruit cocktails. They'd spent the first morning sightseeing where they visited a local museum and then revelled in some quality downtime together, lying companionably on white sun loungers by the pool. The sun smiled at them from a cloudless sky as a warm breeze caressed their bodies. It was a million miles from Brynderwen – and Mum.

They had covered Catherine Fiorelli's strop when Elin came back from Finland, the reconciliation, and the happy time at New Year's Eve; also, news of a mother-daughter trip at Easter to see the Northern Lights. 'Sounds fab, Elin.' Jenny had told Elin all about her plans for Australia and her new life down under and Elin had promised to visit. Then they got on to talking about work.

'The problem with being relatively young and ambitious–' Elin took a delicious sip. Pineapple and coconut. So refreshing.

'–And a woman.'

'–is the mindset of some of the oldies. They think because they've been there for years, they should automatically be given a chair. Some of them haven't published anything for years.' She took another sip. 'I need to make sure when I present my findings everything's as good as I can make it. No room for error, no gaps in clarity.'

'Maybe you should do the presentation in that bikini.' Jenny winked at Elin and stretched over to put her glass down on the low table between them, her wavy copper-tinged hair making a halo around her heart-shaped face. She could do mischievous despite her appearance.

Elin spluttered and coughed on her drink. 'Oh, God, Jenny, you are wicked. I'll miss you so much when you go off to the other side of the world. Screw all that for now. Let's enjoy our holiday.'

It had been brilliant, and they were determined to make it even more enjoyable because it was their last together.

Although she loved the research, Elin enjoyed working with the students too and sharing her passion about the importance and applications of her research specialism – well-being for everyday life. That morning she made her way up to Seminar Room

One on the first floor overlooking the carpark where a group of second year undergraduates waited for their tutorial session. An expectant buzz surrounded them, excited chatter filled the room and then calmed as Elin began with the usual opening notices and pleasantries.

The session was soon in full swing. 'Don't ever be afraid to express your opinion, even if you disagree with anything you've read in a research paper or book. Just because it's published doesn't mean it's not open to debate.' Elin beamed with enthusiasm encouraging them to respond. One or two students smiled back, and someone asked a question about one of the points she had presented on her slides. 'As long as you can support your arguments, then please, feel free to disagree. It's good for you and helps crystallise your thought processes.'

Elin was proud of the learning environment she created. This satisfaction was something she tried to explain to her mother during their many disagreements on the path her life should take. Mum could never see it. She'd only worked for a short while and stopped after she married.

At the end of the session, Elin spoke to two students who wanted to tell her it was difficult to get hold of one of the books she had recommended. She said she'd liaise with the library and pointed them to key extracts she had already placed online as resources for the assignment.

The second group that morning were post-graduates and Elin hurried to repack her bag and head off to meet them in another wing of the building. They filled the small seminar room, radiating energy and enquiry. Elin was delighted to see them again after her three months absence, greeting them by name and wishing each a Happy New Year. They wanted to know all about her research trip; a good rehearsal, she reflected, for the afternoon's research meeting.

This year's group were the usual mix, some straight from their first degree, some her age or older, who had been professionals in other fields before changing course. Elin sometimes went out for a drink with the postgrads but always insisted on no personal questions. Despite, or perhaps because of this, the students liked and respected her, and she was often party to confidences she would have preferred not to have heard. Most she was able to keep to herself, although sometimes more action to support was needed. Her role as an academic was demanding and varied and carried a weight of responsibility. One of the reasons why she loved it and found it so fulfilling.

'Hey, Dr Fiorelli, it's really good to have you back, it is. Bit different since you scarpered off to Finland.' The girl grinned and winked. 'What do you think of the new Dean? Bit of a change, eh?' Bethan Jones was a good student, well-rounded in every sense, on the plump side with an inclination to use too much make-up, eyes ringed with charcoal eye-liner and bright blusher inexpertly applied.

Elin felt a little breathless at the mention of Michael's name. 'Yes. The new Dean. I met him briefly when I got back to the university at the end of last term. I'm sure Professor Hardwick will do his best for the university.'

'Well, then. You've gotta think he's a bit of a looker, don't you now? Silver fox. Tasty though. Looks after himself, I'd say. Fit.' Bethan laughed her raucous laugh and winked again. The others just smiled or tried to ignore the comment.

The rest of the session passed, with some searching questions about how she had managed in such an isolated setting – and, shock horror, without Wi-Fi. Elin was soon in the swing of things with the group and made a mental note to thank the colleagues who'd taken the class while she was in Finland.

The last group of the morning had a different vibe. Final year students who had assignments, as well as dissertations to complete. It was a tense time for them as every mark at this stage counted towards their final degree classification. Elin noticed a couple of unfamiliar faces as well as a few omissions from her original register. 'Where's Annabel Richards? She should be in my tutor group this year?'

'Oh, she's deferred for a year. Expecting.'

Elin sighed at that news, knowing Annabel might not return. There were always one or two who dropped out for some reason, finance, family, health – or pregnancy. She was surprised at Annabel's lack of foresight, but these things happen. With a quick final scan of the students, she checked the register and glanced around the room. One new name: Nicholas Mackenzie. That had to be the lad slouching at the back. He looked a bit unkempt and sullen. His clothes were shiny with dirt and the trainers he was wearing had seen better days.

'Right. Let's get started. I want you to work together in pairs. I'd like you to exchange information on work experiences you've had. Any work experience,' she added. There was a general appreciative murmur.

Elin knew many worked part-time to support themselves. She'd met her students over the years working in bars and restaurants, health clubs, cinemas and the theatre. A lively discussion was soon underway, and Elin flitted from pair to pair joining in their conversations and at times asking questions, prompting them to make connections between work experiences and their dissertation topics.

She paused by Nicholas Mackenzie. 'We haven't met, have we?'

'No. Transferred this year. Frae Glasgow.' He avoided looking her in the eye.

Elin heard a Scottish burr to his voice, and she could also tell he was a smoker by the stale air around him. Amongst other odours.

'That can be difficult. I hope you're settling in okay.' She smiled hoping to encourage him to open up, but he didn't respond, other than a brief glance up from his notes.

'Aye. It's all right.'

After that he seemed to be watching her, almost every time she looked up his eyes were fixed on her. It was a little unsettling. At the end of the session, he waited until the room was nearly empty and then he came over. One of the girls from the group, Cerys, Rubenesque figure and pink cheeks, stood in the doorway, waiting, as he spoke to Elin.

'Can I have a word? Got an extension on my essay but I kinda need a wee bit more help before I hand it in. I dinnae know what you want, see.'

Elin paused. There was something strange about the way he avoided eye contact and his expression that she couldn't quite pinpoint. 'Sure, that's fine. It can be tough moving university. I've no time just now, I'm afraid. You'll have to make an appointment.'

'But it's important.'

Elin's smile faded as she took in his scowl. With a quick glance at the clock, she replied, 'And my meeting is important to me. Please email me, and I'll send you an appointment to see you as soon as I can. I'm happy to help. Now, if you'll excuse me, I've some urgent work to do.'

Elin's tone was sharper than usual, and she could feel her body tense. She needed to get to the conference room to check her PowerPoint was loaded and ready. The student made no attempt to leave and stared at Elin.

Cerys, still waiting by the door, intervened. 'Come on, Nick. Dr Fiorelli will sort it later. Come on.' She pulled on his coat sleeve. Nick scowled but allowed her to steer him away.

Elin hurried back to her office, closed the door and felt her body relax. Time seemed to be racing as she sat at the computer and checked her slides one last time. The Department research seminars were well attended. Although sometimes there was fierce debate, there was never any real animosity, and it would be good practice for presenting her research at the TechSWell conference in the spring. Elin was looking forward to that and to being inspired hearing about others' research in the field. The social aspect would be fun, too, meeting up with Wolfgang, Professor Lars Nordin and others again.

With the final check of her appearance, Elin straightened the jacket of her suit and applied a little tinted lip gloss. She had a bottle of water ready to take with her. Her mouth always went dry before she began a presentation. She ignored the flutter in her stomach. Once started, she knew it would be fine. Her nerves would disappear, as she went into performance mode, confident that she had prepared as thoroughly as she could.

The conference room filled rapidly with colleagues greeting each other. 'Happy New Year' or '*Blwyddyn Newydd Dda*' chorused across the spacious room. Unlike the seminar and teaching rooms, this had more of a sense of grandeur, a bigger scale. A long table, formed by joining several smaller ones had been created in the centre and there was a low stage at one end of the room.

Geraint, the chair for the meeting, arrived. A big man with ruddy cheeks and broad shoulders, he looked as though he would be more comfortable on the rugby pitch. His jacket stretched across his ample waistline, and he pushed a strand of thin grey hair out of his eyes as he called for order. Elin's presentation was the first on the agenda. Geraint's voice boomed across the room; the Welsh lilt unmistakeable. 'Well, now, folks, welcome back and a very Happy New Year to you all. I'm sure you've noticed that this pretty face was missing last term.' He waved an arm towards Elin, 'It seems she was on an extended holiday, called research. She's here to tell us all about it and show us her holiday snaps.'

That provoked laughter in the room. From anyone else the introduction would have sounded like an insult, but Elin had already spoken to Geraint about the best way to preface her talk and had agreed on this light-hearted approach. It was Geraint's way. And in fact, the first slide looked just like a holiday picture, showing the study house in Finland framed against a clear blue sky and surrounded by snow.

Elin scanned the room before she began to speak, feeling more at ease as she saw colleagues' familiar faces. 'This is the study house where I spent three months in isolation with another researcher from Germany.' She flicked to a photograph of Wolfgang, tall, blond and unsmiling. 'As some of you know, the TechSWell project was set up to study the effects of technology and social media on mental health and well-being in our modern society. It's an ongoing project with international connections, part funded by Fonetym, the technology company.'

Elin paused and looked around. She could see from the nods that most of the audience had heard of Fonetym, though one or two of the members of staff frowned in puzzlement. 'We're grateful to Fonetym for their substantial financial contribution to the research. At this point I'd also like to express how much I owe to Huw for providing the rest of the money to cover my absence – and to acknowledge my appreciation for his years of commitment to the development of his staff. I'm also indebted to colleagues who dealt with some of my workload while I was away. I owe quite a few favours.'

'See you in the bar after,' someone shouted, and there was another wave of laughter.

Nods and smiles indicated Elin had started with the right approach. She'd been so lucky to have Huw's blessing and financial backing, like others in the room, and was glad to have said that at the start of her talk.

'So, the project hoped to prove that technology was essential to our well-being and...'

A commotion at the back of the room halted her speech as a tall figure entered. Elin was horrified to recognise Michael Hardwick. She hadn't expected him to attend. Her mouth felt dry when she tried to swallow, and she was aware of a sensation of butterflies in her chest. She looked down at her notes to keep her place. A few coughs and mutterings followed his entrance as people shuffled chairs to make room.

'My apologies, Dr Fiorelli, please do continue.' Michael's well-modulated voice held no hint of apology as he took a seat directly in front of her, his unsmiling countenance a distraction.

Elin could feel the flush in her cheeks as Michael's eyes met hers. There was no warmth in those eyes as he shifted his gaze from her to the screen. A slight frown creased his brow and Elin took a sip of water before she resumed.

'As I was saying, Fonetym's expectations were that without modern technology, our computers, phones and the ability to interact through social media, we would report feeling isolated with other negative health effects, such as mild anxiety and depression. I spent three months in this controlled setting with my research colleague, Dr Wolfgang Richter. We had a technician who came to bring us food supplies and to undertake health tests such as blood pressure and fitness levels – otherwise we were removed from society. We recorded our activities and thoughts in research dairies.'

At this point, Elin held up one of the volumes to show the group. 'As you can see, these are handwritten.'

She felt a thrill of adrenaline as she got to the heart of her talk. 'My stay in the study house had interesting, and surprising, outcomes. Far from feeling isolated, I felt at one with nature and more relaxed than I had been for years. My fitness levels increased, my blood pressure dropped, and I slept like a baby,' she paused for effect, 'without the help of a glass of wine at night.'

There were a few muted laughs and smiles. As Elin glanced around the room, she was aware of one or two, like her, who sometimes had difficulty with stress-related problems and difficulty sleeping. Sioned Morgan for one, over by the window, was commenting to her neighbour, Alan Fisher, who nodded.

'So, Dr Fiorelli,' Michael's voice cut through the murmurs, smooth as melted chocolate but scalpel sharp in tone, 'are you saying that Fonetym wasted its money sending you off to the wilds of Finland? After all, they probably assumed that your findings would be in harmony with their company policy.' There was a tense silence. Michael paused, before he added, 'No multi-million company would give money to someone who disagreed, fundamentally, on everything they stood for.'

Elin could feel her heart beating faster. Her palms felt clammy. 'I... I beg your pardon, Dean. What is your question?'

'It's not so much a question as a statement, or even an observation.' He folded his arms and added in a mild voice, 'You've received a great deal of money, both from Fonetym and this university, to show how in modern times we need, and can use, technology for our well-being. That's correct, isn't it? The premise of the research.'

Elin nodded, unsure of what was to follow.

'Now you're telling us that the money was wasted. You had a wonderful time without technology.'

A few nervous laughs from some of the other academics punctuated the tension in the room.

Elin could feel the fury building inside her and it took all her willpower to maintain a cool exterior. 'On the contrary. That's not quite what I said. My research diaries point towards an increase in well-being, certainly.'

'Qualitative research, which is, of course, highly subjective.' A clipped response and shake of the head from Michael showed his irritation.

'And the health screening also indicated an increase in fitness. Quantitative. The numbers add up.' Elin countered. She'd expected searching questions, challenges even, but not this fusillade from the Dean.

Michael's expression was stern, and his eyes narrowed. 'And

how do you think Fonetym will respond to that? Do you expect them to offer more funding? I think not, Dr Fiorelli. This needs further frank and thorough discussion.' With that Michael Hardwick got to his feet and strode out.

There was silence for a moment, broken by Geraint's comment, to no one in particular. 'Well, I don't think our new boss is very happy, is he now?'

Chapter Ten

Elin

Elin spent a restless night, tossing and turning, and woke early, bleary-eyed and listless. She'd seen Michael Hardwick from a distance at conferences over the years and had always steered well clear of him. It had been a shock, nevertheless, to meet him at such close quarters the previous day; and the last thing she expected was the public and aggressive grilling she'd received. She was hurt and puzzled. If anything, she'd expected him to offer general pleasantries, to ease the awkwardness. What the hell was behind his unexpected attack? His approach was bordering on harassment, downright rude. And the summons to his office this morning... One thing she knew for sure was she'd have all her facts and figures prepared when she met him later.

Elin rose and stretched, pleased to get up at last. After her shower she chose her clothes with care, a black trouser suit and pillar-box red top with high-heeled boots, even though she knew Michael, at six foot, would still tower over her. She had a light breakfast of yoghurt and fruit and was at her desk by half past seven. She spent an anxious hour checking and re-checking everything with meticulous care. By the end she was confident she had it all ready. She'd be able to defend herself, explain her findings properly to Michael. If Professor Lars Nordin, her project team leader, had no misgivings then why in heaven's name had the Dean erupted in that way? And most people in the research seminar had appreciated what she had to say. Damn Michael Hardwick.

At twenty past nine, as she gathered her papers, she noticed a chip on the nail of her index finger. Annoying. Too late to do anything. She checked her appearance in the mirror and tried to ignore the fluttering in her stomach. She was prepared to defend her research.

On Elin's arrival at the Dean's suite, Jodie looked up from sorting mail and indicated with a nod towards the inner door. 'He's expecting you.'

Elin searched Jodie's face for any indication of Michael's mood, but she had begun to tap on the keyboard. Despite herself, Elin felt the familiar churning in her stomach when she knocked on his door.

'Come in.' Michael's voice was as deep and attractive as she remembered. Its rich, well-modulated tones could be seductive or scathing. He was behind the desk and looked up when she entered and stood, straightening his tie to greet her. She noticed at once, however, that he was serious in expression and addressed her in formal tones. 'Ah, Dr Fiorelli. Please close the door.'

A little breathless, she observed at close quarters how Michael's hair was now a distinguished, iron-grey at the temples and there were laughter lines round his mouth and eyes. He was more solid, more settled in the world, than when she'd known him. An unexpected flood of emotion went through her, a sadness for what might have been.

Michael indicated the conference table with a hand. 'Do sit down, please. Would you like some water or tea, coffee?' A jug of water and two glasses were in place.

'No, thank you.' Her voice was clipped, polite.

He took a seat opposite, poured himself a glass of water, leant on the table and steepled his fingers, his dark eyes assessing her. 'Thank you for coming to see me today.'

As if there'd been a choice. Elin just wanted the meeting to be over as soon as possible. 'I've brought in the PowerPoint slides and an overview of my research for you, with some of the emerging findings. I appreciate you didn't have the opportunity to hear the beginning section of my presentation yesterday, or the ending–'

'Let me stop you there if I may. I have something more pressing to discuss with you before we talk about that. There's the issue of your application for a chair as a starting point.'

'Yes. I was told by Huw, the previous Dean, that my research should–'

'But things have changed. Huw is on sick leave and no longer in charge. Your application needs my approval.'

Elin frowned. Where was this going? She was surprised but tried to persevere in the face of what she felt was Michael's antagonistic attitude. Perhaps if she managed to explain about the research, things would improve. 'I'd like to allay your worries about the research programme I've been undertaking in Finland. I thought that was the reason you wanted to see me.'

Michael adjusted his cufflinks and turned towards the window for a moment. Drifting up from her memory she recalled this habit of his, when dealing with a difficult situation. It gave her a premonition that this wasn't going to be an easy meeting, even though she'd already expected some difficulties.

'I've asked to meet with you, because as a senior colleague, we need to discuss the basis of funding research in the Department,' said Michael. 'It's an important and serious matter and goes well beyond the research you've been doing in Finland. The previous Dean gave considerable support and facilitated your research–'

'And we're extremely grateful to Huw. He's been tremendous, a rock, in supporting us,' Elin hurried in to say, clasping her clammy hands together, 'and I feel, due to his mentoring, we have been able to build the Department's reputation and research profile.'

Michael hesitated, looking down before responding. 'Yes, you and your colleagues have been relatively successful, given the nature of this institution.'

'New university or not, you know yourself, that research feeds teaching and brings things to life for the students. If you'd seen the responses from some of my groups–' Elin rushed on.

'I'm sure they were bubbling with it,' he said, with a tight little smile.

The touch of sarcasm in Michael's voice annoyed Elin. She resisted the temptation to thump the table, digging the fingernails of one hand into the palm of the other, out of his sight, on her lap. She wouldn't let him get under her skin. The arrogance of the bloody man. His whole career spent in top-notch universities where research was a key funding stream. Did he still hold negative views about new, post-1992, universities? Surely not, now that he'd experienced the verve and enthusiasm of many staff. She looked across the table. Michael seemed to be weighing his words carefully, pausing to take another sip of water before he spoke.

'I have to tell you, despite this modest success, all research funding in the Department will have to be withdrawn, with immediate effect.' Michael didn't meet her eyes, instead put his glass down on a Welsh slate coaster. The glass made a click as it met the grey stone. Otherwise, there was a momentary silence in the room.

Elin leant forward and steadied herself by putting both hands on the smooth wooden surface of the table. Her head was a kaleidoscope of nightmarish thoughts. This was even worse than she'd imagined. 'What? Why?' she asked. 'I don't understand why there's this complete change of direction. It wouldn't be fair to Huw if he returns, when he returns, to...' Elin struggled for words, 'to decimate the Department's research strategy in this way.'

Huw would never block her career in this sort of way. A nauseous feeling grew in the pit of her stomach. What would happen to her application for the chair now? She struggled to take in what Michael was saying.

'It is not a matter of choice, I'm afraid.' His voice was low, emotionless.

Elin shook her head in disbelief as she looked across the table. Michael's expression was difficult to read. His jaw was taut, and a muscle twitched in his cheek.

'And all this is confidential. I must stress I do *not* want any other members of staff to know about our discussion at present.' His tone was firm, as he continued. 'We must save a substantial amount if the Department is to remain solvent. I don't know how much you know about the finances here, but they're in a dire state and it's my responsibility to take charge and find solutions – some of which will be highly unpopular.'

Elin tried to comprehend. She knew the Department didn't receive much funding beyond their core business, unlike some, which attracted commercial or research monies. She hadn't realised the problem was so bad, even after Sue's warning. Universities didn't go broke, did they?

'I had no idea that the Department was in such a crisis,' she said. 'I'm bringing in substantial research money.' She paused as the implications struck her. 'And I can't possibly stop in the middle. It's run on a two-year basis, and we've just concluded the first phase of data collection.'

'Well, that's an area which could help us, certainly. Fonetym is a massive outfit and I know they're interested in engaging with the university sector. That's a plus point.' He paused and held her gaze with his dark eyes. 'You can appreciate why I was concerned yesterday about the tenor of your findings, reporting those sorts of negative outcomes.' He shook his head and pursed his lips, pausing to adjust his cufflinks again. 'In fact, that's the second reason I wanted to see you. I suggest you think again, very carefully, about your current line of enquiry.'

'What do you mean?'

'If you persist in it, you're inevitably going to deter Fonetym from supporting us in a meaningful way, during Phase Two. You can see, can't you, how that would be a disaster in the present situation, for you personally, and for the Department?' His eyes held a challenge.

Elin couldn't believe her ears. Was he holding the promise of her professorship as bait? Was the Dean actually suggesting that she change her findings in order to please their funder? Compromise her integrity? 'But,' she stammered, in her haste to make the point, 'my findings are based on meticulous data collection over a period of months–'

'There are different ways of cutting the cake. And I'm sure you could present your material in a more... nuanced way.'

'Professor Nordin would think it very strange if I drew different conclusions than those I've already sent in my first report–' Elin countered, but the flow of words carried on.

'So, I'm strongly advising you to take my direction and re-evaluate your material, to give a more favourable perspective on the role of Fonetym in twenty-first century well-being.'

In the silence that ensued, Elin could almost hear her heart beating. What he was suggesting was unprofessional, and unethical. Of course, he was aware of this. She scanned his face. There seemed no sign of guilt or misgiving. Unbelievable. The nerve of the man.

'Absolutely not. I am, unequivocally, standing by my research data and the veracity of my findings.'

With that, Elin picked up her papers, thrust her chair back, and marched to the door, slamming it behind her without a backward glance. She almost ran down the corridor, storming past Geraint without a greeting, hardly seeing him. She was incandescent with rage, her mouth set in a grim line, eyes staring ahead as she rushed to get away.

Chapter Eleven

Elin

O nce she'd left the management suite behind, Elin paused and leant against a wall to catch her breath. Her chest was tight with anger, her muscles trembling. How dare he speak to her like that? Michael Hardwick was a brash, unfeeling individual.

She headed up to her office, her heels beating an angry rhythm on the wooden floor. Her mind was a jumble of thoughts. It was too awful to be true. As she turned the corner to her office, she was surprised to see the same unkempt young man who had been in her tutorial group the previous day, Nick Mackenzie. She was in no mood to deal with impromptu counselling sessions.

'Ah, didn't I ask you to make an appointment?' Elin asked, in a terse voice.

Nick ignored both her question and its tone and stood blocking her way. 'I need tae talk to you 'bout my essay.'

'Not now. Make an appointment, please.'

'I emailed this morning. You didnae reply so I've come up to see you.' He stood arms crossed and legs planted in front of her door.

Elin glowered at him. She opened her mouth ready to fire off a sharp reply, but his stance, and the way he clenched his hands, made her pause. 'I appreciate you're anxious. You've an extension, though, so there's enough time. How about making a start at writing the essay and then bring me a draft?'

Nick narrowed his eyes. He looked unconvinced and made no effort to move.

'I'll read it and give you some verbal feedback. That's the best

I can do. Now, I suggest you email me and make an appointment for Friday morning, before eleven o'clock. Okay?'

With a small nod, Nick unfolded his arms and moved away from the door. A repulsive mix of body odour, cigarettes and stale alcohol wafted towards her. He slouched off but not before his mumbled words, 'Stuck up bitch,' drifted back to her.

Unsettled so soon after the meeting with the Dean, Elin entered her office, locked the door and flopped down on a chair. She covered her hands with her face.

How was she going to deal with Michael Hardwick? If he expected her to sacrifice her professional integrity, he could get stuffed. Impossible. Maybe she could get a job somewhere else... But, Mum... She needed her nearby, a weight of responsibility on Elin's shoulders as an only child.

After a while, Elin sat up, switched on her computer and started planning the next week's lectures. When the phone rang, she jumped, startled out of her concentration.

'Is that Elin Fiorelli?'

'Yes?'

'Oh, Dr Fiorelli. It's A and E here. I'm afraid your mother's had a fall and she's a little confused and upset. Could you please come over to the hospital and speak to her?'

Elin felt as though she'd been winded. 'What? Is she all right? I'll be over straight away.'

'Ask at reception. Someone will direct you. Thank you, Dr Fiorelli.'

Elin's fingers shook as she picked up the phone to ring Geraint. He'd have to cover for her. No reply so she left a message on the answerphone, hoping he'd pick it up before the lecture started.

'Bit of a crisis. Mum's in A and E. Got to go there now. Tell my students to plan their essays. I'll sort something else after. Thanks.'

Elin grabbed her keys, coat and handbag and ran to the car, driving the short distance to the hospital as quickly as she could through the rush-hour traffic. A fall. She'd always thought those oriental rugs on the wood block floors were lethal. Or had it been another dizzy turn?

After she found a parking space in one of the multi-storeys Elin hurried across to A and E. The hospital had been built in 1971, a sprawl of high blocks across an extensive site, with a duckpond in the middle. The emergency Department was the other side of an access road to the multistorey carpark. Busy, as always, with ambulances arriving and leaving at frequent intervals and people gathered outside chatting in hushed tones or smoking.

An older, overweight receptionist, with red manicured nails and lipstick to match, sat behind the screen, a latte and muffin next to her. She was kind, but firm.

'We're extra busy today. I'll pass on your details, and someone will call you. Please take a seat.'

Elin squashed herself into an empty space between an elderly couple and a young mother with a baby who screamed nonstop. She found herself drumming her fingers on her bag while she waited for news. After what seemed forever, a nurse came through and called for her.

'What's happened to my mother? Do you know how she fell?'

'Sorry, lovely, I've not been dealing with her.' The middle-aged nurse, kind face full of weariness and heavy-eyed, patted Elin on the arm. 'Your Mam's in that one, over by there.' She pointed to a cubicle partly concealed by a blue curtain.

Elin gazed over to where her mother lay on a trolley with her eyes closed. Catherine Fiorelli's face was pale, even her lips dry, chalk-like, as she lay still. Her whole figure seemed to have shrunk so that Elin wouldn't have recognised her from a distance. She approached and touched her mother's hand, caressing the soft, wrinkled skin. Mum's fingers were icy cold.

Elin exhaled with relief when her mother opened her eyes with a disorientated, almost glazed look. Then a flicker of recognition.

'Oh, Elin, dear. You're here. It was so stupid of me. I'm sorry.'

A young, energetic doctor arrived, bobbed his head to indicate for Elin to follow a little further down the corridor. 'You're Catherine's daughter? I'm Viraj, the doctor looking after your mother. She's had a bit of a fall.' He rubbed his nose, as if thinking how to proceed. 'We've just had the x-rays back. She's fractured her wrist and possibly cracked a couple of ribs.'

'Oh, no. Poor Mum. Do you know what happened?'

He hesitated, looking at his notes. 'She's a bit confused about that and doesn't seem to know if she tripped over something or not. She also says she's been having dizzy spells?'

Elin nodded.

The doctor scrutinized her face. 'Was that a concern to you or your mother?'

A good question, and Elin was unsure how to tell this young doctor, without appearing uncaring or callous, that her mother was always complaining about some ailment or another. 'My mother's had a number of minor health concerns, especially since my father died. I'm never quite sure how serious these ailments are, or how much I should be concerned.' Elin looked at his name badge. Dr Mukherjee.

'I see. Okay, we'll put that wrist in plaster and then she can go home, although I understand she lives alone?'

'Yes, but I can stay over while she recovers.'

'I think that's a good idea. We'll get her sorted and then you can take her home.'

Elin returned to where her mother was lying, eyes still closed, and moaning in pain. A cheery porter brought a wheelchair and took her to the plaster room to set the wrist, while Elin waited in the corridor outside. When that procedure was finished, Elin was glad to see Mum's cheeks had a little more colour. The porter wheeled her back to the emergency unit and they waited again for what seemed a long time.

'Right, Catherine.' A plump dark-haired nurse, with eyes crinkled at the corners, bustled up and spoke slowly to her, in a loud voice. 'We'll see you in fracture clinic in a week's time. It's busy just now, see, lots of people falling on ice. That's what winter does for us, eh? Now, lovely, we'll get you some painkillers to take home.'

Elin waited for the fireworks, the demand to be addressed as Mrs Fiorelli, but Mum said nothing and stared into space.

'Can you walk now, Mum?'

Mum pursed her lips and said, 'I think so,' in a hoarse whisper. She rose to her feet and gripped Elin's arm to steady herself. 'Oh, oh dear.'

Elin tried to hold her, but her mother's dead weight was too much for her as she slid to the floor in a faint. The nurse called out, and Dr Mukerjee, speaking to the patient in the next cubicle, came to her aid. They propped a pillow under her head, and within a minute or two, Mum was conscious again, dazed and sitting on the floor like a child.

Dr Mukerjee bent over and took her mother's pulse. 'Mmmmm. A bit fast. I'd like to keep you in for observation overnight. Now, let's get you up from here, shall we?'

Between them they lifted Catherine to her feet and on to a chair. The doctor turned to Elin. 'Are you able to stay until we find a bed? It could be some time.'

'Yes, of course.' Elin went back and sat by her mother, watching as she seemed to drift in and out of sleep. 'Mum, they're going to keep you in tonight for some tests. Once you're in the ward, I'll zip over to Sully and get your nightie and wash bag. You'll be more comfortable when you're in a proper bed.'

Mum didn't protest and her eyes were still closed, even when Elin patted her hand. Those last few words were more for her own benefit, as she twisted the signet ring on her finger.

Chapter Twelve

Elin

Elin managed, somehow or other, to cope with her mother's demands over the next few weeks in Seaview Close. Aunt Anne came to stay for the first few days, which helped ease some of the tension, before she had to go back to Kent for work appointments. Mum's friends in the village sat with her when Elin had to go to meetings or teach classes. Sue had been great, dropping by with chocolates, a book or magazine now and again. But it was Elin's idea of hell. They had been pleased with Mum's progress at the fracture clinic; while, of course, at home she was more demanding than ever. That morning she had complained about Elin's need to go to her flat in Cardiff Bay when the plumber came to fix the shower. Elin just hoped Mum would be well enough soon for them to return to normality, thankful the next hospital appointment was that afternoon.

As soon as she got into her flat, Elin went over to the big windows and slid them wide open to let in gusts of cold salty air off the Bristol Channel. Seagulls screeched their warnings as they skimmed the overcast skies, swooping down when they spotted something of interest. What a relief to be back to her own patch and a little bit of sanity in the chaos of her life at present. As the plumber worked, Elin cleaned. Tidy environment, tidy mind. She couldn't think straight otherwise.

She was just paying the plumber when she saw a call coming in from Aunt Anne. She shut the door and flopped down on the sofa.

'Darling.' Aunt Anne's husky voice had an instant cheering effect on Elin. 'How's our patient doing?'

Elin could imagine Aunt Anne raising her eyebrows in the teasing way she had. 'I've escaped for an hour or two. You know–'

'Oh, don't I just! How did you get on at the clinic?'

'Mum's appointment isn't until this afternoon.'

'Keep me posted. Got to go soon, pack for my China trip.' The jingle from Anne's bracelets accompanied this casual statement. 'I hope it goes well. She seemed more cheerful yesterday.'

Elin heard the note of concern in her aunt's voice as she rang off. Aunt Anne's way was to distract her sister with a joke or tell one of her tall tales about her travels abroad. The one about the pick pockets in Marrakesh... classic Aunt Anne. That had even got Mum laughing. Good to have Aunt Anne on your side, cheering you on.

'This way Mrs Fiorelli, Dr Fiorelli.'

A male nurse, all friendly smiles and efficiency, led them down a corridor to one of the consultation rooms in Outpatients.

'Dr Rashid will be with you in a moment. Please, take a seat.'

Elin and her mother were left alone in the small room, which was windowless and felt claustrophobic. A bead of sweat trickled between Elin's breasts. Why were these places always so hot and oppressive? A table, two chairs and a couch had been shoehorned into the space, making the room even more cramped. Elin perched on the couch, its paper covering rustling as she did so. A trace of disinfectant or bleach completed the clinical atmosphere as conversations drifted past outside the room. Neither Elin nor her mother spoke. Mum sat, seemingly engrossed in a poster on the wall warning that abuse of staff would not be tolerated. Elin rose when the young doctor arrived, feeling it was impolite to sit on the examining couch, although there was nowhere else. With an awkward movement, still struggling with her injuries a little, Mum rose too, a woman always aware of social niceties.

The doctor's young, unlined face gave nothing away, but his soft brown eyes focused on Mum. 'Thank you for coming in today.' He offered a small smile. 'My name is Dr Rashid. I'll be your first point of contact, Mrs Fiorelli. Please sit down.'

Mum dropped down onto the chair with relief.

Elin perched back on the edge of the couch as Doctor Rashid pulled over a chair and they sat in triangle formation, a small island in the space. Elin's eyes flitted back and forth, between the doctor, the wall and her mother who sat, back upright, staring at the doctor, shoulders squared, one hand clasped on her handbag, the other still in its sling. In the corridor outside people passed, muffled voices filtering through the door.

'Is there something the matter?' Elin asked. 'The fracture clinic said they were pleased with my mother's progress.'

The doctor paused and looked at Elin, checking his notes, then her face before looking down again. He clicked the top of his pen a couple of times. Why didn't he just get on with it?

'I'm afraid there is something of concern,' he replied at last. 'As you know, we've carried out some further tests to investigate why your mother might be feeling so dizzy and unwell. That's why we've had you in and out for scans and tests, Mrs Fiorelli.' He spoke in a deliberate manner, his slight Yorkshire accent just discernible.

Then he flipped open the file to consult the detail. Elin had the distinct feeling he was buying time and felt a flutter of anxiety begin in her stomach.

'I'm very sorry to have to tell you,' Dr Rashid finally said, looking directly at Catherine with sympathetic eyes, 'that the tests have shown you have an advanced cancer.'

Elin's breath stuck in her throat. Oh God, no, no, no. Her hand grasped at the paper on the couch, ripping it. Her mother stared at the doctor then blinked twice, as if not quite comprehending what he'd said.

When Catherine did speak, her voice was quiet but calm. She met the doctor's eyes, a steady gaze, almost glazed. 'Ah. That's why I've been feeling so ill.' She gripped the handle of her smart leather handbag, where it sat on her knees, her knuckles white.

'I am so sorry.' He glanced from one to the other of them. 'The symptoms you were displaying could have been related to a number of issues. That's why we've had you back in a few times to check things out. But the tests are quite conclusive. The series of blood tests, X-rays, scans. The results all give the same answer.'

'What does this mean?' Elin struggled to speak, her throat constricted.

'We are looking at an end-of-life situation. There are possible treatments to prolong life, if we had discovered the cancer earlier, but at this stage...' His voice trailed away. 'We can and will provide pain relief, of course, but I'm afraid it's too late for any other viable intervention.'

Mum seemed placid, almost vindicated, while Elin struggled to comprehend. Through a fog of emotions, she could hear Mum's voice, impassive.

'How long have I got?'

'We can never be sure about the progress of a cancer, but I suspect we're talking weeks rather than months, certainly less than six months. It's difficult to say. The cancer is aggressive and has already spread to other organs. I am surprised you have not experienced more symptoms. You must have a strong constitution.'

Mum nodded and turned, with her beautiful cornflower blue eyes towards Elin, like a child wanting reassurance or something else.

Dr Rashid followed her gaze and looked towards Elin, while addressing them both. 'When you've had a chance to speak together, we'll arrange another meeting – about next steps and what your wishes are. I realise there's a lot to take in, so I don't want to bombard you with information at this point. You will have a lot of questions, I am sure. In the meantime, let me give you...' Dr Rashid passed over a small business card, 'the details of your palliative care nurse. She'll be able to help you, explain options and answer questions. She's very experienced.'

Elin swallowed trying to keep her tears back. The lump in her throat felt huge, like a rock that had lodged in her chest.

'I'm so very sorry it's bad news,' Dr Rashid said, to Mum, who put the card into her bag, her hand trembling a little. 'Please know we are here to help and will do everything we can to support you and keep you as comfortable as possible.'

The rest of the meeting passed in a daze. As they left Mum leant on Elin's arm, and they made their slow way back to the car in silence.

❧

Later that evening, when Mum was asleep, Elin rang Jenny.

'Hi there. How's tricks?' Jenny's voice was full of verve.

'Not great. It's Mum.' Elin couldn't go on.

'Driving you nuts again? I thought the pain in her arm would have eased but I bet she's–'

'She's got cancer.' Elin's voice trembled, tears threatening. 'Terminal. I... I don't know what to do.'

'Oh shit.' Jenny's shock was clear in the rise of her voice. 'That's awful. I don't know what...'

There was an awkward silence as Elin tried to find her voice again. 'Nothing to be said. I... I just needed to tell someone. I'll have to ring Aunt Anne but...'

'God, Elin. I wish there was something I could do to help. I'm here for you. Just pick up the phone if you need someone to listen. Any time.'

'Mmmm. Thanks, Jenny. I will. Got to go, sorry.' Elin put the phone down and blinked back the tears. She couldn't start crying now or she'd never stop.

Chapter Thirteen

Michael

'Michael!'

The Vice Chancellor's clipped tones were unmistakable. Michael spun around to greet the VC, thrusting his work clothes back into the locker as he took out his towel and shower kit. Early Friday morning was his favourite time, and often his only opportunity, to get to grips with the treadmill, weights and rowing machine in the university gym. He worked out in the attic at home where he had some weights, of course, but the sociable side of the university gym was a bonus.

Michael had particularly enjoyed the workout that day. It was good to sweat off the Christmas and New Year excesses and to shake out some of the stresses and strains of the new job. God knows there were enough of them.

'So, how's it going over there in the Department?' The VC had an easy-going manner, yet with a presence, even as he stood there in his blue swimming shorts. He looked relaxed, too, much more than Michael felt.

'And the family, settling into life in Cardiff? Your wife's Welsh, isn't she? Remember what I told you? There will no escaping once you get dug in here.' Although the VC looked different without his trademark horn-rimmed spectacles, his tone of voice and stance, legs apart, arms folded, displayed the confidence of a man in charge of a university.

'Yes, John, it's all going well, thanks. Of course, there are the usual surprises.'

'Well, you'd expect that, wouldn't you?' The VC smiled urbanely, dismissing the remark with a wave of one hand before stepping towards the swimming pool.

As Michael let the warm water wash over his body, lathering with peppermint and tea tree gel, he reflected on the funding possibilities of Fonetym. He knew a couple of guys there. He could do something himself, with one or two key staff from the Department. Share out the bounty, so to speak. What was wrong with Elin Fiorelli anyway? No business was going to pay out big bucks to have their key mission rubbished. Was she really that naive?

Refreshed and feeling a pleasant glow after the exercise and shower, Michael walked back to his office. A passing thought about Nick went through his mind. He'd looked a wreck. Must find out whose tutor group he was in and get him sorted with counselling as soon as possible. But first, he had other fish to fry. The six-monthly report for the University finance committee was the biggie. Sue should be sending him her analysis on staffing by Monday. Michael appreciated her proactive approach. Showed ambition. Unlike Elin Fiorelli's negative attitude.

Michael frowned. Elin couldn't still be holding a grudge, could she? After all this time? He still remembered the intensity of their passion. Her hair had been longer then, and she'd dressed in a more casual student style. He sighed, straightened his shoulders, smoothing his hair back and preparing to do some reading for his next committee meeting, distracted for a moment by memories. Old history, life had moved on. Another time, another place, and it might have been different. But, anyway, he was happy and settled with Anwen and the boys.

The thought of his wife and children made Michael remember the funny story Iolo had told him that morning about his friend at school. He smiled. Good that they were so settled in Cardiff. Michael resolved to speak again to Elin when the time was right. She held an important key to solving the Department's problems and if she was still angry with him after fifteen years, well, it was about time she got over it.

He picked up his phone and got Sue Deacon's answerphone.

'Sue? Give me a ring back, will you? We need to talk through the staff analysis you are doing for me, for the financial report.'

He was in the thick of reading documents on a case of harass-ment being brought by a student against a member of staff, when the phone rang.

'Michael? Sorry I wasn't able to pick up. Got major probs with the electricity at home and was trying to sort it out, you know. The landlord was supposed to do it, but hey. I need to go back to the house this afternoon to see if I can get something organised. Why do these things always happen on a Friday, or over the weekend?'

Of course, she lived on her own, as he understood it, and wouldn't want to be without electricity over a dark winter week-end. 'I'm sorry to hear that. Have you had any luck getting help?'

'Yep, managed to find somebody. Hoping he'll turn up later. Those figures you want, I'll work on them at home. My report will be ready by Monday... Or, tell you what, if you wanted, you could drop by later and we could spend an hour on it.'

'Good call. Give me the address and we'll do that.' Michael put the details in his phone, reckoning, with all the pressure on him to get the finance strategy sorted, that would buy him some valuable family time over the weekend.

Chapter Fourteen

Michael

Sue's semi-detached bungalow was in a cul-de-sac. Michael checked the address again. Number forty-four, Clos Y Nant. The little houses all looked the same in the dark, pools from the streetlights leaving shadows on the ground and few numbers visible. He was in the right place but – no lights on? Maybe the electrician hadn't come after all.

He hesitated, then parked by the road. The drive was just long enough to accommodate two cars. A blue Fiesta was already in place. Michael had no idea if it was Sue's or a friend and he wasn't staying long. He walked up to the bungalow, gravel crunching under his feet on the short driveway while somewhere close by a dog barked a warning. An amber halo glowed around a full moon as it sailed out from behind a bank of dark clouds. It seemed everyone here was settling down to a cosy Friday night in.

The doorbell rang like the distant trilling of a bird. He heard muffled footsteps and then the door opened. Sue stood smiling, welcoming him. Behind her he saw candlelight and dancing shadows on the walls.

Before he could say anything, she opened the door wider and greeted him with a torrent of words. 'Oh, hey, Michael. You found me. The lights have gone again – think a fuse has blown or something, you know. I had a sort of flickering light until about an hour ago. I rang the electrician, but he can't come until tomorrow.' He saw her chew her lip for a moment in annoyance. 'There's heat from the wood burner, and I've lit candles. It's a bit like a shrine in the lounge, you know. I hope we've enough light to work with. Come on in.'

'Thanks.' Michael hesitated briefly again. Sue was flushed and dressed in a loose tunic top and wide lounge pants and something about how she looked rang vague alarm bells. She moved out of the way so that he could enter, her musky perfume heavy in the air. But if she had all those figures ready for him... God, it would be good to see some real progress.

They went into a compact lounge where everything was neatly arranged, with enough space for a small sofa piled high with cushions and a tub chair, a bright Aztec style throw draped over the back. At the heart of the room was a wood burner, placed in the original chimney breast, its flames flickering and glowing behind the viewing panel, offering a faint smoky aroma. It radiated generous heat and created its own shadow dance on the white, woodchip painted walls. There was also a low table, where a group of candles was placed beside a set of papers. Michael could see a spreadsheet on the top of the pile with scrawled notes circling names and numbers.

'Here, let me take your coat.' She went out to the hall and hurried back in. 'Glass of wine? I always find it helps me deal with problems, you know. Not in work, of course.' A sudden giggle.

The bottle was just over half-full, so she'd already made a start. Michael cleared his throat, about to respond.

Sue prattled on as she poured the deep red liquid into a glass. 'This is a Gigondas. The man in the shop said it was a good one. Are you hungry? I don't suppose you've eaten.'

'No, not yet.' Michael said. Anwen would have made something, though they weren't having their usual Friday takeaway curry. 'My wife will have something prepared.'

Sue seemed oblivious to the reserve in his tone. 'There's cheese and biscuits too. I had soup earlier. There's some left I could heat up if you'd like? Thank goodness there's a gas hob otherwise I'd be down the chip shop.'

Michael's collar was uncomfortably tight around his neck with the heat and the strange situation. Sue's behaviour was unusual, odd, her voice going on and on. Was she already drunk? Maybe. Disappointment flashed through him that he'd miss another bedtime with the children, but the job was important to all of them. He accepted a glass of wine, nodding his approval and sat down on the sofa leaning back against the cushions as he took the first mouthful. 'Mmmm. Good choice.'

The wine was a perfect temperature and a deep flavour, peppery and plummy. Michael savoured its richness as he swirled the liquid around his mouth before swallowing. He relaxed a little, loosening his tie, and moving the small mountain of uncomfortable cushions from behind him; then tensed, remembering where he was. The candlelit atmosphere felt too informal; still, the main thing was the budget and the sooner it was sorted the better.

He gestured towards the papers. 'Complicated, isn't it?'

'Yeah. We've made *some* progress though. Cutting the research budget has helped, you know, but we're still a long way from balancing the books. We've a couple of research bids which are pending.' Sue perched next to him on the tub chair beside the sofa.

'We can't rely on those.' He was leafing through. 'They may not come to anything. Facts. What we've actually got to work with, that's what we need, not figures picked from the air.'

Sue nodded, 'Yes, I realise...'

'Have you looked at everything? Staff overtime? Part-time hours?'

Sue sipped her wine then chewed a fingernail. Michael grimaced.

At last, she spoke. 'There's only one way left to cut down on outgoings. You know what that is, and so do I.'

Michael met her gaze. Sue had paled and gulped down the rest of her wine. Michael was surprised to find he'd drained his glass too. He poured another. Bugger. He closed his eyes and exhaled. When he spoke his voice was low, holding a hint of disappointment. 'Job re-allocations across courses, course rationalisation and... Have staff been informed of the situation in any way?'

Sue shook her head. 'People know there's something going on. Rumours flying. Gossip and that. But I don't think anyone is really aware that their jobs...' Her eyes filled with tears. 'What that does to people. I... I know what losing your job can do to families. It's devastating and scary.'

Michael nodded. 'My job is to sort out the finances. I can't let personal considerations take priority. If I don't tackle it, they'll just bring in somebody else who will.' He drank some more of the wine, enjoying the fruity richness of it, picked up the papers again. 'No getting round it. It's going to be a pretty rough ride.' He leant forward, scanning the staff list Sue had prepared. 'Okay, let's hit it. We'll start with those likely to be leaving in any case and then work out how much the payoff will cost against the on-going salary. That should give us some ballpark figures.' He ran a hand over his eyes, as he tried to focus on the paper, straining to see in the poor light. When he looked up, he saw Sue was brushing a tear away. 'Are you okay?'

Sue gulped the wine, still with tears in her eyes. 'Just reminded me again, you know. When my dad got the sack, it was... He sank into depression and drink. My brother got into trouble.' She paused before she went on, her voice wobbling. 'He got two years for assault. Beat up some teenage kid when he was pissed out of his head. I came to Wales to get away.' She hesitated. 'And... other reasons... It wasn't a good time.'

She gazed at the glow from the wood burner, swirling the wine around in her glass. 'I... I haven't been back. This job, well, it means the world to me, you know.' She glanced across at him. 'A proper career, like. I want to make something of myself.'

It seemed natural to lean forward and put a hand on her arm to comfort her. She blushed at the gesture. 'That sounds awful. But it's behind you now. *Your* job isn't at risk. We need your expertise.' Michael tried to cheer her up. 'You've been invaluable in getting to grips with things. This is very challenging, I know. Looking on the positive side, some of these people may be gasping for a change of direction and...' Michael shuffled the papers like a deck of cards, 'we've no choice.' He took another mouthful of wine and then let out a groan of exasperation. 'It all takes so bloody long in universities. Nothing happens quickly, not like in the real world.'

'Yeah, too true.' Sue nodded.

'It'll probably be the end of the academic year before we get it sorted. On that basis, I'll do the summary report but hold off on the detail. Gives some of those in the front line the chance to get out before they're pushed.'

Sue emptied her glass and swayed a little as she went to the kitchen to fetch a second bottle. For the next hour, they pored over the figures and discussed options.

At last Michael sat back and ran his hand through his hair. 'The way I'm seeing it, we have to lose at least three full-time senior posts, possibly more. How flexible is HR here? Do you know?'

Sue shook her head. 'We are in the University sector here. We need to work out the figures first, see what's viable, and talk to them after.'

Michael frowned. He stared at the ceiling and then down again at the array of papers. 'I hope something else turns up before it comes to that. Large-scale disruption is very bad for morale and leads to all sorts of further problems. I should know – been there before.'

'I'm sure if anyone can sort this out, you can.' Sue's blue eyes glimmered across at him in the candlelight.

Michael glimpsed, as she leant forward, how her top gaped open, displaying her ample cleavage. He tried to ignore this distraction, pondering the Department's pressing problem. 'What we need is an injection of research money. Some project with megabucks attached.' Michael skimmed down the lists of figures, puzzling over the problem, and sighed.

Sue struggled to her feet, a little unsteady. 'Oh, damn it. Need to change.' She dabbed at her wine-stained top. 'Sorry, Mike. Bit tipsy. Gotta sort this out.'

She made for the bathroom while Michael put the papers down and closed his eyes. He was wrung out. Constant pressure and not enough family time. Maybe he should take them all away for a weekend? Escape the pressure for a couple of days. Or a weekend in the Cotswolds with just him and Anwen? Some little pub with rooms, hidden away.

He heard a rustle and looked up as Sue came back, wearing a long silk dressing gown, split at the front. It was obvious there was nothing much underneath. Sensing the change in tone and the jeopardy, Michael struggled forward from the clutch of the sofa and rose to leave.

'Look, I'd better go, Sue. We can return to this first thing on Monday. I need to get home to my family now.' He hoped the mention of his children would have a sobering effect on her.

She was swaying and slurring her words. 'Don't go. Please, Mike. Not yet.'

She slid her arms around his neck, nuzzling close to him. Her perfume was lingering, seductive, and he could feel the warmth of her body through the thin fabric. He was tempted – for a second – then gently, he disentangled himself from her embrace.

'Sue, I'm flattered, but we've both had far too much to drink. I'll call a cab.'

When he got home, Anwen was waiting for him in the front room and he noticed, with a pang of guilt, how strained she looked. Her shoulder length dark brown hair was mussed, as if she'd been scrunching it while worrying and her eyes were dark with shadows beneath.

'Michael, where on earth have you been? I... I thought there'd been an accident or something. You said you'd be a little late. It's after nine now. I got really worried. The boys were in bed ages ago.' Tears filled her eyes, and she blinked in an effort to hold them back. Her arms were wrapped tight around her body.

The taste of wine was still in his mouth, stale now, and his stomach knotted when he thought how close he'd been to disaster. He paused, trying to clear his head.

'Anyway, you're here now.' She moved closer. 'The beef casserole you like is in the oven and...' She stopped and sniffed. 'You've been drinking. Where've you been? Michael?'

He tried to put his arms around her, but she shrugged him off, her body stiff, unyielding. Oh, God. How was he going to get out of this mess? 'I had to go and see a member of staff on my way home. It was urgent – about this bloody budget report. I thought if I could sort it tonight then it would be more time for us over the weekend.'

Anwen narrowed her eyes and tilted her head to one side as she scrutinized his face. 'What member of staff? And if you were working on a report, how come you've been drinking? And where's your car? That was a taxi, wasn't it?'

Michael squirmed, examining the pattern in the woodblock

floor, and becoming aware of a pain over his left eye as Anwen continued her interrogation.

'Was it a woman?'

'Anwen, my love. It wasn't like that.' Michael tried again to hold her, but she backed away. 'Look. I've got the figures here in my briefcase. I can show you exactly what I was doing. We had a glass of wine as we worked, well more than a glass. Nothing else. That's why I got a taxi home.'

'You've been out drinking with a woman on a Friday evening under the pretext of work.' She folded her arms and asked. 'Who was it?'

'Sue Deacon, the Finance Officer.' He struggled to meet Anwen's gaze. 'This six-month review is crucial, you know that.' He observed the conflicting emotions cross her face, suspicion but understanding, too, in the tightening of her jaw and the tense angle of her head as she took in what he was saying.

'The blonde one. Bit brassy? You've been with her?'

'Working on the figures–'

'And I can guess whose figure too.'

How could he convince her nothing was going on? Anwen knew all about his past, his reputation. He'd found happiness with her and would never risk that. Surely, she understood? 'Okay. I get it. You're mad at me. I don't blame you. But I swear on everything that's dear to me, you, the lives of our children–'

'Don't–'

'I am *not* having a fling with Sue Deacon.' Michael put his hand over his heart. He couldn't lose her. His family was too precious.

Anwen scrutinized him for what seemed like hours. Then she relaxed her shoulders a little. 'Okay. If I didn't love you so much...'

He felt relief flood through him as she came over and put her arms around him. Her hair smelt of flowers and cooking.

'I was so worried. I kept imagining the car in a ditch or something–'

'I know. You're right.'

'You should have rung.'

'I should. I'm sorry.' He held her close. 'I'm a selfish bastard. Tomorrow will be all family time. I promise.' The niggle of worry gnawed at his conscience as they ate. He should have known better than to go to a woman colleague's house on a Friday evening. What the hell had possessed him? And how was Sue Deacon going to react? What a bloody mess.

Chapter Fifteen

Elin

Time seemed to pass in a blur. When Elin woke one Saturday morning, she felt disorientated. Instead of the dappled shade from a blind, which she normally woke to in her flat, she was in a darker, unfamiliar setting. As she drifted from sleep back to consciousness, she recognised the floral curtains and canary yellow walls of her bedroom at home when she was a girl; half expected to hear Mum calling from downstairs, telling her to hurry up and get ready for school. Was she wasting time reading again?

Then she fully woke up and the dislocated feeling she'd experienced since the news of her mother's illness hit her hard. It was surreal and yet raw and painful at the same time. Aunt Anne's comment, pithy as always, from some talk years ago came to her, 'Life's a bitch – and then you die.'

Elin put on her old red terry towelling robe, still hanging on the back of her bedroom door, and went to see how Mum was doing. She was asleep, looking peaceful, eyes closed and her hand to the side of her face. It was heart-breaking to see how her English rose complexion was fading as the illness ate her up from inside, diminishing her daily, little by little.

With a soft sigh, Elin tiptoed out of the room again and went to the kitchen to make a cup of tea and some toast for them both. This had always been her mother's domain. Creating recipes and preparing meals in her bright and airy kitchen was where she was at her happiest. Not that she'd been doing much cooking recently. The windowsills were dusty. Pots and pans hadn't been put away.

Nothing was as pristine as it once had been. It was yet another task in a list of things Elin had to try and do.

She'd just finished preparing a tray and was on her way to the bedroom when she heard Mum call.

'Elin, are you there?' Her voice sounded weak, but bore that familiar, querulous tone, absent for the last few days.

Although over the years it had been the prelude for an argument, Elin was pleased to hear it. She tried to appear upbeat, despite a heavy heart, as she entered. 'Yes, Mum. I've brought us some tea and toast.' She bent to put the tray down on a side table, then straightened, ready to take the plate over to the bed.

Catherine was pulling herself upright and lost no time in complaining. 'Why did you use those cups? I suppose the ones I usually have are in the dishwasher.' She sniffed in disapproval. 'And I don't want toast.' Wearing her pink fleece bed jacket, she leant over to reach a brush from her toiletries bag on the bedside table, before Elin could help her and began combing her hair with fretful strokes. 'So, that's it for our family.'

'Mum–'

'And I won't have any grandchildren.' She paused putting her brush down and fixing Elin with one of her aggrieved looks. 'Do you have any idea how much I've done for you? How much you've cost me?'

Here we go again. Elin braced herself. A worn record played over and over. It was pointless to argue back.

Mum said, 'Yes... yours was a traumatic and difficult birth. Emergency Caesarean after two and a half days.' Her voice was quiet now and she seemed to be talking to herself. 'The doctor came to me afterwards, after I had lost all that blood, and told me I wouldn't be able to have any more children.'

'Mum,' Elin said, her voice tinged with amazement, 'you never told me. I thought you *chose* not to have any more children.'

'Why would I do that?' Her mother snapped back. 'Your father and I loved children. But that was it. You were the precious apple of his eye, and I was the wife who couldn't have any more. Not that Angelo wasn't proud of me.' She was in a reverie, eyes turned toward the window shrouded in their blue and pink chintz curtains. 'We had some marvellous times.' Tired with the effort of talking, she closed her eyes and soon her breath was slow and even, interspersed with soft, whistling snores.

Elin couldn't bear to stay. She picked up the tray and crept back to the kitchen, closing the door with a quiet click and leaning against it for a few moments. She couldn't manage the toast and gulped down the lukewarm tea with a throat that felt raw with emotion.

It was oppressive in the large house and airless, but she resisted the temptation to open the windows. Mum might get a chill; God knows she was fragile enough. It was as if the diagnosis had given her permission to let go any pretence of enjoying life, as though her grieving for Angelo could go free now. In between brief moments when her old feisty self showed through, Catherine was waiting to die.

Although Elin was glad she was there to help, she just couldn't stay indoors all day. She was used to a full and busy life, even at the weekends: work, research, marking, admin; going to the gym; meals out with Sue or other friends; more work. She opened her laptop and looked at her emails but couldn't concentrate; though she saw the Dean had asked to meet with her again.

She had to get out. A run to blow away the cobwebs and energise herself. She'd head down to the beach and pop in to see Sue on the way back. Elin figured that should help to put her in a better frame of mind. They hadn't spoken yet to the palliative care nurse or talked about the future. It was as if life was in suspended animation. But the conversation with the nurse needed to be arranged soon.

Outside, the usual Saturday morning life in the village was starting. Elin waved to her mother's neighbours, a young couple who'd recently moved in, as she jogged down the street. It was a beautiful morning. The air was crisp with blue skies, fluffy clouds and the sun danced on the waves by the beach. After ten minutes or so, her spirits lifted as she felt the blood pumping around her body.

What next for Mum's care? Elin knew she wouldn't be able to stay through the week in the long term with all the pressures of her job. They'd have to arrange nursing help – if Mum would agree. Then there was the research project. Preparation for the second phase was starting in a few months. So exciting, though how the hell was she going to manage that on top of everything else? The immediate problem was the conference and team meeting in Brussels. She couldn't miss that. Or could she? Nothing was clear anymore now that Mum's time was limited.

As she ran, Elin remembered the last conversation she'd had with Michael. She'd forgotten all about that. As her feet pounded the pavement, the image of his irritated face came to mind. Maybe Fonetym was why he wanted to meet again. Well, he would have another thing coming. He could go and jump in the lake. If Fonetym had concerns, they'd have contacted the project director, but... Lars Nordin was happy with her findings. It seemed Michael was playing a power game, trying to manipulate her. No way was that going to work.

Elin was close to the cul-de-sac where Sue rented. It was quiet there, mainly pensioners who stayed indoors in the colder weather. Her place was just around the next bend. The smell of the sea was fresh and invigorating. Elin stopped and took a lungful of it, revelling in how her body tingled with the exercise, feeling alive. Her mind was clearer too. She'd have a coffee with Sue, a bit of a heart-to-heart with her about Mum, and then a brisk walk back. Elin rounded the corner and came to a sudden stop, almost tripping over. There, parked in front of Sue's bungalow, was a black BMW.

Chapter Sixteen

Elin

Elin stood at the corner, heart pounding, feeling as though she'd been punched in the stomach. Michael Hardwick's car outside Sue's house at ten on a Saturday morning could only mean one thing. If Sue was sleeping with Michael, then God knows what she'd been discussing with him. Work and sex made for a toxic mix, especially when the lover was the Dean of the Department, with power over a lot of people's lives. That pillow talk could be lethal.

As Elin stood transfixed, her head was working overtime. Michael's betrayal all those years ago had changed her whole life. Sue could be too naïve, too trusting, but Elin recognised a streak of something familiar as well. She could see her own desire for advancement mirrored in Sue's hardworking attitude and the blurred lines that could arise then between personal and professional. It hurt. She had counted on Sue as a friend.

And the professorship. Was that at risk? Elin had sacrificed everything, the chance of a happy marriage and a family; and her relationship with her mother had been tainted with the drive to prove that she was as good as any man. Not just any man. One particular man. Otherwise, what had all the hard work to forge her own path been for?

Michael's words to her at the beginning of their affair echoed in her head. 'The trouble with you, my sweetheart, is that you expect everything to be perfect. Life isn't like that. My marriage is far from perfect. I've learnt the hard way that life is what you make it.'

When he'd left for that job in Scotland, Elin knew it was a way for him to escape the tangled mess their lives had become. If anyone had found out about his involvement with her, as his student, he could have been dismissed. Yet, here he was with everything, a career, a new wife and a young family. He'd gone from strength to strength, while she... And now – this.

Perhaps she should have given Sue a stronger warning about Michael's unscrupulous nature with woman. God, if she was having an affair with him now... it didn't bear thinking about. Elin wondered how long it had been going on – and the cut in the research budget had been such a blow.

She turned and half-ran, half-walked back to the house, sweating and out of breath when she arrived. Mum was, thankfully, still asleep so she had time to compose herself. She stepped into the shower and stood under the refreshing spray until she'd calmed down a little, feeling the water on her face mix with the salt of her tears.

She dressed in jeans and an oversized green sweater and drank a glass of water with hands that still trembled. When Mum next woke, Elin knew she'd be occupied with reading to her and helping her to eat a little. For the moment, she tried to untangle her thoughts and emotions.

What to do? Elin held her hands to her head as the questions tumbled over one another. Ignore it? Carry on as normal? Confront them? It was really none of her business.

She looked out into the garden with unseeing eyes as she sat slumped, her body limp, alone.

'Elin. Are you there?' Mum's voice disturbed her thoughts.

For once, Elin was glad of the distraction. 'I'm here. Can I get you anything?' She hurried to her bedside. She could see Mum was becoming weaker and thought her pale skin was tinged with yellow. The cancer had probably spread to her liver as the doctor had predicted.

'I'm thirsty.' Catherine rubbed her lips together as though she'd applied lipstick and was trying to spread the colour. 'Dying is hard work.'

Elin filled a glass of water, unable to say anything. They both knew it was true. Mum was weaker, thinner, lacking in energy and with little appetite. Weeks of worry and guilt had taken their toll on Elin as well. When she looked in the mirror, she saw that her skin had lost the honey glow and dark rings showed under her eyes. Restful sleep evaded her, and, in any case, she was often called on in the night to help. She was finding work a blessing and a curse. She needed its distraction but trying to balance everything was almost impossible.

After a light lunch of creamed rice and fruit juice, Mum slept again, and Elin got out her laptop to do some work. The TechSWell research report was almost ready in preparation for Brussels at the end of April. With a sinking feeling, Elin realised it would be impossible to go. She couldn't leave Mum, not now. Elin had already asked for annual leave to cover the conference, adding a couple more for sightseeing. Nothing had as yet been approved. Just as well. And this business of Sue and Michael. She still couldn't believe it.

Deep in thought, Elin was startled when the doorbell rang. She opened the front door to see Sue standing there. The cheek of the woman. Had she no shame? Sue wore dark glasses and seemed subdued and lacking her usual vivacity, standing there in worn jeans and a navy-blue puffer jacket. Elin searched for signs of discomfort or even satisfaction after her night with Michael, but apart from dishevelled hair everything seemed as usual.

Sue lifted her sunglasses, showing red and tired eyes, and held out a bunch of roses and a packet of chocolate biscuits. With a slight lift of the lips, she said. 'These are for your Mum and biscuits for you. I thought you probably needed some distraction. How's she today? Alright?'

With a curt nod, Elin opened the door wider and directed Sue towards the kitchen. 'The same. Sleeping a lot more. She's just dropped off again but will probably wake up soon, as she's due her meds. The nurse will call this afternoon too. They come to turn her and check that she's comfortable. That sort of thing.'

Arranging the pink roses in a vase, allowed Elin time to avoid meeting Sue's eyes. Forcing herself to be polite she said, 'Tea?' and moved the laptop to one side of the table.

'Please.' Sue scanned Elin's face as she dropped her bag onto a chair. 'You look awful if you don't mind me saying so, Elin.'

Elin lifted her head in a swift movement and faced Sue who was still talking.

'I know it's a difficult time. And, on top, you're working all the hours God sends. There's more to life, you know. Isn't it all a bit overwhelming with everything you have on?' Sue blushed under Elin's steady stare, biting a fingernail. 'I mean, have you never wanted anything else besides work? Marriage, a family?'

What timing – insensitive and naive of Sue to ask after... Elin turned away again, not responding. In the pause, she felt her eyes well up with tears. God, everything was getting to her. Grabbing a tissue, she hesitated before answering. 'Once upon a time, perhaps. Then other things happened, and I decided to concentrate on something I knew I was good at. I love my job, the research, the teaching, making a difference to people's lives and I've been lucky, so far.'

'You sound as though that's all over. Maybe you need some time off. This is hardly the way to relax over the weekend, is it?' Sue gestured to the open laptop.

Examining Sue's face again, Elin didn't reply, but those guileless blue eyes met hers with concern.

'What's the matter, Elin? You seem a bit edgy. Have I done something to upset you? Sorry if I'm intruding. Maybe you'd rather be with your Mum.' Sue bent to pick up her bag as if getting ready to leave.

Elin blurted out, 'Did you have a good Friday night? Do anything interesting?'

The question was out of context and Sue seemed startled, dropping her bag. She paled, then blushed. Elin watched her fidget in her chair then look out of the window, at the garden and beyond.

'I... it... was alright.'

'Just alright? I'd have thought Michael Hardwick was better than alright.'

'How? What?' Sue stared back at Elin, her mouth open in surprise.

A tight ball had formed in Elin's chest. Sue sat, her eyes wide, locked on hers. Elin's voice was full of hurt and accusation. 'I went for a run this morning. I thought I'd pop in to say hello. His car was parked outside. How long has the affair been going on?'

Appearing dazed by the unexpected attack, Sue couldn't answer.

'I told you he was unscrupulous. I thought you'd see past the charisma. I didn't think you were so stupid.' Elin stopped, realising she could have been talking to her own younger self.

The only sound for a moment was the fridge freezer humming in the corner as they stared at each other.

'It's not what you think.' Sue's voice was a whisper as she dropped her gaze down to her hands. She looked shell-shocked, shaking her head and gulping. 'I didn't sleep with him. We... we were working on an urgent report, we drank too much wine and I got... He didn't stay the night. I made a pass at him, he–'

'Really?' Elin tone was incredulous.

Sue's face crumpled and her voice was forlorn. 'Yes, Elin, It's true. He was charming, saying I was attractive, but his marriage came first. He seemed... oh, I don't know.' A hiccup. 'He couldn't wait to get away, you know. I'm so ashamed. I don't know how to face him on Monday morning.' She put her face in her hands.

Elin sighed, her anger and confusion deflating as she sensed that Sue was telling the truth. 'I see,' she said, 'maybe I was too...' She paused, trying to explain. She was so wound up with everything, seeing Michael's car had been a trigger, something else to fuel her overwrought emotions. And she had taken it out on her friend. 'I'm sorry–'

Sue was already leaving, with a last look back at Elin that seemed to hold reproach. The kitchen door clicked shut, followed by the heavier sound of the front door. Elin closed her eyes. Everything was unravelling and she didn't know how to stop it.

Chapter Seventeen

Michael

Two weeks had passed since Michael left Sue Deacon's bungalow late that Friday night. He'd seen her in the corridor a few times, and on the odd occasion, she'd come into his office with papers for signing. She acted as if nothing had happened, just a bit quieter than usual and didn't hang on his every word with those baby-blue eyes. But he was still uneasy. It could all go belly up.

He sat every now and then over those two weeks, in between emails at his desk, and berated himself. What a bloody fool he'd been. Idiot. What if she decided to make a fuss, accuse him of stuff? One glass of wine would have been excusable, sociable even, but... He groaned inwardly every time he thought about it. Having to leave his car and go back for it the next day smacked too much of the bad old days. What if someone had seen it? Put two and two together and made six? If only he hadn't been so focused on the damn detail. Thing was, Sue was the only staff member, apart from himself, who had the full overview. If it wasn't for that, he'd never have been there.

As the days turned into weeks, Michael began to hope he might be in luck, be able to put it all behind him. And now there was progress on the finances too. He'd identified three senior members of staff, who, if they went, would make a considerable impact in the Department's deficit. One of them was Elin, a situation he regretted, though there wasn't any wriggle room. Her belligerence over the research had shown she wasn't a team player – didn't want to play his game. Still, he'd speak to her once more.

Give her a chance for old times' sake. She was a talented research-er, and the students gave positive reports, yet, the salary saving...
and he couldn't let sentiment rule his head.

'Has Elin Fiorelli got back to you on those couple of dates I suggested for a meeting?' Michael asked Jodie later that morning.

'No. Nothing yet.' Jodie was busy tidying her desk for a half day's leave, meeting her fiancé to go over their wedding plans. She was entitled to the time off, but it didn't stop him feel another prickle of irritation. She was much more enthused and committed to her life outside work and it showed in lots of small ways. For now, he'd let her be.

'Ring her up, will you, please, before you go off and get a meeting fixed up. I need to see Dr Fiorelli as soon as possible.' Michael sensed, rather than saw, Jodie's aggrieved expression as he turned and strode back into his office.

After a couple of focused hours reading up on risk assessment and management for a meeting with the VC's special working party, Michael glanced at his watch. He'd arranged to pick up Gareth from school and take him to football practice. It would be a welcome change to spend some time with his boy and not think about work for a while.

When Michael arrived, a straggle of parents was already lining the pitch, assembled near the concrete path and trees that ran alongside the playing field. A cold wind gusted across the park and threatened to send some of the lighter equipment the coaches had laid out spiralling to the no man's land in the centre of the field. Intermittent spitting rain added to the bleakness. Most of the spectators were wrapped up warm for the duration, some with folding chairs and thermos flasks.

Michael approached the group, nodded to one or two he knew and then caught up with his brother-in-law, Osian, greeting him with a friendly punch to the arm. 'Haven't missed much, have I? Didn't realise they were playing a match today.'

'Oh, it's just a friendly. Gives them a bit more motivation than skills practice. Haven't seen you for yonks, mind you.' Osian stamped his feet to keep the circulation going.

Michael wrapped his tartan scarf closer round his neck, appre-ciating its warmth and softness. 'Yes, Anwen's been bringing the boys.'

'Busy at work?' The glance Osian gave him was searching.

What did Osian know? Had Anwen said anything? 'You could say that.'

They stood on the side-line watching their sons play. Since coming to Cardiff, Michael had got to know Anwen's younger brother a lot better. Not a bad bloke, Osian. Reminded him of her, same dark Celtic looks, and he was interesting to talk to, footie and cricket. Osian's hobby, or obsession, Anwen said, was collecting antiques. He'd taken Michael to a couple of auctions, and they'd gone for a few bevvies after in Michael's local, The Horse and Groom.

'Pass! Pass!' Osian screamed downwind to his son and then another glance sideways and up at Michael. He raised an eyebrow. 'Full-on, is it? You look a tad troubled, old son. Something brewing?'

Michael half-smiled, smoothing his hair back where it had been ruffled by a blast of wind. 'Whatever makes you think that? Couple of potentially sticky situations, you know the score...' His voice trailed off as he considered how much to divulge. 'To be honest, I'm not quite sure how the job's going, or what I'm doing at the moment. Has Anwen spoken to you?'

Osian shook his head so that the grey bobble on the top of his blue wool hat bounced. 'Just that it's all busy, busy. But that's you, isn't it, mate?' He nudged Michael with his elbow. 'You know I'm here as a sounding board if you want to talk through anything.'

'Thanks, appreciate that,' Michael hesitated, 'though it's all a bit hush-hush. I probably shouldn't talk to anyone outside the university.'

Osian laughed and shrugged his shoulders. 'Hey. I'm a solicitor, remember, as well as your brother-in-law. Any secrets would be treated in the utmost confidence – unless you've committed a murder, of course.'

Michael forced a laugh. More likely he'd be the victim if Sue Deacon told Anwen about that evening. 'Actually, I would welcome a chat through. How about we meet up for a pint at the weekend and I could run the scenarios by you?'

'Sure.' Osian peered up at Michael, holding his rain splattered glasses in one hand. His eyes were hazel and almond-shaped, ringed by dark lashes, almost the same as Anwen's. 'Doing the usual, are you? Pitching in and saving the institution? Getting rid? God, I'm glad I never worked in one of your departments.'

'That's a bit harsh.' Michael narrowed his eyes at that remark, even though it was couched in friendly, male banter. 'You don't know the half, Osian. I went through hell with the last lot. Anyway, thing is, this one's more complicated. For starters, I want to stay here. You can see how happy Anwen and the boys are. And this job could lead to more things in the university . . .'

He watched his son sprint down the pitch. Gareth was a promising player. Michael cupped his mouth against the wind and shouted. 'Great goal, well done!'

There was a whoop and cheer from the team as the match ended. They'd won. Osian put his hand on Michael's arm to share the pride before he joshed in his usual bantering way. 'Next weekend then. I hope I can provide absolution, or at least a possible solution, to your problems.'

They'd collected their sons and were heading towards the car park, when Michael noticed a couple getting up from a bench a little way ahead. They seemed an odd pairing. The girl was dark-haired and attractive, but the man – with shoulder-length hair – looked as though he'd slept rough. They walked slowly, holding hands, and absorbed in conversation.

Something in the young man's gait and overall appearance jolted Michael's memory. Could it be Nick? He looked again and was sure. The girl was steering Nick along in a way that made Michael wonder. He hadn't been able to check with the counselling service to see if Nick had taken his advice and sought help. Confidentiality. He'd just have to hope for the best. At least Nick had kept his word and stayed out of the way, and out of trouble.

Michael saw the boys were drifting further off into the middle of the park, as the wind skewed their passing shots. He didn't want to catch up with Nick in the park where anyone and everyone could hear what was going on. And he certainly didn't want to risk another awkward encounter with Nick while Osian was there pricking up his ears and reporting back to Anwen.

'Gareth, come here,' Michael shouted, and waved to the boys.

They dashed back, panting and laughing, buzzing after having won the match. Michael took a sharp left towards another exit out of the park and almost nudged Osian over in his haste.

'Steady.' Osian shoved him back. 'Where's the fire?'

'Quicker this way.' Michael hardly paused to see if Osian and his boy followed. As they got to the edge of the park, he draped an arm over Gareth's shoulder and pulled him closer. 'Nice one today, son. You did great.'

He had an uncomfortable sensation, as they went through the gate, that Nick had recognised his voice and was watching.

Chapter Eighteen

Elin

Evidence that the year was turning surrounded Cardiff Bay as Elin gazed down from her apartment window. It was a peaceful scene where a few swans floated on the still water and a couple of sailing boats could be seen in the distance. The sky blushed pink and seemed a little lighter with each passing day. Snowdrops had made an appearance and the other spring flowers, crocuses, daffodils and tulips were bursting their way through the earth towards the light.

She flopped on the sofa, relieved to be home again. Her welcome safe haven. She'd given a cheery wave to Rhys, the concierge, on her way in. He always seemed to be about, watchful, at the door to his office, waiting to talk, offering to help as she carried bags back and forth from the car. Stocky with a bent nose and chipped front tooth he was the sort vagrants or drunken revellers wouldn't argue with, but he was soft at heart. She'd told him about her mother's illness.

'Nasty thing, cancer, it is.' His full lips gathered spit as he talked. 'My Mam went that way too. Hard to watch. Don't you worry about your flat, Dr Fiorelli. I'll keep an eye, as always, I will now. If you need someone to go in and check on things, just let me know.'

It was good to have words of support. The cancer had Catherine in its grip, devastating her body, turning her sallow-skinned, thin and fragile. Elin could feel her mother's bones through her clothing when she helped her to sit up in bed and saw how every

movement was difficult. She longed to be able to relieve her suffering and thought back to what Dr Rashid had said. 'It's a stage
four. One of the most aggressive cancers I have seen. Nothing we
can offer except palliative care. I'm so very sorry.'

Elin's whole world had rocked and his words echoed in her
mind as a terrible refrain. The rapidity of the disease had shak-
en her, made her duty-bound to prioritise this last time with her
mother, whatever other demands she had on her. She couldn't
ease Mum's pain, but she could sort the best nursing care and give
her as much time as possible, squeezing in her work, and all its
pressures, as and when she could.

She called into the house in Seaview Close every day. It
was a huge emotional strain – on top of which she knew Mum
would like her to be there full-time. But she avoided that for
now. It hurt too much to see her once-feisty mother deteriorate.
Meanwhile, her job was a guilty relief, a distraction. While she
was engrossed by that, the nagging grief and worry receded for
a little while.

Elin worked from her flat as much as possible with her mobile
on the table, ready to jump into the car at any moment if the nurse
called. Apart from other tasks, at this time of year there were large
numbers of assignments to mark and she spent hours assessing
essays online. It was time-consuming and she had to concentrate
in bursts, but she was slowly getting through it. Most of the results were good which pleased her as she was reading through.
The work generally showed an interest and commitment to the
topic. Only a few of the essays she marked were poor, one in particular, and she thought a long time about the grade. She read
through the piece again, very much a borderline case, looking for
evidence of reading and reflection on the topic. After some time,
deliberating, she typed '42' into the spreadsheet and emailed it
to the Examinations and Assessment Office. Tick. Another set of
assessments completed.

Time to inform Professor Nordin that her presence at the Brussels conference was impossible. She drummed so hard on the
keyboard it sounded like tap dancing on a wooden floor, giving
frenzied vent to her pent-up anger and frustration:

I'm sorry I can't be at the conference, as my mother is dying.
My boss wants me to lie about my stay in Finland and say
that I really, really missed having emails bombard me every
waking minute. He also wants me to tell you that my life on-
line is more important than what I do from day to day.

She read it back and laughed with a touch of hysteria, slumping back in the chair, her emotion spent. Well, I can't send that. The last step towards my professorship and it has to be thrown away. God, Mum, why couldn't you have picked a better time to die? Elin had never missed having a sibling growing up. Now, with her mother so desperately ill, she wished she had someone close to share the burden of her worries. Not some faceless person from a charity, as the doctor had suggested.

'Get a grip. This isn't the time to fall apart. Be strong. Get on with things. Focus.' Her solitary voice seemed to echo around the room. She slouched at her kitchen window, hands cupped round her coffee mug, looking out at all the people milling around in the Bay, busy leading their lives. How easy to imagine no one else in the world had her problems. But it was time to stop feeling so sorry for herself. With a determined movement, Elin straightened. Mum was her responsibility and, however difficult it became, she'd do what she could to make her death an easier journey. Except... do what exactly? All she could do was be there with her when it came to the time. Mum was right, dying was hard work.

The phone rang. A welcome disturbance. She got to her feet, and answered, while looking over the water below. 'Elin? 'Sue's voice sounded hesitant. 'Elin? Are you there? I need to speak to you.'

'Yes, sorry. I was miles away. Is something the matter?' A pigeon landed on her balcony fixing her with a beady eye and then flying off again.

Sue's voice seemed quieter than usual, subdued even, as if she was afraid of being overheard. 'Look, I know things haven't been good between us –'

'It's a very difficult time... with Mum. I'm–'

'I understand and I'm sorry to bother you. I hope I can have a chance to explain stuff . . . when things settle a bit. But, well, that's not why I rang. I thought I'd better warn you.'

Elin frowned. 'Warn me?' she repeated. 'Has Michael made a pass at you? Or harassing you because of, well, you know?'

'No, no. Nothing to do with that. Something else, very confidential and I shouldn't even be talking about it but, well, we've been friends and...'

'For God's sake. What the hell is it? Spit it out.' Elin clenched her jaw, wishing she could see Sue's face.

At last, Sue answered, although her voice sounded taut and nervous, 'You remember what I told you – about the Department's money problems?'

'Yes, and stopping the research budget with all the other cuts sorted it, didn't it?'

A silence followed. Elin blinked as an awful thought occurred to her. She should have realised. 'Oh, my God. He's going to reorganise and lose posts. Don't tell me your job's going? Oh, Sue. How awful. That's shocking.'

Sue coughed before she replied. 'I think *my* job should be okay. They can't really do without a finance officer. No, it's... There're other possible changes. No one's safe, you know. I just wanted to warn you. There'll have to be further cost-savings. Staff who teach a lot are probably alright, but it might not be like that for everyone.' Sue's voice sounded almost panic-stricken. 'I just wanted to warn you. You mustn't say a word to anyone. Promise?'

Elin's heart was beating faster, and it took an effort to respond. 'I promise, of course. I won't breathe a word to anyone. And Sue, thank you. I owe you.'

There was a grunt of acknowledgement at the other end of the phone before the click indicating the call had ended. Elin's head was spinning. Her legs felt weak, and she sat down before they gave way altogether. Sue wanted her to know how serious the situation was. She'd taken a risk phoning her at all. Maybe they had a shortlist already of vulnerable personnel; people who were likely to leave, or who ran unviable courses, or whose salaries would make a good saving. Maybe her name was already on there. She was a senior member of staff and with all the stuff about Fonetym... Elin felt her stomach heave. She had to speak to someone. Aunt Anne was abroad until next week.

She dialled Jenny's number and prayed she could answer. She should be on her lunchbreak.

'Hello? Everything all right?' Jenny answered straight away.

'Oh, God.'

'What is it? Your Mum—'

'No. Oh, Jenny' She was trembling, hand shaking. 'Something else I've just heard. Sue told me they're cutting jobs.'

'So,' Jenny said, 'you think Sue was hinting your job might be at risk?'

'I'm sure of it. She's been working with Michael Hardwick and HR for weeks and...' Elin gulped. 'I think she's got insider knowledge – pillow talk, sort of.'

'What? You mean...?'

'I saw his car outside her house. She denied it but we both know what he's capable of, don't we?'

'Typical.' Jenny paused a moment. 'So why did she tell you this? Can you trust her?'

'Um. Don't know.' Elin put a clammy hand to the base of her neck as a wave of panic washed through her body. 'I can get another job but not at the drop of a hat and I can't worry about this now.'

'How *is* your Mum?'

'Declining fast, but she has good days and bad days. The carers are amazing.' Elin bit her lip and sniffed.

'Don't beat yourself up. You're doing the best you can.'

Elin remembered those words as she lay staring up the ceiling in the early hours. Even though there'd been whispers of job losses floating around, Elin had ignored them as scaremongering. People liked to create dramas out of nothing. Now it all looked different. She had a hefty mortgage on the flat and what she thought was a successful career. Her life since... well, it had been devoted to work but now it seemed everything was crumbling. She recalled her recent conversations with the Dean, and, shuddering, felt sure her name was on that list of staff at risk. Michael had been the cause of shattering all her dreams when she was younger. Blighting her career was just another, different, way of destroying her life. But she'd be damned if she'd give that up without a fight.

Chapter Nineteen

Elin

I t was a fine Sunday evening, and the hazy light of dusk was
just setting in as Elin returned to her flat in Cardiff Bay. The
hyacinths were coming into bloom in the pots by the main entrance, their tender blue flowers opening towards the light with
their delicate fragrance. How many weekends had she been doing
this run? Felt like forever.

Elin began the climb up to her flat noticing the communal
stairs seemed extra clean. Somebody must have seen to that after
the residents' committee had complained. She dumped the shopping and weekend case in the hall, put lights on all over the flat
and went to fill the kettle.

Blast. The papers she needed were still in the car. She stopped
midstride, leaving the coffee jar open on the draining board. Grabbing her keys, she ran downstairs and out to the car. In the short
time since she'd arrived, it had gone from dusk to dark. The wind,
blowing off the sea with a salty tang, made her shiver; her coat
left upstairs in her haste. Elin knelt on the back seat, leant over to
collect her papers and briefcase and felt the muscles in her lower
back twinge; an old injury and another outcome of going backwards and forwards to Mum's and not taking enough care of herself. With a faint groan of discomfort as she eased out of the car,
she made a mental note. A visit to the gym one lunch hour that
week was called for if this punishing schedule was to continue.

Straightening, with some difficulty, while clutching her bag
and papers ruffled by the wind, she heard the sharp crack of a

twig nearby. Elin froze for a second, sensing there was a figure in the shadows to one side of her car. When she turned to look properly, though, there was nothing to be seen. Adrenaline coursed through her body. It was almost too quiet. But then she shook herself. There was no one there. A cat or fox perhaps, prowling in the undergrowth in search of food. Tiredness was making her jittery. Elin looked towards the bright lights, glowing globes on the path leading to her building, and hurried back inside, into the warm lobby.

Once in her own flat, she switched the television on and poured a glass of wine, leaving the boiled kettle to cool. To hell with coffee. She needed something stronger. She crossed to the window to pull down the blind and glanced towards her car and the spot where she thought she had heard someone.

Nothing. She was imagining things and it showed how she was way too tense. With a wry smile, she turned to the television and tuned into some celebrity reality piece. She kept it on mute as she often did, just there for background company. Her store of well-being, which had been so well-stocked during the three months in Finland, was depleting fast. An aching back and twitchy nerves were sure signs that she was in a far from good place, mentally or physically.

Being aware of the problem wasn't going to solve it and there was too much else happening anyway. Elin put the cool wine glass to the centre of her forehead above her eyebrows where a headache was beginning. Ever since her mother's prognosis, she had been in a sort of dream-like state. Mum had always been so strong, with an iron will, as though all the things she complained about were irritants, rather than something that could harm her. But now it seemed Mum wouldn't see another spring.

Elin curled her legs up on the sofa, put the volume up and tried to watch the television. She couldn't concentrate. In her mind's eye, she relived incidents from the last few weeks. The everyday and mundane features of their time together was boring and painful, but they both knew it was precious; the last time they would do these things. In fact, they hadn't spent so many hours in each other's company for a very long time. Elin asked herself how that had happened, and the answer was simple. She was always so busy, and Mum didn't like leaving the house for long, or going away on holiday. Their Scandinavian trip to see the Aurora Borealis would never take place. It was all too sad to think about.

Elin took a large swig of her wine and spoke to herself in a firm tone. 'It isn't all my fault. We're just two very different people. There's no getting away from that. And she's been a bloody nightmare at times over the years.'

Then, another vivid memory, of Mum trying to raise a skeletal arm to brush her hair. She'd always taken such pride in herself. Elin found she still had more tears from the well of her sorrow, although she'd cried so much over the last weeks. They coursed a salty stream down her face, and her heart ached as she remembered.

A few weeks before, they were sitting in the kitchen. The evening sun was glowing in and tinting the room with an amber glow. Elin sat with her back to the window and the shape of her bob was outlined against the light. She'd been almost startled when Mum put her hand out to follow the curve of the cut.

'I like that style, Elin,' she said. 'Where do you go for your hair now?'

'Oh, this was at one of the salons in town,' Elin had said, putting her mug down on the table. Having a good haircut was one of her luxuries and she always went to a top stylist. 'Now that Tony's retiring, I needed to find somewhere else, and the new stylist suggested I grow it a bit longer.'

'I'd like to have my hair done again soon,' Catherine said, 'it's in such poor condition now.'

That had been the cue for Elin to take Mum to the hairdressers and at the time it had given her a boost. Mum always liked salons and beauticians. After they got home though, she collapsed with exhaustion, and they had to call a doctor out, a locum on emergency cover. When he took Mum's pulse, he frowned and told her not to overexert herself.

'But I can rest all I want when I'm dead,' Mum had retorted, with an echo of her previous spirit.

It was all so difficult. Elin wiped the tears off her cheek and channel hopped. She was doing the best she could, but there was no
point pretending either of them had become different people.
Elin's default position had always been to steer towards superfi-
cial things like clothes, hair and fashion. They had such profound
differences of opinion – politics, gender roles and why Elin didn't
have a husband and children. Not that Mum held back when the
mood was on her, Elin recalled with rueful and irritated love.

After finishing her glass of wine, Elin took out her laptop. She
was enjoying writing her book on well-being and the influences of
nature, using a more general and accessible style than in the many
research papers she'd written. It was almost a type of therapy,
a change from routine, a way to escape from pressing thoughts.
And somehow, despite heavy eyelids, she managed to finish her
preparation for the morning too.

But when Elin closed the computer and stretched, she realised
just how tired she was. She padded into the bedroom and stood
by the window ready to draw down the blind. With a shock, she
thought she saw someone standing by her car and staring up towards her flat. Dark clothes, pale face. She leant forward to get
a better view, but the figure disappeared into the shadows. Her
breath came in shallow waves, and she put her hand to the wall.
Once the blood settled and she felt steadier, she drew the blind
down. Was she imagining it? She needed to get a grip. It was just
somebody parking. Or maybe there wasn't even anybody there.
It could have been a shadow from the trees, a reflection from one
of the other flats perhaps. Despite this reasoning, she shuddered,
annoyed with herself. She wasn't usually spooked, thinking she'd
seen things. Elin got ready for bed and set her alarm, but the uneasy feeling persisted. As she switched off her side light, she tried
to shake her mind out of a sense of foreboding and premonition
by remembering some of her adventures when she was in the
wilds of Scandinavia. The Elk Incident had been pretty amazing.

That had happened a couple of weeks after she'd arrived. She
was in the kitchen, making her lunch, when she heard heavy foot-

steps approaching the back door. She'd been nervous then, too. But that was hardly surprising in an unfamiliar place; and getting used to being without technology. The surprise came when she'd gone to the door to see who it was and opened it, the sight of a huge deer, its bulk filling the whole doorway making her gasp. She'd never seen such a large, wild animal at close quarters before. It stretched its head forward towards her, looking at her enquiringly with large, soulful brown eyes.

Then from behind, Wolf had shouted, 'Elk. Quick. Close the door. Hurry.'

She'd slammed the door shut with a strength she didn't need in her everyday life. Elks came sometimes into gardens in search of food at that time of year, Wolf had said, and they could be dangerous; she'd been lucky it hadn't attacked. He showed her afterwards where a shot gun was kept securely inside a cupboard in the boot room. He told her it was there to be used in emergencies – such as to scare off bears. Elin had nodded but decided that was not something she'd try, never having handled a gun in her life. But their visiting elk had wandered off through the snow after rooting around in the garden and they hadn't seen it again.

Sleep was elusive as Elin lay in her bed, in Cardiff Bay, trying to distract herself with this memory. In the end, she managed a restless night, slipping in and out of sleep, images of the elk, her mother and shadowy figures mingled together in her mind.

Brrrrrrrrr!

The alarm woke her the next morning, its insistent ringing disturbing her dreams. Dragging herself from sleep to silence it, she saw she'd slept through the original call and now was late. She snatched a quick glass of apple juice and a piece of fruit on her way out. Rhys was at his office door but, as she hurried past to the car, she only had time for a rushed, 'Got to dash. Late.' Maybe she'd mention the figure she thought she'd seen last night when she next caught up with him.

The delayed start led to more stress, as all the way across Cardiff, there was heavy, queuing traffic, exhaust fumes clogging the air – and then she couldn't find a parking space on campus. She went around and around and ended up in a very tight spot, with the passenger side inches from a wall. 'Great. This day's getting better and better,' she mumbled under her breath. High heels clicking, she hurried up to her office to grab a couple of things before her lecture. As she got closer, she could see a piece of paper stuck into the door jamb. Taking out her swipe card she pulled the note from the door. She supposed it was from John Lopez, the visiting academic, warning her about something – computer maintenance, or the new shelving that was due.

The typewritten note in capitals said: I AM WATCHING YOU.

Chapter Twenty

Elin

It was bad enough being late for work. Elin tutted. Really, what now? She frowned as she read the words. Was it for Charity Aid week, some weird way of raising money? That had sometimes resulted in bizarre stunts like 'wrong trousers day' or that time when students abseiled from the top of B block. Or was it someone's idea of a sick joke? What stupid nonsense. She scrunched the note into a ball and threw it into the wastepaper bin. God, how she hated to start the week in the wrong mood. The office smelt musty again, so she opened the window, letting a cold draught whisk around the room, a couple of papers flapping in its path. Five minutes should refresh the stale air and help get some of the bad temper out of her system.

Elin moved back to the door, which she had left open, and peered up and down the corridor. 'Hello. Anyone there?' Her voice echoed. She checked for evidence of paper sticking out of any of the other doors. Nothing. The hairs on the back of her neck stood to attention. She was alone. All her colleagues seemed to be out. Should she tell anyone about the note? Some staff would be teaching, of course, and others working from home. Walking to the end of the corridor, Elin peered over the balustrade. There was no one to be seen. Then the slam of a door and whistling, becoming fainter, as an unseen figure retreated. Whoever had been in the building had left. And probably it was nothing to do with the note.

When she returned to her office Elin retrieved the paper, read it again, and with a snort, crumpled it even smaller and threw it back into the bin. Best place for that. She pushed the unpleasant words out of her mind as she settled down to the day's tasks.

There was sifting work to be done on her diaries from the Finland trip. It was illuminating to look at them retrospectively and Elin sighed while recalling how relaxed and alive she'd felt during that time. She found the place where she had started to code her entries in the diary to help her see which activities had produced a more calm and grounded state. Life without technology had taken on a different pace and focus in the study house. But coding was a time-consuming and absorbing process so she decided not to dive into that just now. She needed to read through the reports from other members of the research groups first. No doubt Wolfgang Richter's account would paint a different picture from hers.

Elin smiled while recalling how he'd almost leapt on his mobile phone as soon as it was returned to him. He'd simply waved when she left, being already too busy chatting away on his phone and swiping screens. However, in a few days, once settled back into his normal work and life routine, he had been in touch to talk about their joint research paper. She wondered if the addictive nature of technology would form part of the project's findings. It was almost inevitable. She suspected it would feature strongly as a negative, but that could also be a highly contested issue, given the usefulness and 24-hour access of technology for people such as Wolfgang. Brussels was going to be interesting.

Her mind moved on to the staff meeting in the afternoon. These meetings left her with a sinking feeling in the pit of her stomach, dreading the tedium of it all. Too many people who, as far as she was concerned, liked the sound of their own voices. The staff members fell into two groups. In the first were those who argued every point and talked non-stop regardless of their audience. The second group tended to display their boredom by either working on their tablets, doodling or doing the crossword in the paper. A couple of staff had even fallen asleep on occasion and had to be prodded awake. Elin usually said as little as possible. She'd learnt a lot about her colleagues by just observing them.

❖

At two o'clock most of the staff were gathered in the lecture theatre. Nearly everyone seemed to be present and there was an anticipatory buzz, people chatting and moving around finding somewhere to sit. The email summoning them had been worded to stress the importance of this particular meeting and attendance was obligatory. Elin noticed Sue near the front with a sheaf of papers. She was biting her nails and shifting in her seat, no doubt on edge in case she was called on to speak. Some people hated public speaking and Sue was one of them. Elin would have liked to whisper a word of encouragement but preferred to sit near the back where she could watch and blend into the sea of bodies. Poor Sue was in the spotlight.

Most folk seemed quite relaxed. Elin squeezed in beside Geraint and noticed the smell of cigarettes coming from his clothes and peppermint from the gum he was chewing. He'd told her he was giving up smoking on doctor's orders.

'Everything alright? Do you know why he's called us all?'

'I've a bit of an idea, *blodyn*, but he's keeping his cards close to his chest. I... well, we'll see now, won't we?'

He was a bit fidgety, and Elin's body responded to his tension. She twisted the ring on her finger and tried to breathe slowly, like in yoga classes. Elin hadn't seen Michael, as Dean, in a formal setting like this before. No doubt he'd exude charm and charisma, as well as power.

At two minutes to two, with a flurry, Michael Hardwick entered the lecture theatre. A few people nodded or smiled at Michael as he made his way down the steps to the front of the room. The podium stood in the middle of a raised platform and a huge screen was the backdrop with the university logo of two swans and a tree in the corner. He took his place on the stage and waited, glancing around the room. Squaring his shoulders, he rested his hands on the podium and, at two o'clock indicated, with forefinger raised, for the door to be closed. An expectant hush fell over the crowd. The hum of conversation ceased as all eyes turned towards the stage.

Apart from a couple of coughs, there was silence. Elin could see people sitting up, eyes front. When he was certain he had everyone's attention, Michael began to speak. He used the microphone, and his voice was clear, articulate, reverberating through the lecture theatre as he spoke.

'Well, good afternoon, colleagues. Thank you all for coming this afternoon. I apologise for insisting so strongly on attendance, but this is a vital meeting and will affect the future of the Department.'

Michael paused for a moment. Despite herself, Elin had to admire his timing and presence. He had control and was prepared to use it to his advantage. He was brimming with confidence. She could see he knew just how to work a large audience.

'The first thing is to inform you that Huw Bevan, the Dean, is making a good recovery. I'm aware of your concerns for him and know you will be relieved at that news.' A general hum of approval greeted those words, but Michael was just starting to deliver his message. 'I'm also aware of rumours and gossip about the workings of the Department. I was brought in to deal with the severe financial difficulties, and so far, we have been able to make some savings by cutting the research budget and pausing promotions.' A murmur followed that with a few people exchanging comments with their neighbours. 'Unfortunately, those cuts have not been sufficient to pull us out of the red. Let me show you.'

Geraint made a sound somewhere between a grunt and a groan.

Elin nudged him with her elbow. 'Are you okay?'

He turned bleary eyes towards her and made a half-shrug. So, he'd been expecting something like this. Elin inclined her gaze towards the podium again where Michael was demonstrating, by PowerPoint, the seriousness of the situation.

With a click of the button a graph appeared on the screen behind. Michael stood to one side, using a laser pen to point at the graph. 'Here we have the projected income for the next year,' he moved the laser, 'and here the deficit. As you can see, our projected deficit is a worry. We are still in the red and by quite a margin. It's not a problem that is going to be solved easily but it must be addressed for the sake of the future of the Department.' He paused with one or two final slides, ready to conclude his presentation and take questions, but before he could move on, he was interrupted.

'What does that actually mean? Are there going to be job loss-es?' The union representative, Maelog Griffiths, stood up from his place in the centre of the theatre and glared across people's heads at Michael. His grey hair flopped into his eyes, and he pushed it back with an impatient gesture as he asked his questions.

Michael looked levelly at the union man, drawing himself up to his full height. His glance took in the rest of the room. 'I appre-ciate your concern. The bottom line is if members of staff leave, they're unlikely to be replaced under the recommendations I've made to the board. As I have repeatedly explained during this meeting, the financial problem is huge, much more serious than we first thought. Our biggest expenditure is staffing costs – which is why as a further measure there will be no promotions for some time, even for those who were in the process of being upgraded. This will, of course, be reviewed as we monitor the situation.'

Elin heard a few disgruntled mutterings and there was an air of discontentment in the room that was almost tangible. Some people shook their heads, while others turned to the union rep-resentative to see his response. He was taking notes, scribbling in his notebook.

It was incredible. Elin gritted her teeth. All her hard work, years of study, research bids and the promise of the professorship gone in a flash. It was her turn to react with a sigh. Geraint seemed to be sinking deeper into his seat.

But Maelog wasn't to be easily dismissed. 'So, are there go-ing to be job losses?' He spoke, with a deliberate slowness and slapped his notebook for effect, glaring at Michael.

It seemed as though everyone in the room took a breath at the same time. A shocked silence was followed by murmurs and shuf-fling, while people exchanged alarmed glances. Michael's eyes met Elin's for a few seconds, then he looked away.

'I can't say for definite at this moment. The report has been presented to the board and is in the process of being approved. We won't have further details until after the Easter break, but we'll work closely with HR and the Unions should job losses be involved.'

'Why can't you answer? Maybe you won't answer. You were

brought in to be the hatchet man. I'm going to ask you again. Are there going to be job losses?' In a state of agitation he was wagging a finger at Michael, his notebook flapping in the other hand, and he seemed to be unable to stand still.

The pleasant smile had left Michael's face replaced by a bland expression, and Maelog, despite his insistence, seemed to have paled as he waited for the response.

Michael continued to explain the cuts to the budget. 'If I may continue; in addition, if new teaching is required in the future, due to increased student numbers, for example, or new courses, we shall look to redeploy staff. If we do need to recruit from outside the Department then any new members of staff will start at the bottom of the scale. We shall implement performance management so there may not be automatic incremental increases in salary. These are some of the recommendations I have made.'

Most voices were raised in protest, and it looked as if chaos would follow. Geraint groaned, louder this time. Elin knew he was hoping for promotion as he was on his second marriage and had two families to support. Michael Hardwick stood still, his face betrayed no emotion, as if knowing it was unwelcome news, yet seeming prepared for the battle. Elin thought he'd make a good politician, having managed to avoid answering the question by giving them enough information to create a scene, a distraction. Maelog was taking more notes, scribbling and shaking his head in disbelief. Elin felt a shiver cross over her. She was sure Michael knew more than he was saying. Had Sue's warning been more than just a friendly gesture? Did Sue, too, know more?

Elin had a growing premonition she was in the firing line. She had felt it when Michael's eyes met hers in the lecture theatre. Damn the man. She'd have to fight for her job, would she? Well, she was no longer a naïve student to be used and manipulated. She'd show Michael Hardwick just how much she'd changed.

Chapter Twenty-One

Elin

As the computer screen blinked in front of her, Elin closed her eyes for a moment and sighed. She considered the email she'd just opened from Lars Nordin. The final schedule for Brussels and list of papers were exciting. They showed the TechSWell programme was already delivering on its aims, and the project conference provided the ideal forum to discuss and debate the issues. But there was no way she could get to the meeting. This was the first time she could ever remember that she hadn't been able to attend a planned conference or research meeting. People joked about it, about her dependability. Once, in Vienna, with a broken ankle, she still managed to hobble up to the lectern, on crutches, to give her paper.

But that was then. Now, it wasn't about her. Every day, it seemed, Mum was getting weaker and weaker. Elin had been called to Sully early the previous day. The nurse said Catherine was agitated and seeing her daughter might help soothe her, calm her down, so she'd driven like a maniac to her mother's bedside. It meant that Elin hadn't got back home to her flat, ready for an early start at work the next day, until after eleven. Exhaustion and disappointment caused her to sigh again and she rested her head on her hand, staring at the computer screen.

Her roommate was in the office for the day, a rare occasion. John Lopez, early thirties, earnest, with a square jaw and physique that revealed his prowess in basketball, heard the sound and looked up from his computer. The passing sound of footsteps in the corridor outside and the buzzing from the computers hadn't masked the sigh. 'You okay?' he asked, concern in his voice.

'So, so. It's hard going just now with my mother and work. All too much at times. I'm going to take a break. Do you want anything from the students' union?' Elin stretched. She got to her feet and picked up her bag. She glanced at the clock and then at her colleague. 'Got to get some caffeine into my system. Want to join me, or shall I bring one back?'

'No, thanks.'

Elin was relieved. Joining her or bringing a drink back up might encourage conversation she could do without. Her colleague seemed subdued. His research hadn't been going well and he was set to return to the States soon. He'd hinted to Elin that he could arrange for her to do some guest lectures at his university. But the timing was all wrong. Another opportunity lost. There were moments she'd been glad of John's presence in the office, although more often she just wanted to be alone. Like now. Perhaps she should get her coffee and then take it outside, have a walk around the campus to clear her head.

The students' union bar was throbbing with conversation, a low beat of music and dull chatter from several television screens. Students sat in groups, some reading but most chatting. The smell of greasy food was overwhelming. To her surprise, Elin spotted the Dean. He was about to pay for a cup of tea and a sandwich. Elin grabbed a coffee, and with apologies to a couple of students, moved up to stand behind him in the line.

'Hello, Michael.' A chance to speak to him. Maybe find out a bit more after the hints at the presentation.

He spun towards her and gave an unexpected, friendly smile. Its openness left her a little disorientated and she struggled to smile back. He seemed different from the urbane and distant figure at the podium in the lecture theatre. And the hostile figure at the research meeting. This Michael was more human, the man she remembered.

'Hi there, Elin. Braving the lion's den?' Michael waved an arm to indicate the horde of students sitting around. In groups, they did look rather predatory. Elin examined his face. She'd heard on the grapevine there had been disquiet, in some quarters, about his management. Up close she could see signs of the strain. Fine lines mapped his forehead and there were shadows under his eyes. Still, she was glad he had smiled. It made things simpler for her.

'I'm more surprised to see you here, Dean. I thought you would have everything brought to you.'

It was a pointed remark, but Michael seemed to take it in his stride. The smile didn't fade as he explained his presence. 'I needed a change of scene, to get away from my computer screen for a bit. Now, I'm not so sure it was a good idea. Loud music and even louder conversation do not help with brain space. I expect you feel the same but needed an espresso fix.'

He nodded at Elin's cup and then their eyes met, for longer than necessary.

That was unsettling. She remembered the days when he used to tease her about her addiction to coffee. She could feel the warmth in her cheeks as she rushed on. 'Actually,' she said, 'I'm really glad we bumped into each other. Is there any chance I might come and see you today for a chat?' Elin knew she was pushing it, but she really needed to tell him as soon as possible about her situation at home.

Michael hesitated. 'I'm–'

'It's important or I wouldn't ask. It won't take long.'

'You can come up in about twenty minutes if you like, while I'm having a bite to eat. Otherwise, it's back-to-back meetings until the end of next week.' He didn't look overjoyed at the prospect of talking to her, but at least he hadn't refused.

'That'll be great. Thanks. It is an urgent matter.' With a brief smile she left. No doubt Michael would think it was about the meeting on Monday. She knew he'd been bombarded by a steady stream of people coming into his office since then, looking for reassurance. Maybe he thought she'd changed her mind about Fonetym.

Twenty minutes later, when Elin arrived, Jodie was on her lunch break. She knocked the inner door and heard his voice, 'Come in.'

She entered to see Michael eating a sandwich at his desk while peering at the computer screen. Every time she came into the Dean's office there were more stacks of paper than the time before. It appeared that Huw, lovely as he was, had left things in more than just a bit of a muddle. Now that she was in the room alone with Michael, Elin had a fluttering feeling in her chest. She didn't know what sort of a reaction she'd have when she talked to him about home. Once, she could have gauged his moods, but the man in front of her was a different creature, familiar but also unpredictable. 'Is this a good time? Shall I come back in five, when you've had a chance to eat?'

Michael shut his laptop, pushed his half-eaten sandwich into its carton and said, 'No, no. It's fine. What can I do for you?' He indicated the chair on the other side of the desk.

She sat, perched on the edge and hands clasped together on her knee. The smell of his tuna and sweetcorn sandwich filled the room. Mixed with the aroma from the bergamot and lemon diffuser the effect was repellent. For a brief moment she closed her eyes before she spoke. To have to ask for something, after their clashes over the Fonetym research, grated. 'I need to ask for compassionate leave. I don't know if you've heard, but my mother is terminally ill. I... I need to be ready to take leave to be with her as things deteriorate. We're not quite at that stage yet, but well, it won't be long. I'd rather be prepared.'

'I hadn't heard, Elin. I'm very sorry. I'm glad you've come to see me. Of course, we'll do everything we can to support you. Geraint, knows about this, I assume?'

'Yes, I've told him.' So far so good. That wasn't all she needed to say. 'The thing is this will have a big effect on the Fonetym project. There's a meeting in Brussels coming up soon. I won't be able to attend that. Then there's all my teaching. It was end-loaded so I could take the Finland sabbatical in the Autumn Term. I hate to let myself and the University down.' Elin felt her throat tightening and gulped, trying to keep the emotions in check.

Michael interrupted her, holding a hand up, white cuff bright against the golden tan of his skin. 'Okay. Let me stop you there and reassure you. You don't need to worry about work. That's my problem. You've got enough on your plate.' Michael's voice was soft, sympathetic. With his reputation for ruthlessness, and her antipathy towards him, it was not the reaction Elin had expected. His voice continued in a calm, soothing tone. 'We can sort everything out. The main thing is to look after yourself and your mother.'

There was something about the way Michael leant forward and looked at her, something familiar, masculine and reassuring, that reminded her, for some strange reason, of Papa. 'It's been a nightmare. Ever since I got back from Finland it's been one thing after another. And now my mother...' Through a blur of tears, she saw Michael pass her the box of tissues from the table. Taking a couple, she wiped her eyes and blew her nose.

'Sorry.' She smiled a weak and watery smile, then looked down at the floor, vulnerable in his presence, almost like the PhD student she had been so many years before. But they were different people now and she was grateful for this support as her Dean, when the struggle was so gruelling with Mum and everything else.

'I'll get Geraint on to it immediately.' He was making notes as she spoke, the ink flowing across the paper in that familiar scrawl. 'Most of the undergraduate teaching will be finished soon but you've got post-grads I assume?'

'Yes. I can deal with that remotely. I just can't keep everything going for much longer.' She sighed, overwhelmed again at the thought of the impossibility of juggling teaching, research and being needed at Seaview Close. 'And then there's the Brussels trip...'

'Well, that's another problem. What goes on in this Department is my concern, however, I rather suspect you've scuppered any chances of further funding on the TechSWell project, with Fone-tym, anyway.' The sympathetic tone was replaced by something between resignation and resentment and Elin flinched. 'We'll talk again about Brussels, but at this moment try not to worry about all that.'

'I wondered if someone else could go and deliver my paper at the conference. The flights and accommodation are already paid for, and I've prepared...' She stopped, seeing Michael's lips tighten and his eyebrow lift.

'I think you need to concentrate on more pressing matters, like your mother. That's your main concern, isn't it? There are times when family comes first. This is one of those times, Elin.' He stood up. As he did so there was a ping as a meeting reminder popped up on his screen.

'You're right. Mum's needs come before everything. Thank you for your time.' Elin stood, too, and moved towards the door.

'Don't struggle on alone. Keep me, and your colleagues, in the loop.'

As she left the office, Elin remembered she hadn't asked about how the changes in the Department might affect her. And the Brussels conference was left unresolved. Another golden opportunity to further her career gone.

Chapter Twenty-Two

Elin

It was Friday at last. The end of a long and tiring week. Elin had her bag packed in the car with all the things she needed for the weekend with her mother. She'd got into the habit of leaving a set of items, including casual clothing, in the house in Sully, so the bag contained only the essentials, such as her washbag and change of underwear.

Elin could hear her father's voice. 'You're lucky. You work Monday to Friday. I work every day.' If only it was Monday to Friday. The pile of marking to be completed over the weekend made her groan, inside. Oh, how she missed Papa. Her mother's illness had magnified everything. She was always in the wrong place and not doing anything properly, her mind and body laden with physical and mental exhaustion. No wonder she'd broken down in Michael's office. He had been so kind; so unexpectedly kind. Perhaps she needed that compassionate leave more than she thought.

Compared to the beginning of her week, Friday was a quiet day. Elin checked through her lecture notes for the session and read an article just published by one of her TechSWell colleagues to ensure she was up to date with her references. She marked another abstract to follow up when she had more time. It looked good. The whole project was fascinating and the picture being built up by the research team was beginning to show new evidence about the impact of technology on health and well-being.

At ten to eleven she gathered her notes together and threw

them into her briefcase, just remembering to put her purse in before she set off. Sue had asked Elin to join her in the café for lunch. Trying to build bridges again. They had exchanged few words since their misunderstanding where the trust between them had been broken. And Elin still harboured some suspicions, reservations about Sue's motives. On the other hand, Sue had been kind enough to call and see Catherine, at times when Elin wasn't there. And they had both been so busy.

The lecture hall filled up quickly. It was cold in the room but would soon warm up once the mass of bodies crushed in together. Elin waited, watching as the students shuffled into places. A mix of piano and water sounds played in the background, providing a soothing start to the lecture. She saw Nick Mackenzie, sitting in the front row, scowling until his girlfriend, Cerys, touched his arm. He twisted around to look at her with such warmth that it transformed him and he looked almost handsome. A memory flitted through Elin's subconscious. Young love. He'd moved all the way from Scotland to be with his girl. A romantic gesture. Elin hoped it was worth it. Cerys seemed to have given him some stability as he had a less disordered appearance.

When everyone was in place, Elin switched off the music, beaming at them. For the next step, to engage the group, she asked them to take a few deep breaths, counting in and out, while being aware of how their bodies reacted. She found that mindfulness techniques, like these, at the beginning of a lecture often resulted in more awareness and enlightenment with the topic. Sometimes, she showed a series of photographs of nature to create an ambience of relaxation and tranquillity. Some of her colleagues thought she was a bit avant garde with her methods, but if they worked, she could take their teasing.

Using the research findings from the Finland project, Elin began by raising questions about well-being and technology. She also asked that the students put away all technology during the lecture, promising that full notes would be available online. There were some mumbles of surprise and protest, as she had anticipated.

'Well then,' she said. 'Think about it. What does this reaction tell us about society? Is technology an addiction? Is it on par with drugs and alcohol? I wonder how many of you would have had much fun being out of touch with most of the world as I was in Finland.'

'Do you think it's an age thing?' One of the mature students, Ffion Evans, had asked the question. She was in her late twenties, a single mother, round-faced, hair dyed red and on the plump side. Intelligent and outspoken, she had come back to university after her daughter started school.

Elin wasn't quite sure how to respond. 'Could you explain what you mean by that? Are you suggesting that older people, like myself, are not as tuned in to technology? Maybe not as interested? I certainly don't carry my phone around as a child would a comfort blanket. Lots of students do. Is that what you mean?' Elin laughed. She must seem ancient to some of these youngsters. She didn't think of herself as old but maybe that was how she appeared.

Ffion considered the issue. 'Mmmm, maybe. I'm the eldest in my tutor group and I switch off my phone when I go into lectures. I do it out of respect and to avoid distraction. But some of the others are forever looking at their phones, or tablets, during session, and it's not research either. It's usually social media. I think it interferes with their learning.'

There were a few mock groans but some of the other students seemed to be agreeing judging from the way they listened to Ffion. Elin was grinning, as she watched the responses; a wonderful way to ensure that debate was meaningful.

Now that she'd started talking, Ffion launched further into her viewpoint, 'And another thing, I don't want to live my life online or know what my friend had for breakfast or which guy she shagged last night. Some things are best kept private.'

There were a few embarrassed giggles. Elin shrugged. 'That's an interesting point, Ffion and one we can discuss further afterwards. Now, phones off, please.'

As Elin launched into the lecture, with the photographs of Finland to start, she heard a ping. Someone hadn't switched off. She stopped speaking and glanced around the room. No one made any attempt to apologise or retrieve a device. She drummed her fingers against the podium. Another ping. Close by. 'I asked you to turn things off. That was for a reason. If that is your phone pinging, please switch it off. Now. Unless, perhaps, you'd prefer to leave.'

There was an embarrassed silence as the students looked at one another, shrugging shoulders and shaking heads. Elin resumed speaking when a third ping sounded, loud in the silence. She heard a hissed voice, 'Nick' and Cerys nudged him with her elbow.

'Please switch your phone off now, or I shall ask you to leave, if you'd rather.' Her tone of voice was cold, humourless.

Nick glowered at her. Despite his appearance being more presentable than the last time she'd seen him, he still had attitude. With a slow, lop-sided grin he took his phone out of his pocket. It pinged again. Elin stood rigid, her lips pursed, waiting.

'Dinnae get your knickers in a twist, woman. I'll do it.'

There was a gasp from a couple of the students at the front who heard the exchange and a giggle from the row behind. Nick took his time, turning the device to locate the button and then, eyes locked with hers, he pressed. 'Are you happy now?'

Elin turned away from him and carried on with the lecture, but he'd spoilt the ambience and there was a tension in the air. She tried to build back, making the presentation as interesting and interactive as possible, asking questions and encouraging an exchange of ideas, to add to a feeling of collaboration. A shared experience. After a while she felt the initial warm response return and towards the end of the session, she stopped and looked around the hall.

'So, folks, you've had nearly an hour without your mobile phones, laptops and tablets. How many of you are itching to get hold of those devices and contact your friends? Come on, now. Be honest.'

Nearly all those present raised their hands. Some had already delved into bags and pockets to bring out their devices and were clicking away, including Nick.

'I don't know if it's age related or whether the pace of life and expectations have changed. I'm currently doing some research into it for my book on well-being so if anyone would like to answer a questionnaire then that would be great.' She waved a sheaf of papers in the air. 'I've some links online for the survey and background information, ethics et cetera. Or you can have paper copy and return the form to me in the box outside my office. All information will, of course, be confidential. Lots to think about, I hope. Thanks for listening and for the comments. I hope some of you will help with the research.'

Despite the fraught start to the lecture the students were buzzing as they left the hall, and a few said thank you. Some gathered around her at the end to ask questions about the lecture, their assignments and further reading on the topic. Others collected questionnaires. As usual, some wanted to discuss grades. It was impossible for Elin to have a quiet word with Nick to indicate that his behaviour was out of line. He'd scarpered as soon as the lecture finished and she didn't want to call after him and single him out in any way. God knows how he would react to that.

It was ten past twelve by the time the last student had gone. Elin gathered her things together, grateful that the next lecture wasn't until mid-afternoon, and dashed down to the café. She almost bumped into Sue at the door.

The aroma of chips and curry mixed in the air with coffee and cake. Background chatter in the room sounded like a flock of magpies exchanging greetings. Some of her students were clustered together, laughing and glancing towards her or perhaps beyond.

'So sorry I'm late,' Elin began. 'Students asking questions. They'd have my blood if I let them.'

Sue laughed. 'Don't worry. I had a telephone call just as I was about to leave, you know. I swear someone waits until I open the office door before they ring. Can I get you something? My treat. I asked you to join me.'

'I'm not very hungry. I think I'll just have a coffee.'

Sue sighed. 'Are you still pissed off with me? I told you–'

'Not here. I'll find us a seat somewhere quiet.' Elin scanned the room and, finding a corner unoccupied, zoned in on it and sat down. She knew she shouldn't have bitten Sue's head off like that, but really. Did she have no discretion? A pang of guilt hit as Sue approached, weaving between tables with the tray.

'I know you said you weren't hungry, but I got you a fruit scone. You need to eat.' She plonked the tray down on the formica table and sat opposite. 'I'm really sorry, you know. I've been an idiot and you've got a shedload of problems.' She glanced around this time, seeming to realise she should make sure no one was listening, 'There was nothing going on with... I made a mistake, and I don't want it to destroy our friendship.'

The statement was disarming and Elin could see by Sue's candid gaze that she was telling the truth. It must have been difficult for her to make that confession and to stretch out the hand of friendship again after their earlier disastrous misunderstanding. As Elin opened her mouth to respond, a gale of laughter exploded from a table in the middle of the room. Then, a student turned and pointed at her. What the hell was going on? Or was she just feeling neurotic again? Sue was talking but it could have been in Mandarin for all Elin knew. Her concentration was shot to ribbons.

Ffion Evans stood up suddenly and left the group, approaching Elin and Sue. There was a worried expression on her face and she held her phone in her hand. After a fleeting glance at Sue, she spoke to Elin. 'I'm sorry, Dr Fiorelli, but I thought you should see this. Someone's posted it on the Department intranet, see, and it's not very nice, is it?'

She handed the phone to Elin who stared and then passed it to Sue who giggled.

'It's not funny, Sue. Not funny at all.'

Someone had pasted her face onto the body of a Jersey heifer with the words, "Look at this cow. Scary."

Elin was in a state of shock.

Chapter Twenty-Three

Elin

The murmur of voices from lunchtime diners, the clatter of plates, knives and forks and all the busy images on the large screens seemed to recede as Elin stared at the picture which Ffion had now forwarded to her.

'You're right.' Sue peered across at the image, 'Sorry. It isn't funny. It was just a surprise, bit of a shock. You should report this, you know. Some student's sick idea of a joke. Way over the top.' She spread her hands wide, offering support. 'Hey, at least they haven't posted to the whole University. I heard about one lecturer who had her head photoshopped onto a porn star's body. I don't know if it was true or one of those stories you hear.'

Elin didn't take in Sue's chatter.

'Are you okay?' Sue seemed to notice how quiet Elin was. 'I'm due at my next meeting, but I can cancel if you like.'

'No, no. I'm fine.' Elin managed to say, feeling numb, detached.

'Alright, if you're sure. Find Geraint, you know. Tell him. It's part of his responsibility with the Staff Student Liaison Committee to keep an eye on things. He'd rather hear it from you than see it himself.' Sue patted Elin on the arm and hurried off.

Elin finished her coffee which had gone cold and left the cafeteria on weak legs. She climbed the stairs and walked in a daze along the corridor towards her office, passing students and colleagues, but hardly registering who they were.

She wanted to delete the image, wipe it clean. But the damn thing was already out there, like the genie from the bottle. Steady.

Keep cool. A silly joke? Combined with that note on her door, it seemed she was a target for someone's anger. Thinking back, she shouldn't have thrown away the note. Too late now.

On reaching the second floor, she met up with a small clutch of students.

'Hi, Dr Fiorelli.' Suzy Marshall seemed to be the spokesperson. 'Hope you don't mind us waylaying you, but we wondered if we could have a word about our assignment; arrange with you to go over some more details? We're not sure about some of the criteria.'

Elin felt a rush of affection for their energy, commitment, and youth. One student with a grudge shouldn't destroy the joy she felt for the work she did. The group were so enthusiastic about the course and she'd enjoyed reading their assignment pieces. 'Sure. Happy to do that, although I can't talk now. You know I've put lots of stuff up on the university intranet for you?' She coloured, wondering if any of them had seen the offending image, but was met with candid gazes.

They had seen the teaching materials and guidelines, but they wanted to check on some finer points. Despite feeling distracted, Elin said she'd go over the criteria again and take questions in the next lecture. They parted, and Elin walked at speed towards Geraint's office. The sooner she got the incident reported, the sooner she could get off to Sully. As she rounded the corner, she almost collided with the burly figure of Geraint Eynon. 'Good heavens, *blodyn*, what's the rush? You nearly had me over.' His eyes filled with alarm. 'What is it, Elin? Is it your Mam?'

'No.' Elin looked at Geraint. His rugged, concerned face with its deep worry lines, his kind eyes and his nose, slightly off-centre from his rugby-playing days, were what she needed.

As if reading her mind, Geraint steered her to his office, opened the door and said, 'You'd better come in and tell me what's up.'

People had often said that Geraint was the natural successor to Huw, although others were of the view that he didn't have the necessary killer instinct. But now that things were difficult with the new Dean, Geraint was more popular than ever. Elin sat down on the battered brown leather sofa Geraint had along one wall of his office, away from the impressive clutter of papers around his desk.

'It's really unpleasant, Geraint. Nothing like this has ever happened to me before.' Elin struggled to sit upright on the sagging upholstery. If she leant back into its ancient folds, into the sofa's capacious embrace, she'd be lost.

'Tell me what's going on, Elin *bach*.' Geraint put a strong, pudgy hand on her shoulder, as though she was one of his daughters, before sitting down. 'I can see you're out of sorts and no wonder–'

'There's been a couple of incidents. I don't know who it is or why, but I'm being targeted by someone with a grudge.'

'Never.' He looked at her in surprise. 'Though you wouldn't be the first, mind you. What's happened?'

Elin took her phone out of her bag, scrolled through to find the picture and handed it to Geraint.

'*Duw, duw,*' he whistled. 'No one would have dreamed of pulling a stunt like that against a tutor when I was in college.' He handed the phone back, 'And you said there were other things?'

'Well, there was a note on my office door a while back. It said, "I am watching you". I thought it was a student prank and I threw it in the bin.' Elin could feel her cheeks redden as she said this.

Geraint nodded. 'That it?'

It did sound rather pathetic now she had voiced her concerns, but there were the other issues. Should she tell him? 'And outside my flat last week,' Elin added, 'I heard a noise near my car when I got home from Mum's on Sunday evening. But I didn't see anyone.' She hesitated. 'Later that night, I thought I saw somebody in the shadows looking up at my flat. I told myself it was my imagination playing tricks. With all that's been going on, I'm pretty stressed out.'

'No wonder, *blodyn*.' Geraint frowned. 'But if there was someone outside, that is a serious matter. We can't have anyone being harassed or bullied, staff or students.'

'By my flat, I just don't know... And with other things, it could have been some of my students. But why?' Elin brushed a hand across her face in a wave of frustration. 'They certainly chose their time.'

'Yes, indeed. But that might be it now, a couple of students letting off steam.' Geraint shook his head. 'You know how it is, after a few pints in the Students' Union bar or pub crawling down the Bay.'

'It might be,' Elin said, her voice lifted. 'It's a bit weird. You think we should draw a line under it – unless anything else happens?'

'No nuisance phone calls or emails, nothing on social media?' Geraint leant forward.

'No, the two incidents on campus... and I'm really not sure about that thing by my flat. I'm very tired and maybe my mind's playing tricks.'

Elin thought Geraint looked relieved. Decisiveness was not his strong point, as she had discovered over the years – and he wouldn't want to involve campus security or the police if he could avoid it. Things got into the papers and that was bad for the university's reputation.

'I feel better now I've told you. Puts it into perspective.' Elin added, 'Is there any way we could find out who did it? Have it removed from the intranet?'

'Oh, I don't know about that, *bach*. I'll have a word with the IT blokes. Should be able to get it removed, but anything else, well, that's another question. I'll chase it up, now.'

'You understand?'

'Course, I do. You take care of yourself, and my guess is we won't hear any more now. A couple of stray incidents I bet. It's not personal. You can be sure of that.' He beamed at her reassuringly from under his bushy brows. 'You're one of our most liked and respected academic members of staff.' He patted her on the arm. 'Try and put it out of your mind, *bach*.'

How could he think it wasn't personal? As she walked out to her car later that day Elin was relieved, for once, to be heading to Sully. Even with Geraint's reassurances her flat was no longer a sanctuary, not in her present state of mind. A shiver passed through her, like a cold wind on a winter's night. She had the feeling she was being watched and glanced around. But there was nobody to be seen.

Chapter Twenty-Four

Elin

'Elin, Elin. Where are you?' Mum's voice seemed stronger than it had been earlier in the week. Elin went into the bedroom and was surprised to find she was already sitting up. Her eyes were bright, and her cheeks flushed.

'I'm here. I've been out in the garden. It's a beautiful day. Do you feel well enough for a little trip out?' Elin half-expected her to decline, it was just a sudden thought.

Mum agreed. 'What a lovely idea. I do feel a little stronger today. Some fresh air should help. Where's that nurse?'

'She'll be here any minute. We can check with her if she thinks it's okay.' Elin tried to sound upbeat, even though she felt weary. She was surprised at the little burst of strength Mum was showing today and determined to make the most of it.

When Nurse Angela shouted 'Hello' and came in, Elin remembered the first days of the care regime. Mum had fixed her eye on one nurse who started out calling her 'Catherine' and declared, 'I don't like all this informal nonsense. I don't like strangers calling me by my first name. It shows a lack of respect.' The nurse had exchanged a glance with Elin, who had difficulty hiding her twitching lips. Her mother was feisty and determined that she was not going to be treated as an infirm patient before it was necessary.

'Mrs Fiorelli seems perky this morning.' Angela said, after she had helped Mum with meds and personal care. The nurse's beaming smile enveloped Elin and her mother. 'She says you're going out. What a lovely idea.'

Elin, relieved at the approval of her plan, responded with enthusiasm, 'I don't want to put her at risk, but it's such a beautiful day and so warm. I thought a little jaunt out might cheer her up.'

Angela patted Elin's arm. 'Yes, indeed, anything that gives you pleasure, isn't it, Mrs Fiorelli? Within reason, of course. No partying, mind.' This was accompanied by a belly laugh from Angela, who turned to whisper to Elin, 'You'll find she tires easily. Make sure she keeps warm. Getting a chill wouldn't be wise.' Then a generous thumbs up to them both. 'Enjoy yourselves. I'm on duty later so you two ladies can tell me all about it.'

Mindful of Nurse Angela's words, Elin put a rug and hot water bottle in the car. When Mum was wrapped up and ready, she told her of her suggestion to drive to the esplanade at Penarth, the nearest coastal town and a favourite place.

Mum was delighted at the suggestion. 'Oh, yes, dear. That would be lovely.'

Elin's heart lifted that she'd got it right. You never knew.

'We used to go there so often on holidays and high days when you were a little girl.' Mum carried on, gasping a little as she tried to get her breath. 'Do you remember?'

Elin nodded, concentrating on the traffic as they headed towards Penarth on Lavernock Road.

'One day your father got you an ice-cream and it dropped out of the cone right onto your new shoes. Goodness, what a noise you made. Papa scooped you up in his arms and took you to a café where you had some great concoction of jelly and ice-cream in a dish. Knickerbocker Glory it was called. Such a silly name for an ice-cream dessert. I thought it would make you sick, but you ate every bit.' She reminisced, 'Oh, they were good days, weren't they?'

Although she didn't remember that incident, Elin agreed. It had been a happy childhood, if a little lonely at times. Elin had always taken solace in reading and the characters in her books had been her friends. It was as she grew up and became more independent that things had gone downhill. Mum became ever more critical of Elin's desire for learning and of her career taking the place of a husband and children.

They drove down to the esplanade and Mum sighed as they

passed the pier with its new façade. Elin had intended to take her into the café, but there was nowhere to park close enough. The choppy water looked grey and dismal, despite the sunshine, with bobbing plastic bottles and debris floating near the shoreline as the tide receded.

'I remember there used to be a multi-storey car park here,' Mum recalled. 'It's a pity they've taken that away. It might make things more open and attractive, but not as convenient. Papa liked it here. Goodness only knows why. In the old days it was quite run down...'

Mum seemed content to be driven slowly along the esplanade reliving old memories, but Elin was racking her brain to think of somewhere they could go and enjoy the sun. 'Shall we go to Cosmeston, Mum? There's a little café there and if it's not too windy we can sit out and watch folk walk around the lake.'

'Whatever you think, dear. I'm just glad to be out of the house. It's been lovely to have your company. I know we haven't always seen eye to eye, but you've been good to me since your Papa died.' It was a telling remark, unexpected.

'I'm your daughter, what do you expect?' Elin smiled, but they both knew it hadn't always been plain sailing.

'I didn't expect you to spend so much time with me.' Mum gave her that direct gaze she kept for when something was important. 'You've never been very good with illness; your own or anyone else's.' She gave a wry laugh. 'I know you are only doing your duty, but I do appreciate it.'

'Mum.' Elin had difficulty speaking. She was shocked at how perceptive and sad these words were. She touched her mother's hand, a butterfly touch on the papery thin and blue veined skin. 'Don't be like that.'

Mum squeezed Elin's slightly, then pulled her hand away with a small shrug. 'I know you care, really. It's just the two of us are sometimes...'

Elin swallowed back tears. The words didn't need to be voiced.

It was busy at Cosmeston Lakes but Elin found a free disabled space just yards from the door to the centre and café. Mum walked very slowly, her stick thumping the ground and her other hand clutching Elin's arm.

Elin felt how frail Mum's body was, birdlike bones, and how much effort each step took. 'Are you alright? Are you in pain, Mum?'

'A little, dear, but it's alright. Just a bit of backache. Nothing to fret about. Shall we sit outside? It's so warm for March, or is it April? I've lost track of time.'

They negotiated their way to the little deck where they could have their snack, while viewing the lake and the boardwalk. It was a cheerful sight. Ducks swam amongst the reeds, gentle quacking punctuating the air. Families with dogs and children swarmed around the lake, laughing and chattering as they enjoyed the blast of spring sunshine, so welcome after dreary winter rains. Elin settled Mum, tucking the rug around her and went off to get a pot of tea and cake. When she brought the tray over, she saw Mum had her face tilted to the sun, lips slanted upwards, eyes closed. A gentle breeze lifted her hair, now thin and wispy, making a halo around her drawn face.

'Did I tell you Aunt Anne's coming down this week? She's going to stay for a couple of days.'

'She wants to see me before I pop my clogs.' Mum crossed her hands over one another and played with her wedding ring, now loose on her finger.

'Mum. That's a terrible thing to say,' Elin said, in mock horror. 'I'm sure Aunt Anne doesn't think that.' But it was good to see Mum's eyes were twinkling. Elin poured their tea.

'Perhaps. We have to face facts, though. My number's nearly up. We all know it, so why pretend otherwise?' She stretched a thin arm out for the teacup, the cup rattling on the saucer as she drew it near. 'I'm looking forward to seeing Anne in any case. She has such zest for life.'

'That's true.'

'Now,' Mum added, 'that looks a particularly good Victoria sponge cake. Perfect choice.' Although she attacked the cake with enthusiasm at first, she only managed a few small mouthfuls and they sat in silence for a little while, sipping their tea and people-watching.

She seemed content but Elin was aware how much just being out of the house was exhausting her. The drive back took longer, with heavy traffic, and Elin was glad Mum dozed. When they arrived in Sully, Mum woke, yawned and looked out of the car window at the house, seeming disorientated before she remembered where she was.

'Thank you, dear. That was such a lovely day. I'm glad we went out. You're a good daughter.'

Later as she helped Mum to the bedroom for a rest, Elin noticed again the tinge of sallowness below the makeup. It wasn't a good sign she knew, but it was wonderful they had managed the little outing. Spring had arrived at last, and Elin felt more optimistic than she had for a while. This calm and pleasant day was a gift, a counter to the difficult times they'd so often had, the misunderstandings and quarrels. Life was hard but there was always hope and this interlude had given Elin a much-needed boost to carry on helping her mother in every way possible.

Chapter Twenty-Five

Elin

A knock on the door around five forty that afternoon was unexpected. Elin kept the door a little ajar unless she didn't want to be disturbed. It helped the room feel less claustrophobic and was an indicator to students that she was available. But by this time most students were either deep in their books, getting ready to go out or off to work. Muffled sounds of campus life, shouts across the quadrangle, revs of battered cars starting into life drifted in now and again through the open window. A puff of wind blew a strand of hair into Elin's eyes, and she blinked as Cerys Williams peeped around the edge of the door.

'Am I disturbing you, Dr Fiorelli?' Her dyed crimson bob flopped over one eye as she stood on the threshold, waiting, uncertain.

'No. It's nice to see you.' Elin waved a welcoming hand indicating for Cerys to enter. The eldest child from a farming community, Cerys was passionate about well-being, both people and animals. What did she want? It must be important as the girl looked nervous, hanging onto the strap of her shoulder bag like a lifeline.

She edged into the room. 'May I?' One hand on the door pushing it closed.

Elin waited as Cerys stood, rocking on her feet, as if unsure what to do or say.

'It's about Nick... Nick Mackenzie–'

'He hasn't harmed you?' Elin asked, scanning the girl's face for signs of distress.

'Gosh, no,' Cerys was quick to reply. 'Nick's not like that. It's just I wanted to explain.'

'Sit down, and fire away.'

Cerys sat on the edge of one of the chairs and gave a little cough. 'Me and Nick, well, that is, we've been together a while now. I'm the reason he's transferred from Glasgow.'

Elin had wondered as much when she'd seen them sitting together in the lecture hall. What on earth did Cerys see in him? 'Ah. He must be smitten with you.'

Cerys blushed and picked at a blue painted fingernail. 'It hasn't been easy for him. I know he was a pain in the lecture hall and... I'm sorry. But, well, I thought if you knew a bit about why–'

'Does Nick know you're here?'

'God, no. He's very private. Keeps things bottled. Then they explode.' She put a hand to her mouth. 'I don't mean that he's violent. He just gets a bit het up, like.'

Elin didn't know what to say. Perhaps it was best to just listen.

'Thing is, Dr Fiorelli, he's had a hard life in some ways. His parents split when he was little, and his Mam had custody. She had drink problems. Looks a bit like you, she does.' She paused. 'I mean...'

Oh great. Saying she looked like an alcoholic. What a compliment. Cerys was going around the houses, but Elin didn't want to push her to get to the point. 'You're saying Nick has inherited a tendency to addiction? Am I right?'

Cerys bit her lip. 'Yeah, but he's been working hard to deal with it. He gets anxious and...'

'Has he been to student services to get counselling? I can give him a referral if he needs it. Lots of students get more anxious as the exams and dissertation approach.' Elin leant forward her hands clasped together on her desk. 'What can I do to help you both?'

'He's having counselling. It helps but I know he's been a pain in some of your classes–'

'You could say that.' Almost every time she came in contact with him. Nick Mackenzie was troubled. That was easy to see, but how to manage things with him and give him the extra help he needed was more of a challenge.

'He's not keen on women in authority, see. I've noticed at uni and when we were working in the pub. He liked Dr Stevens who was taking your groups while you were away–'

That figured. Elin could imagine why. Phil Stevens knew his stuff but was coasting towards retirement, demanding little and a fan of giving handouts to students instead of engaging them in discussion and debate. His seminars and lectures always ended early.

'–And then things went pear-shaped over Christmas.' Cerys swallowed. She was worrying at the strap of her bag.

'The "happiest time of the year",' Elin made quote marks in the air, 'can be fraught with emotion, and not all of it good.' Like the row she'd had with Mum just before Christmas. Emotions running too high.

'His Mam's bloke doesn't like Nick. There was a big fight. He threw Nick out of the house. Nick was sofa-surfing for a bit until term started and... well, he hit the booze, see.'

Elin sat back in her chair. This explained why Nick was so belligerent at the beginning of term. And, if she reminded him of his mother, God forbid, then he was taking his frustrations out on her. Why hadn't someone warned her about the possible problem before? And what had prompted Cerys to come now? There was a little silence while Elin digested the information and Cerys sat waiting. A buzzing sound in her bag made Cerys shift in her seat.

'Is he still drinking? Why do you think I need to know all this? Has something happened?'

'I was, well, embarrassed really at the way he spoke to you in that lecture and...'

If Cerys didn't stop twisting that strap it would break. And her phone was buzzing in the depths of her bag, again. Someone frantic to speak to her. The poor girl was uptight and so in love she was blinded to the bleaker side of Nick's personality. No doubt she thought she could fix him. Make him a better person.

'If you're apologising for Nick's poor behaviour it isn't your place to do so, or to worry yourself into a state over it.' Elin's face softened as she tried to placate Cerys. 'He needs to be aware that when he goes out into the workplace employers will not be as tolerant as I've been – so far.' She leant forward again. 'Thank you for telling me. It always helps to know why people react the way they do in different situations. He's lucky to have your support but look after yourself too.'

'I... Thanks, Dr Fiorelli. I'd better...' Cerys stood, and with a small wave of her hand in thanks slipped out of the room again.

Elin had the feeling there was more to the story. It was as if Cerys had changed her mind about what she intended to say. What else had Nick been up to? Whatever his girlfriend thought about him, he'd shown he had big problems. Elin hoped the counselling was helping him. His home life sounded grim, poor lad.

Chapter Twenty-Six

Elin

O n Sunday morning Elin was bending down to put soiled sheets into the washing machine and jumped when she heard a tap on the back door. She turned and recognised Sue outlined in the frosted glass. 'Gosh, you gave me a fright. I was miles away.'

'Sorry to startle you.' Sue stood, hesitating in the doorway. 'How are things with your Mum – and with you? I'm just on my way to get petrol and do my Sunday errands in the village, so thought I'd drop by. Just in case there was anything you need.'

Elin noticed Sue looked more rested than earlier in the week. She seemed younger in her jeans and boots too than in the formal wear she favoured for work. Elin put detergent in the soap dispenser, set the machine on and pointed to the kettle. 'Cuppa?'

Sue agreed and seemed pleased to be invited to stay. 'How did you get on with Geraint after?'

Elin told Sue the gist of the meeting. 'So, hopefully that's it.' She put two RSPCA bird coasters out on the table.

'Yes?' Sue sounded doubtful.

'Mmm.' Elin poured hot water into the cafetiére. The rich smell of fresh coffee came up to greet her. 'I still want to know who did it, though, and why. It could be like Geraint said, a bit of a lark after a few bevvies, nothing personal. Or it could be more sinister, targeting me.' Elin set the coffee jug on the table between them. 'Do you think it really is the end of it? I so don't need this now.'

Sue leant forward. 'You're a tough cookie, Elin. You won't let this get to you. You could report it on, escalate it as a complaint, you know. I mean if you're worried about it?' Her voice rose, making the statement more like a question. 'And if they can figure out, who did it and why. I don't want to frighten you, but there are a lot of weirdos out there.'

'The thing is,' Elin said, 'I have this feeling that it's a sort of cry for help. I keep going over names and faces of students in my tutor groups... And it might not be a student.'

Sue raised any eyebrow. 'Oh? Who else then?'

Elin plunged the coffee filter down and poured two mugs. She warmed her hands on her mug, concentrating. 'Well, there have been a couple of things which have unnerved me a bit recently. Nothing definite but when I had time to think it struck me there might be, oh, I don't know. Maybe I'm just imagining things.'

'What? Someone at work?'

Twisting her signet ring Elin said, 'No. At the flat. I don't like to think about it but there's Rhys, the site manager.' She took a gulp of coffee. 'He always seems to be hovering around by his office, wanting to help me with my bags and things. Very sympathetic when I told him about Mum. Offered to water plants and stuff.'

Sue looked doubtful. 'Could just be doing his job.'

Elin carried on. 'Then I thought I saw someone in the trees peering up at my flat one night.' Elin shivered, her eyes dark with worry. 'No. I'm seeing everything wrong. Rhys is a nice man. I've known him for years. And those photos were on the intranet. It had to be someone with access. Probably a student having a laugh at my expense. I don't know why I'm over-reacting to it.' She closed her eyes and slumped back in the chair.

Sue reached to pat Elin's arm. 'You're done in. Working flat out and being here for your Mum, it's no wonder.'

'God, you're right.' Elin put her hands on either side of her head and groaned, 'I've got enough worry with Mum.'

'How is she? Any change?'

'She's having a sleep just now, but we had a very good day yesterday. Went for a drive out to Penarth and then Cosmeston. Sat and watched the ducks. Mum even managed some cake, a couple of tiny mouthfuls but that was good. It's as if she had a little burst of energy. She's exhausted today, though.'

'Bound to be. But it was fab you could go out together, especially now the weather's getting better.'

A silence hung over them both, like one of those misty dews over the grass in autumn. Elin had a sudden memory of the many family meals she'd had there. Her father used to sit in the high-backed armchair where Sue was sitting, as it was 'kind to his back' after long hours at work. On Sunday mornings, he'd spread the papers in front of him on the table, commenting, between ample bites of marmalade and toast, with Mum bustling around. Happy memories and hard to believe that life had gone forever. Sue's voice pulled Elin out of her reverie.

'I haven't told you this before – I don't like to speak about it – but the reason I came to Cardiff wasn't just ambition and building my career.' Sue paused and picked at the nail on her index finger.

Elin knew Sue's family life was complex. She'd spoken about one brother who'd been in trouble with the police and the money problems they'd had when she was growing up. Sue seemed to be the only member of her family who'd made a go of her life. When Sue still didn't speak, Elin gently prompted her. 'Another reason?'

'Yes. His name's Georgios Nikolaou. My first boyfriend. We went to school together and then, after A levels, he went off to work in Birmingham. Anyway, later he came back to London. We took up where we'd left off. The only thing was, he didn't tell me he was married and had two kids.'

'Ah, difficult. And... you broke up with him?'

There was a pause where Sue took a deep breath. 'Yes. I really hadn't a clue, you know. Should've seen the signs but, well, I didn't. When I found out, I ended it.'

'And started a new life in Cardiff?'

'If only it was that simple.' Sue gulped. 'Georgios wouldn't accept it. When I told him it was over, he went berserk.'

Elin could see how difficult it was for Sue. She waited and nodded encouragement. Sue's face was blotchy with emotion. 'In the end a restraining order was put on him, but I was still terrified he would turn up and attack me or my Mum. I moved here and changed my surname to protect my identity. I haven't been home since.'

Elin scrutinized Sue's unlined face and ingenuous blue eyes. How little anyone knows about other people's lives. Work colleagues, neighbours, general acquaintances. 'That's awful, Sue. I'm very sorry. I had no idea.'

'How would you? It's not something I tell people. I only told you because, well, because sometimes these things blow up, you know. Little incidents like you've had can get bigger. So, just be careful. Be aware in case–'

'Elin?' Mum's voice sounded hoarse through the intercom between her bedroom and the kitchen.

'I'd better go,' Sue said, half rising.

'No need. Mum probably just wants a drink, or the loo. Stay a bit longer if you like?'

'Ok, then. Thanks. It's been brill to have a chance to catch up.' Sue looked at Elin with meaning.

Elin added, 'Don't feel you have to stay, either, if I'm not back after quarter of an hour or so – though I expect Mum will carry on resting until lunch time.'

Within a few minutes Elin had helped her mother to the toilet and made her comfortable again. Mum refused the offer of a cup of tea but had a sip of water before leaning back against the pillows and closing her eyes. Then, 'We had a good day yesterday, didn't we?' She opened her eyes again and a weak smile creased the edges.

'Yes. It was lovely.' Elin stroked her mother's arm aware of the bedjacket's voluminous sleeves and how they made her mother look like a child in grown-ups clothing. 'Have another nap if you want and I'll see if you'd like a cuppa and a bit of toast after that.'

'Thank you, dear.'

Elin waited until her mother's breathing grew soft and even before she went back down to the kitchen.

'Is she alright?'

'Very tired. She's not up to visitors today, otherwise you could've popped in to say hello. She's enjoyed your visits.'

Sue looked down at her hands and rubbed her right thumb over her index finger. The nail was virtually bitten to the quick. 'You should speak to the Dean about what's going on, Elin,' she said. 'I know he's not as approachable as Huw was, but I've found him to be fair and supportive. Actually, he was better than Huw when I told him about my problem with Georgios. And... you-know-what is all in the past, thank God.'

Elin thought back to her recent meeting when she'd asked for compassionate leave. At that time Michael had shown a different side, kinder and more understanding than the ruthless go-getter she'd described to Sue. 'I've already been to see the Dean about Mum, and to be fair, he was helpful. But there's more to this than meets the eye, Sue.'

'Oh?' Sue put her mug into the sink and came to sit down at the kitchen table.

'Do you remember when I first found out that Professor Hardwick was to be our new Dean, replacing Huw? When I came back from Finland?'

'Yes. You seemed to be pretty negative about him. Unscrupulous, you said.' She glanced at Elin. 'No one realised how bad the money problems were then. It's his job as the new Dean to try and tackle that. I admire him for the way he's gone about it.'

So, Sue was still enchanted by Michael. 'I suppose that's true, although there are ways of tackling the problem and I don't agree with some of the decisions he's made. I'm sure I'm not the only one either. When Huw comes back, he'll have a thing or two to say about the direction Michael is taking the Department,' Elin said.

'I don't see Huw coming back,' Sue replied in a flat tone.

For a moment, Elin's thoughts went to the nightmare of being made redundant and the mortgage on her flat, but she carried on. 'Michael Hardwick was my PhD supervisor in Bristol.'

Sue looked interested and her eyes were wide and innocent of the implications behind that sentence. 'Was he? I did wonder how you knew him so well. I thought he was about your age, or slightly older.'

'I was the first doctoral student he had.' Elin paused. Could she tell Sue? Would she understand? 'But he was more than my PhD supervisor. We... we had an affair. He was married, with a son. I knew, but he charmed me, mesmerised me. I was his student in the days before protocols on staff student relations. Not that it would've made much difference. We were in love. At least I was, and I believe he felt the same way.'

Sue shook her head as if in disbelief as she waited for Elin to carry on with her story.

'Then, after about a year, he told me he'd got a new job and was moving away. Had to try and make his marriage work for the sake of his son. He wanted us to carry on meeting somehow. But I couldn't. I was heartbroken, completely devastated. They moved to Scotland and, well, we never met again until he turned up as our new Dean.'

Elin felt for her signet ring from Papa, twisting it round and round.

'Oh my God, Elin. No wonder you were properly shocked. But,' Sue hesitated, 'maybe he did love you? It was complicated, with a child and everything. Maybe, you know, maybe he thought it was best to not get you involved in a messy divorce. You were too young. At the start, sort of.'

Elin paused to consider that. It was hard to disentangle everything. A lifetime ago, so it shouldn't still hurt, should it? But it did; his betrayal and all that followed, a constant, dull ache in her heart. 'Who knows? Maybe his wife found out and put pressure on him. Maybe he decided I wasn't fun anymore, getting too serious. All I know is that he ended it. Brutally.' Raw emotion turned her voice to a whisper. 'Michael Hardwick ruined my life.'

Chapter Twenty-Seven

Elin

As the days passed Mum became calmer, the biting remarks less frequent and a sort of serenity taking over. Elin found it became easier to spend time with her as they looked through old photographs, laughing and sharing some memory or other. A bittersweet time.

One afternoon as Elin was sitting by her mother's bedside Mum reached out and stroked her head. 'I worry about you, Elin.'

'Why? I'm fine. It's busy but I'm always busy. You know that.' She held her mother's hand, brought it to rest on the bedcover, and traced the blue veins on the back with her index finger.

'But you've got no one. No partner. No children.' Her eyes were full of sadness.

Elin braced herself. Was the old argument going to resurface?

'Why don't you want children? It's not too late.' Catherine heaved a sigh as she looked into Elin's eyes. 'I dread to think of you with no one to look after you like you've looked after me. It's too sad.'

Elin spoke the words she had sometimes tried, and failed, to speak before. 'I... I can't have babies. I found out a long time ago. I'm infertile.'

'Oh... oh, my dearest girl. Why didn't you tell me?' Her blue eyes were misted with tears. 'I'm so sorry and all these years...' Mum's voice drifted, as the medication made her drowsy.

Elin remembered all the clashes they experienced over the years. If only she'd been able to confess to her mother earlier, perhaps they could have had more of an understanding.

'My poor, poor girl,' Catherine crooned, as her eyelids drooped, and sleep claimed her.

Disengaging herself from her mother's limp hand, Elin pulled the duvet up a little and tiptoed out of the room.

Secrets lying buried deep for years. Nobody had gained from that.

Work swallowed every waking minute Elin wasn't with her mother. It seemed there was an ever-increasing mound of paper to wade through. Life was a non-stop carousel of work, caring and very little sleep. She was glad her Aunt Anne would be arriving soon to stay a couple of nights. It should provide some respite from the constant rush against the clock and the feeling of being overwhelmed.

They were so different. Aunt Anne was the younger one; calm in an emergency, despite being unconventional in many ways. Sometimes Elin wondered how they were sisters. Thinking of them, Elin felt sad to realise how things would be easier if she had a sibling to share the memories and the grief. Her father's death had been so sudden, so unexpected, that there'd been no time to say goodbye. Although he'd been ill, he was optimistic about his future and had made plans for when he would be better. With her mother, it was different and Mum was adamant about what funeral arrangements she wanted.

'None of that mumbo jumbo stuff your father had, Elin. Remember that. And no weeping and wailing. You should speak. Do the eulogy. I expect that.'

Elin pushed that thought to one side. Time enough to deal with it all when the day came. Maybe Mum would last longer than expected? Elin didn't know what to think anymore. Her brain was fogged, stress and exhaustion taking their toll on her body as well.

Meanwhile, at work the presentation for the Brussels meeting on the TechSWell project was one of her priorities. Elin wondered who could go to the meeting on her behalf. Was Michael right? Would Fonetym be concerned by her findings? Perhaps the feeling of elation and release that she'd experienced in Finland was unique to her? Professor Nordin seemed complimentary, and she'd looked forward to discussing things further with him when time allowed. A senior academic would have to take her place that was for sure. The trouble was, who would be able to do it? She ran through the list of colleagues in the Department again but there wasn't anyone. The nearest match was Geraint, so she prepared with him in mind.

The afternoon disappeared in compiling a PowerPoint presentation with the main findings. When she paused to have a break and pop down to the café, she saw Sue hugging a cup of coffee and looking weary, shoulders slumped and heavy-eyed.

'Busy day?' Elin asked.

Sue nodded. 'Aren't they all? I was surprised your Mum was able to go out on Saturday. You know, considering, well...' Sue coloured.

Elin smiled in sympathy. She'd found people got so embarrassed at times. Death was still something they didn't want to talk about. Acknowledging their own mortality, she supposed.

'What you mean is that she seemed chirpy considering she knows she's dying. And it's true.' Elin sat on the seat beside Sue and tilted her head to the side, gazing at a poster on the wall, trying to explain. 'It's quite strange. She's very calm and matter of fact. She wants to sort the funeral herself, which is a blessing, because when my father died neither of us had a clue what he would have wanted. He ended up with all the smoke and whistles, even though he was a lapsed Catholic.'

Elin swallowed, remembering. 'In a way, she seems to be enjoying it all. Don't get me wrong, she's very ill and in a lot of pain but... it's hard to explain. It's acceptance, I think. Time is the enemy. We don't know how long...'

There was a pause and Sue looked uneasy, but Elin was relieved to be able to talk to someone. 'Her sister Anne is coming down for a few days, which is great, gives me time to get this TechSWell project report sorted. I've told them I can't go to Brussels, but Fonetym want their money's worth. You can't blame them. Whoever goes to Brussels in my place will need to be quick thinking and ready to fulfil their expectations – and the rest.'

'Who do you think will go? Geraint?'

'Mmmm. That's what I was thinking. I don't know who else could go. I'm working on that premise and making my report idiot-proof.' Elin giggled, something she hadn't done for a while. 'God, that sounds awful. It isn't that I think Geraint is an idiot–'

'But he wouldn't be your first choice as back up.'

'He'd enjoy the food and beer too much.'

They exchanged knowing glances and Sue grinned. They both liked Geraint, but they knew his weaknesses too. It was good to share this moment and Elin had a little burst of cheerfulness as they went off to their separate offices.

A video call to Wolfgang was her next task. She'd sent an email explaining her home situation but there were other things to discuss. Wolfgang wasted no time in small talk, getting straight to the point in his usual abrupt manner.

'I have read your section of the paper.' His precise manner of speaking was matched by a serious expression. 'I think we have some good discussion points between us. It is such a pity you cannot be here. But I understand.'

'I don't like letting colleagues down but there is nothing I can do. I've a favour to ask as well.'

'Of course. And how may I assist?'

It was hard to resist a smile. He had such an old-fashioned turn of phrase at times. 'It seems, from the programme, I'm down to chair a panel the same afternoon as I was due to present my findings to the committee. Someone will be going to Brussels to give my presentation but... I wondered...?'

'Of course. I should be delighted to perform this task in your place.'

That was a relief. Another box ticked on the ever-growing list of things to think about.

Later, when she rang the house in Sully, Aunt Anne answered, a cheery voice. 'Darling. How lovely to hear your sweet voice.'

'Aunt Anne. What time did you get there? How are you? Good journey?'

'Ghastly. Packed train and delays. I'll be in bed by nine. Thank you, darling, for leaving that sheet with the daily routine and the names of the various nurses. I'm hopeless at names and getting worse in my dotage.'

Elin laughed. Aunt Anne was far from her dotage. In her late fifties, slim, vibrant, a gym bunny she ran marathons and travelled far and wide. She always had tales of the exotic places she'd visited. A tonic to be with.

'How's Mum been since you got there? She's been quite good the past couple of days. We had a lovely weekend together. She was bright and chatty so I'm sure she'll enjoy your company. I'll come after work tomorrow and bring a takeaway and we can catch up.'

There was a moment's silence before Anne replied. 'That would be lovely, Elin. I'll look forward to it. Your Mum's very tired this evening.' Her voice dropped to a whisper. 'I don't like the look of her. To be frank, she seems a lot more poorly than I expected. I've asked if the doctor can call tomorrow. I'll ring you after she's been. Will you be in your office?'

'I've got a lecture first thing, but you can leave a voicemail on my mobile if you like. I'll have it on silent. The number is on one of the sheets of paper I left for you.'

'Yes, yes. I've got that. Not to worry. I'm sure it's nothing to fret too much about. While there's life and all that. We'll see you tomorrow, darling. Now, off you go home and rest. I'm going to sit down with a large G and T.'

Elin stared at the phone for a moment. She'd noticed her mother's wan complexion and wondered, not for the first time, if it meant the cancer had spread to the liver. She turned back to the computer with a sigh. She needed to get the report sorted. If she wrote a long explanation to go with each slide, then, without doubt, Geraint would be able to follow without too much trouble. He was fine with the boys in the pub or a group of students, but with a room full of his peers he sometimes blustered. Maybe that was why he hadn't been appointed acting Dean. Geraint was just too nice for his own good and maybe a tad lazy. Not the smooth and confident operator that Michael presented to the world.

She was deep in thought when her office phone rang. It was after eight, a dark evening after a dull grey day, but academic life didn't follow office hours, so she wasn't surprised. Many of her colleagues lectured in the evenings, especially if they were working on Masters' programmes.

'Elin Fiorelli here.'

Nothing. Silence. A click as the call was terminated. Elin shrugged her shoulders and carried on working. Five minutes later the phone rang again.

'Elin Fiorelli.'

Deep breathing. Silence. Click. Elin slammed the phone down. Was someone playing a sick joke? Who? When the phone rang a third time, she picked it up but said nothing, counting under her breath.

One, two, three, four, five.

Elin could feel the heat rising in her face. Her grip tightened on the receiver. She shouted, 'Who is this?'

Silence.

Click.

Chapter Twenty-Eight

Elin

Elin leant back in her chair and stared at her computer screen, which had gone into sleep mode. 'Feels like the stuffing's been knocked out of me,' she said to the empty room. That's what Papa used to say sometimes after a long day with awkward customers. But he'd come back fighting and his business went from strength to strength. And she wouldn't let whoever it was, get to her either. How dare this person try to frighten her? Elin drew a deep breath and tried to compose herself. She brought up the screen where she had been working on the Brussels report and was beginning to get into the detail of some data when the phone rang. Despite herself her body responded by a tightening in her chest. What was going on? Enough was enough. Clenching her jaw, she grabbed the phone.

'You bastard, you can't scare me!' She shouted. 'Who do you think you are? Just get lost. Leave me alone!'

'Elin?' It was Michael. 'Are you alright? What's happened?' His voice sounded both puzzled and concerned.

Elin's shoulders dropped in a rush of relief, and then she felt her cheeks go hot. Swearing at the Dean, of all people.

'Oh, Michael. Oh, I'm so sorry. I thought... I've had a couple of funny phone calls. Just heavy breathing. It's unnerved me.' She put her hand to her chest, the pounding of her heart slowing as she spoke.

'What? I don't like the sound of that. It's not advisable to be on your own in your office at this time of night, anyway. Remember the lone working policy? I wouldn't want my wife in that situation. Have you told security you're there?'

'Yes, I told reception I'd be working for a couple of hours, but then I got caught up in some preparation and carried on longer than I meant.' It was true. As always, she'd become caught in the buzz of the research and lost track of time.

'Hmmm. I wanted to speak to you about my thoughts on covering your workload during your absence. When I noticed your office light on I wondered if you could drop by now, if you've time. That is unless you have to go back to see to your mother?'

Steadying her breath, Elin replied. 'No, I don't have to go back. That's fine. My aunt is staying with my mother for a few days. There are the nurses, of course, as well.'

'Great. I'll put some coffee on. It sounds as though you could do with the caffeine.'

Elin closed her computer and stood. It was completely dark outside by this time, and she had an uncomfortable feeling that, if Michael had noticed her light on, probably whoever had rung had seen it too. Maybe that had prompted whoever the creep was, to phone – if they were watching. She shivered at the thought, despite knowing that she wasn't alone in the building. In fact, there were likely to be at least four other staff working late in their offices, but academic work was often solitary, and colleagues would not necessarily be aware of each other's presence.

Never before had Elin felt vulnerable working late. She wondered, as she pulled her coat on, whether the senior management team should come back to the lone working policy and do some further adjustments, given the problems she was experiencing. But then, not many women academics would be staying as late in the office, would they? They'd be working from home, juggling professional and family responsibilities. The thought made her feel even more solitary, as she stretched and massaged the muscles at the back of her neck. Too much time hunched over the laptop.

Closing the door to the office with a soft click, Elin made her way down the dark corridor and stairs. Pools of electric light sprang into life, woken from sleep by the automatic sensor, as she approached the dark stretches ahead. She was reassured by the sound of her heels clicking in the relative hush of the building. There was a worry that she might see someone in the shadows and was glad to reach the bright lights of the front reception area. The night security guard was on duty.

'Alright Dr Fiorelli? You're working late.'

'Time flies when you're having fun,' Elin responded, with an attempt at humour. Now was not the time to stop and explain to him about the latest incident.

There were several darker corridors to traverse before she got to the Dean's office in the other wing of the building. A welcoming aroma of fresh coffee greeted her as she rounded the corner. The outer door to the Dean's suite was open so she went in. Through the half-open inner door, she could see Michael seated at the conference desk reading something on his laptop. He looked solid, reliable and in every way like the senior academic and Dean of Department that he was. But he was also the man who had been her lover all those years ago; the only one she could have stayed with. This was the man for whom she had sacrificed so much of her private life. The man who had caused so much pain. The scars were still there, well hidden under a veneer of professional confidence. He heard her approach and greeted her with a genuine smile which made the corners of his eyes wrinkle.

'Elin. Come in. I have the percolator on the go.'

The room was comfortable, cosy even at this time of night. The uplighter and desk lamp cast a glow over the oak grain of the conference table and the room was warm, soothing almost. What a contrast to the last time she was there. Then she had felt nauseous and on edge. Perhaps it was something to do with the different way she was looking at Michael now. However, the impression of relaxed comfort was counteracted by the pleasant, but formal, way in which Michael stood up to greet her.

'Do sit down. Let me get you a coaster for your cup.'

Elin remembered Michael was the product of a public school, with polished social manners.

He poured the steaming liquid into a mug, sat opposite her at the conference table, where his laptop was open, and regarded her with some concern. 'So, what's going on with these phone calls? You seemed really agitated. Mind you, if I'd been a heavy breather, I'd have put the phone down, pronto. You certainly know how to scare the pants off a man.' He laughed, with a hint of admiration in his voice.

Elin attempted a weak smile. 'There've been a few strange things going on. Little incidents really, but this latest was a bit creepy. I'm sorry you got an earful.'

'What things?'

'I had a note stuck on my door, then derogatory stuff on the intranet–'

'What?'

'It's okay. They've been removed. Somebody's idea of a joke I suppose. But tonight's little episode wasn't funny.' She pushed a wayward strand of hair out of her eye.

'No, it bloody isn't.' He frowned. 'Have you reported all this?'

'Yes, Geraint knows.'

'So, this phone call is an escalation of the harassment you've been suffering. I'm very sorry to hear this, Elin. I know how difficult things have been for you at home. You don't need any more hassle in your life.'

'The thing is, what can I do about it? Minor things really. It strikes me that it's not malicious, but at this time of night it's a bit creepy.' She took a gulp of coffee. 'Whoever it is, they're getting themselves into a lot of trouble. Very stupid.' She placed her half empty mug with care on the coaster.

'We can't do anything more at the moment, but when we find out who's behind it,' he shook an emphatic forefinger, 'there'll be trouble. Sooner or later, they'll make a wrong move, and we'll have them. Leave it with me. I'll speak to security and see what can be done.'

That was reassuring. She knew that Michael would follow up with action. Lovely man though Geraint was, she had little confidence he would do anything much. Put it down to pranks and shrug it off. Perhaps that's all it was, some silly prank. She was so weary.

'How's your mother?' Michael's voice cut across her thoughts.

'We're taking it a day at a time. Good days and bad days. Mum's fading, but she has a very strong will. In fact, last weekend we went for an outing to Cosmeston Lake, which she really enjoyed. We used to go there with my father when I was a child.' Her voice sounded wistful, even to her own ears.

'That sounds very pleasant, I'm glad. And how about you? How are you doing?'

Under Michael's scrutiny Elin squirmed. The phone calls had shaken her, and she was aware of how tired she looked, pale and careworn.

'I'm okay. It's a day at a time for me too.' She turned away so he couldn't see the truth in her eyes.

'Why were you working to such a late hour in the office? I thought you were all into well-being. Long hours culture doesn't sit with your beliefs, does it?'

Was that an accusation or genuine concern? She couldn't tell if he was digging at her or being kind. His face betrayed nothing. Elin sat up straighter in her chair. 'There's so much to do before I take compassionate leave. I want to have everything ready.'

Michael lifted his mug to his lips and peered at Elin over the rim. 'I have a couple of proposals to talk through with you on who will cover what. If you don't feel up to it, though, we can do it another time. These phone calls must have shaken you up. You look a little pale.'

She arched her eyebrows at him. 'No, it's okay. I'd like to talk about it now. It would be a weight off my mind. I hate to leave loose ends.' Unlike the tangled ones in her personal life.

'We've some keen young staff, who will be happy to cover your teaching load. We've already agreed you're going to keep in touch with your master's and doctoral students by email and Skype. I must stress you're not to take on too much in this area while you are away.'

He paused. 'And, then, there's TechSWell...'

'Yes.' Elin hesitated. 'I've been thinking a lot about that.'

'It's a very exciting project. I've looked more closely at the data and interpretations you sent me. I think you're really on to something with your line of research. You always had a knack of thinking outside the box.'

The compliment floated in the air for a moment. Despite herself, she felt a glow of pride. His opinion still mattered.

'I have contacts and it appears that Fonetym are really interested in investigating this angle of health and well-being through complementary apps, though not through being isolated from technology, as you were in your fieldwork. Naturally enough that doesn't sit well with their mission. But they're very keen to take the essence of your message and develop it in their offering.'

She couldn't quite believe what she was hearing and was trying to read his face, but he was giving no indication of his thinking. If this was Fonetym's view, that would be excellent and would lead, almost certainly, to more funding in the next round of the project and into the future.

'It could be a really exciting development for the Department, and it would help us considerably on our road to financial recovery.' Michael sounded positive.

'So, you've been speaking to Fonetym or someone in the company? I knew you had contacts but...' She sat back in her chair, considering his comments. She was struggling to process the implications of what he was saying. This change of tune was unexpected, and she wondered if he had an ulterior motive. Michael Hardwick was a smooth operator, and despite what seemed a sincere interest and concern in her welfare, she was still a little wary.

'Yes. I've some contacts there.' He was waiting for her response.

'I've prepared materials and PowerPoint slides for the next TechSWell meeting in Brussels. That's why I was working so late,' Elin explained. 'I had all the materials ready, but I needed to shape them into a pack that somebody else could present on our behalf.' She drew her hand over her forehead and massaged her temples, exhaustion clouding her thinking process. 'I suppose it'll be Geraint – as a senior member of the Department. I was preparing the pack with him in mind.' It was almost a question.

'That's very helpful, Elin. Thank you. I can see this next meeting is of vital importance. We must have the right person to present your work.' He waited a moment. 'No disrespect to Geraint, but research is not his forte.'

'No. His interest in research is limited. I mean, he's a great communicator and very practical but... but, well, Geraint understands about well-being from the bottom up.' It wasn't coming out the way she wanted. How could she explain her reservations while keeping her respect for Geraint obvious?

'That's very true, I'm sure.' Michael pushed the lid of his laptop closed. The soft ping of emails coming in was silenced.

With a sigh Elin continued, 'I don't know who else would do it. Our coverage of this research area is very thin. This has all come at the wrong time.'

Elin tried to think who else, apart from Geraint, could go in her place. Was he intending she would participate through video call? She wasn't prepared to do that. It was impossible to make one's case properly and engage in discussion on that basis. Most of the team would be present in Brussels, sitting together and debating in one room. She'd been in many such similar meetings and those who tried to participate virtually often had a raw deal. She was running all the arguments against such a move when Michael spoke again.

'Well, I have a solution. I hope you'll approve.' Michael ran his hand through his hair. She recognised his nerves. 'I'll go to Brussels and do the presentation on your behalf. It will help you, the Department and–'

'*You*? Go to Brussels?' Elin could hardly believe her ears. Never had she considered that as a solution. Michael was a researcher with a track record in the area, although not in recent years. He was the Dean of the Department. Well-known and respected internationally as a professional speaker in the innovation and engagement field. It might work. She leant forward a little as she waited to hear what he had to say.

'I know you might be worried about my position in the light of our earlier difference of opinion,' Michael continued, 'but as you can tell from our conversation today, I've moved on in my thinking. I'm committed to making the Department a success. I believe your project offers a great deal to us and the university and I want to support you in making the best of it.'

Elin considered his offer. It was good news for her and her colleagues in the Department. It would be even more essential for the project to be handled carefully in the Brussels meeting. On the other hand, she didn't want to lose the core of her research findings, have him dilute it into some commercial offering for Fonetym, despite the opportunity it offered for further development with their support.

Michael shifted in his chair and added, 'I hope to stay in a permanent position as Dean after the end of the year. You may know that my wife's family come from this area and she is delighted that we've come back to Cardiff. Her parents can see more of us and the children are settling well in school. What do you say?'

Elin winced slightly at the mention of Michael's family. Was this really an honest offer? She twisted her ring on her finger and couldn't decide how to respond.

'I'm not unknown to some of the executives. I think this investigation could be the next big thing. If the Department can become more involved then it could save the sinking ship, so to speak.'

Elin had a flash of insight into his motives. She could see now. It was all about Michael and what her work could do for him. Selfish, as always. Her nostrils flared as she said, 'I don't think so. I don't want my research findings changed into some offering to appease Fonetym.'

'That's not what I intended.' He was taken aback by her response, his posture more rigid. 'I'd deliver your presentation as you wish.'

Elin hurried to stand, almost knocking over her chair. 'And talk to people behind my back trying to downgrade my research findings while sucking up to the money boys. No way. I'll find a way to deliver the presentation myself.' She wanted to scream as her eyes flashed at him, but managed to hold onto a veneer of calmness. In a quiet and deliberate voice, Elin said, 'You and this offer can go to hell.' With that she marched out of the door, leaving it swing shut behind her.

Chapter Twenty-Nine

Elin

March

It had been a strange week. Elin flushed at the memory of losing her temper with Michael, replaying the meeting in her head as she swung between animosity towards him and something else. His genuine concern for her safety had softened her thoughts about him. In the fifteen years, since they'd parted, they had both changed but she had still so much grief, loss and anger suppressed from that time. Every relationship afterwards had been tainted by her inability to trust and her own inner demons. She had, through her own volition, made herself into a workaholic. None of that was Michael's fault.

The more she thought about it the more she knew an apology was needed. As her superior, Michael could discipline her for her outburst, rudeness and unprofessional behaviour. And he had been offering a solution to her problem. It was no good. She would have to swallow her pride, accept with good grace and put her trust in his integrity when he covered for her in Brussels. Would an email apology be enough? Probably not. Best to do it face to face.

It was easier than expected. As she headed along the corridor to his office, Michael emerged, a sheaf of document folders in his hand.

Head held high, Elin wasted no time. 'My apologies, Professor Hardwick, for my behaviour earlier this week. I... it was rude... I'm sorry. I've considered your offer to present my findings at the

TechSWell meeting,' she rushed on, 'and if you are still willing to do that...' Elin paused as she saw Michael's eyebrows lift and a quizzical expression cross his face. What? Was he going to refuse now she'd eaten humble pie?

'My pleasure, Dr Fiorelli.' He was smiling.

She remembered that teasing grin.

'And I'm sure any number of people in this university would like to tell me to go to hell. However, I think Brussels will do for now.'

He left Elin standing open-mouthed as he strode off down the corridor with a definite spring in his step. Cocky so-and-so, but at least it was all sorted now. And he would be a million times better than Geraint.

Time to focus on things at home. Aunt Anne was leaving on Saturday and Elin had invited Sue around to share a meal; a thank you for her support. Mum was too weak to join them, often nauseous at the smell of food and reliant on small portions and energy drinks. Anne remarked that her sister seemed to be shrinking by the day; and, knowing it was true, Elin had been grateful for her aunt's presence to lighten the burden for a few days.

By seven thirty Mum had taken her meds and was asleep. Elin checked on her, stroking her cheek and pulling the sheet up over the wasted body. When she returned to the lounge, Aunt Anne, resplendent in an orange kaftan, gestured to the two glasses of wine sitting on the coffee table. In many ways, Anne resembled her sister. She was always well groomed with never a hair out of place, but a little taller and with a more florid complexion. Anne's dress sense was also different. While Mum wore tailored outfits, Anne dressed in whatever gaudy costume she had picked up from her latest travels. Accessories were similarly bright coloured and exotic. But the main difference between the sisters was Anne's manner. Where Mum was quietly spoken, Anne was loud. She filled a room with her exuberant joy of life. She was also untidy. Elin had noticed the mess in her aunt's bedroom as she passed with clothes scattered over every surface.

After she'd ordered a Chinese meal, Elin sent a text to Sue to tell her the food was arriving soon. When Elin opened the door a short time later, she was surprised to see Sue standing on the doorstep, looking upset, with red-rimmed eyes and hunched shoulders.

'God, Sue, what's happened? You look awful. Come in and join us. You look as though you could do with a glass of wine, or even a bottle.'

Elin steered her into the lounge where Aunt Anne was pouring a second glass for herself. An enquiring look passed between them, but nothing was said.

'It's nothing for you to worry about,' Sue said, as she took the wine glass with shaking hands. 'You've got your own problems.'

'Don't be silly. I want to help. Can you tell us? Is it work?'

Sue bit her thumb nail and gulped, one arm across her body.

'Spit it out, girl. We can't help if we don't know what's the matter.' Anne's tone was matter of fact. 'Come on now. Nothing's that bad, is it?'

Sue seemed to be heartened by that and stuttered. 'It's Rick. You know, the guy I met on Tinder.'

'Yes?' Elin tried to remember which he was, now Sue was on a roll with the online dating.

'He... He...' Sue gulped and sniffed, putting her glass down to fish out a tissue. 'His wife came after me.'

Elin's eyes grew wide. She put her arm around Sue, afraid to ask what had happened next. 'Oh, God... he was married. Didn't you know?'

Sue said, 'Yes,' giving a hollow laugh, 'but he said they were separated, you know. We were just having a drink when this huge woman rushes in and throws a glass at me in the pub. She was mad... so wild.' Sue shuddered before she carried on. 'Rick scarpered and a security guard restrained her, called the police.' Sue was trembling with shock, her legs twitching.

'Did the police charge her?' Anne asked.

Poor Sue. No wonder she looked a wreck.

'Dunno. I left as soon as I could. The woman needs help.' With a shrug, Sue swallowed another mouthful of wine.

'That sounds as though the matter is in hand,' Anne said, in a firm tone. 'You're safe, which is the main thing.' She patted Sue on the shoulder and added, 'Tinder, indeed. What's wrong with meeting someone in real life? I've got a few sure-fire dating tips

I'll share with you.' She winked at Sue who seemed more cheerful, the tension gone from her body. 'Now I think I heard a car outside. Hopefully that's our meal arriving. Just as well. I think we all need it. If I drink any more on an empty stomach, I'll be under the table.'

They ate in the kitchen. A bottle of Prosecco helped the evening to go with a swing, and Sue, during the course of the meal, became more relaxed and even laughed, responding to Anne's lively manner and outrageous stories. Elin had ordered a set meal for three with various meat and vegetable dishes and what seemed like a small mountain of fried rice. She enjoyed the evening, too, but it felt almost surreal that they should be so sociable, and even merry, while her mother lay in another room, unconscious, in a drug-induced sleep. She kept an ear tuned in for sounds from the monitor in case Mum called for her.

The conversation continued through mouthfuls of food.

'Did you tell your aunt about the stuff on the intranet?' asked Sue.

'Yes, she certainly did,' said Anne. 'Who would do such a thing? It's all very strange and mysterious.'

'Oh. I forgot to tell you both. I've also had a heavy breather.' As Elin spoke the conversation stopped and two sets of eyes turned towards her.

Sue's eyes widened, but Anne just snorted with laughter. 'Huh! I wish I had a tenner for every one of those I've had. The first time was when I was in my twenties.'

'What did you do?' Elin smiled at her aunt.

'I had a suspicion who it was. I just asked him if he had a cold. I told him he should try Lemsip and if that didn't work, he should see a doctor about his affliction. He didn't ring again.'

They all laughed. Anne had a way of making even the sinister appear funny.

'When did this heavy breather start? And where? Here or your flat?' Sue asked.

'No. In the office. I was working late, and the phone rang. The first time, nothing; then it went again and there was just the sound of breathing. When it went the third time, I asked who it was. But he hung up.'

Sue shuddered, suddenly serious. 'I hope you reported it.'

Elin felt her cheeks flush as she remembered her response to the final call. 'Well, actually, I reported it to the Dean. By accident.'

'By accident? How'd that happen?' Sue's voice rose, and she leant forward, eyes wide.

'When the phone rang a fourth time, I was so angry I shouted something like, "You don't scare me, you bastard," but it was Michael.'

Both Sue and Anne collapsed in giggles. Elin looked at them for a moment and then she too could see the funny side of it and joined in the laughter. It felt good to make light of the incident and she was glad she'd shared it with them, although she omitted the part where she'd told the Dean to go to hell. Her aunt would have revelled in that little gem, but she wasn't so sure how Sue would react. Michael was, after all, the Dean and should command respect. Anne was becoming very mellow and, when they went back into the lounge, regaled them with her experiences abroad.

'Men are all the same. They don't know how to keep their hands, or anything else, to themselves. I had my bottom pinched in the Vatican of all places would you believe?'

Both Elin and Sue chorused, 'No,' in disbelief.

'It's as true as I'm sitting here. He sidled up to me and then pinched me.'

'What did you do? Slap him?' Elin knew her aunt was quick-witted at times.

'I pinched him back. You should have seen his face.' Anne's raucous laugh filled the room. 'One of the guards saw me. I thought I was going to be arrested or something, but he just winked and then turned away as if nothing had happened. The bum pincher went off.'

'So, tell us what other horrors happened on your travels.' Elin loved to hear her many adventures. Aunt Anne's trips abroad were always action packed.

'Well, when I was working in Sydney, I had a huge bloke come up and demand a kiss. He was completely pissed and could hardly stand he'd drunk so much. He kept on and on, and finally, to get rid of him, I said I'd rather he came to my apartment and wrote an address on a piece of paper.'

'You didn't give him your address?' Sue was incredulous.

'Don't be so daft. No.' Anne was laughing so much she was spluttering, 'I wrote down the address of my boss. An absolute cow of a woman. A real bully. I just wish I'd been there when he turned up.' Anne held her stomach, bending with laughter as she recalled the incident. 'She came in the next day in a fury and demanded to know who had given out her personal address. I just played innocent and pretended to be horrified that some huge drunken lout would call on her. It was hysterical. Catherine thought it was awful, of course, when I told her what I'd done.'

At the mention of her mother Elin stood and went to check on her. Mum was sleeping soundly but stirred a little as Elin put her arm back under the covers. Even the loud laughter hadn't woken her. At least the drugs allowed some respite from the pain. When Elin went back into the lounge, Anne was still in full flow, right in the middle of another dramatic story.

'...Hands everywhere. All I wanted was to enjoy the film in peace. Ah, Elin, I was just telling Sue about my experience in the cinema. I went alone and this bloke sat beside me. No harm until he put his hand on my knee and started moving it under my skirt. I gripped the hand and whispered, "If you don't move your hand, you'll be singing soprano. I've a black belt in judo." You've never seen a man move so fast.'

'Were you ever afraid or felt threatened by anyone?' Elin asked. 'I mean, I swing between anger and unease with these strange goings on. I don't know who it is, or who would have such a grudge against me. Or maybe I'm just paranoid.'

'Hmmm. I've felt uneasy a few times, but I don't take risks. I'm aware that a woman travelling alone seems easy pickings to some men, but I've usually found that a sharp tongue and a confident air works. Try not to worry, Elin. You've kept people informed and you haven't been physically harmed, so let's hope he gets bored and buggers off to annoy somebody else.'

Anne got to her feet staggering a little. 'Oh, dear. I've an early start tomorrow.' She yawned, and with a wink, said to Elin and Sue, 'It's been a lovely evening, girls, but I must get to bed. My beauty sleep, don't you know.' She turned to Sue. 'I think you should stay here tonight. There are more than enough rooms. It's raining and blowing a gale. Besides, there's at least half of that delicious bottle to finish.' She hugged Elin to her ample bosom. 'Courage, my sweet. There's always a lull before the storm.'

Elin wasn't sure what Aunt Anne meant by that, but she held onto her with a surge of affection and gratitude.

When Anne had gone, Sue stood up to get her coat, but Elin said, 'Aunt Anne's right. We have plenty of space. The airing cupboard is full of fresh sheets, so let's make up a bed for you. You'd be soaked walking round to your place in this.' She saw Sue's shoulders drop with relief; and not just at the offer of staying overnight.

'That's kind. I didn't wear my waterproof as I wasn't thinking straight when I came round.' Sue blinked. 'The meal was delicious, and I really needed a good laugh tonight. Your aunt's a scream. It's hard to believe she's your mother's sister, you know. They're poles apart.'

'Aren't they just? Anne always brightens things up. She used to bring me the most inappropriate gifts when I was a child. Lipstick and perfume from Spain. Satin French knickers from Paris. A fertility doll from Africa and a phallus keyring from Majorca.'

'No!' Sue gasped.

'Oh yes.' Elin was shaking with laughter. She remembered Mum's face when she saw the keyring. 'Auntie Anne is always good for a laugh.'

The evening had been a welcome interlude from the stress and strain of the previous weeks, and as she got into bed that evening, Elin thanked her lucky stars for the support of her aunt and that she was back on good terms with Sue. It had been a relief to have some respite from thinking about the hard road ahead.

Chapter Thirty

Elin

April sunshine streamed in through the window and Elin sat to one side of her desk leading a tutorial with a group of third years. This Wednesday afternoon was one of the last meetings before finals and an urgent sense of acceleration towards completion was in the air. She had arranged a question-and-answer session on the group's dissertation topics. In the cramped space the heat soon became overwhelming from the combined effect of the bright sunshine and seven people in a confined space. The students were fanning themselves with paper and Elin could feel her hands becoming slick with perspiration.

'Open that, will you, Joanna, please?' Elin indicated to the student sitting closest to the window. 'We won't be able to get any work done, if we don't get a bit more oxygen in.'

The group shuffled on their chairs to avoid the direct beam of sunshine as it moved round dazzling them, but it was fresher with the waft of spring air, and soon there was a lively conversation underway. Elin had worked with all the students during previous years; the exception in the group being Nick Mackenzie. He was also the one she was most worried about. She knew she would have to be careful how she spoke to him, having noticed, on more than one occasion, that his main means of communication seemed to be a leer, or more usually, a scowl.

They had already received Elin's comments on their drafts before the tutorial and she was pleased with how their studies were developing – working on individual topics within the broad area of young people and well-being. Their enquiries spanned a wide range of personal choices in the area: mental health in adolescence, the role of social media in identity development and anxiety around body image. Elin shared some of the material from her current research for the TechSWell project and suggested further reading. Questions were asked, and answered, and the students were engaged in sharing ideas and issues. Nick, though, sat in the furthest corner, surly and unresponsive, occasionally shifting impatiently in his seat.

'So, well done, everyone.' Elin smiled at them, drawing the session to a close. 'I think that's as far as we'll go today. I'll be in touch by email with more guidance about the submission process. Good discussion. Thank you.'

The students gave thumbs up, mumbling thanks, as they edged out of the small office; all, that is, apart from Nick. He remained seated, legs apart and body slouched in the chair, continuing to look at her with a challenging and unpleasant expression. Elin anticipated trouble and was reassured by hearing her colleague's voice in the next office, and a sudden burst of laughter from his dissertation group.

She left the office door open after the last student had left and went back to her chair. 'Did you want to speak to me?' She had nothing pressing in the next hour, so was free to give him some time. He clearly needed it, judging by his dissertation draft. But he had had a haircut and trimmed his beard and certainly smelt fresher, so perhaps he was turning things around. She hoped that was the case.

'Yes.' He slapped his dissertation draft with the back of his hand, like someone swatting a fly. 'Why have you put all these negative comments? I looked at some of the others and they didnae have anything like that.'

'Well,' Elin chose her words with care, 'there's more to be done if it's to meet the standard required.'

'What dae you mean? I did all it said I needed tae do in the dissertation guidebook.'

It seemed there was a big gap between what he thought was required and the actual level of work he was producing. It happened sometimes. Weaker students failed to distinguish between dropping undigested quotations into their work and engaging in a critical dialogue with the authors they were quoting.

His tone was belligerent, and he stared at her with eyes narrowed in anger. Despite increasing uneasiness, she maintained a calm and steady tone as she attempted to explain. 'If you look again at the dissertation guidelines, you'll see that an important element is engaging with the literature, reading around the topic and showing ability to critique ideas.' She glanced across at him, but his frown did not lessen. 'You've done very little reading, it seems, and so you are currently not able to engage in a deep enough way with the topic.'

'What do you know about it? Your lectures are nothing but a rehash of other people's work.' He leant forward from his slouched position and put his hands on his knees. His expression was increasingly defiant. 'You've made up your mind tae fail me 'cos I've come in late – and I'm no one of your favourites.' He almost spat the words at her.

Elin was startled at his venom. It was impossible to reason with him. His breathing was heavy and forced, as if he was about to unleash his fury. She could see a vein in the side of his throat throbbing and the hairs on the back of her neck stood, prickling in response. Was he dangerous? 'Look, Nick. I can see that perhaps you feel at a disadvantage–'

'Too right,' Nick interrupted. 'I know the score. I know when I'm being treated unfairly.'

'–so, I think the best thing is for you to leave now, and for us to meet again, when you've had a chance to calm down. We can go over the dissertation together and I'll give you some further guidance on the best way forward. I am more than willing to help but when you are willing to listen.' Elin stood up, indicating the meeting was over.

Nick also stood. In the small office, he towered over her, his aftershave overpowering. 'I'm no leaving until this is sorted. You're not going to blow me off again.' He scowled at her, fists clenching and unclenching.

The adrenaline was pulsing through her veins. Drawing on her inner steel, she held her hand in front of her, palm facing him. 'I must ask you to leave. You're harassing me. I will talk to you another time.'

Nick stood far too close for comfort, his breathing heavy. Sweat beaded his forehead. The anger was ready to explode in the tense way he held himself. She had to get him out of this confined space before things escalated. With a show of confidence she didn't feel, Elin moved to the door and opened it.

Nick made no attempt to leave and glared at her, large fists clenched by his sides.

Elin hoped she sounded more in control than she felt. 'Okay. In that case, we need to speak to one of the Senior Management Team. We'll see if Mr Eynon is in his office.'

She led the way, not waiting to see if Nick followed her or had closed the door. She could hear his heavy footsteps pacing behind her all the way to Geraint's office, her heart beating too fast. She knocked on the door, relieved when his voice boomed, 'Come in.'

Elin had intended to go in first to explain the situation, but she didn't have the chance. Nick followed close on her heels and stood next to her, chin jutting out, ready for a fight with his splayed legs and crossed arms.

Geraint turned from his computer towards the two of them eyes flitting from one to the other, obviously assessing the situation. He was on the Student Staff Liaison Committee and used to hearing student complaints through formal and informal channels. 'A visitation. What can I do for you, Dr Fiorelli, and... Nicholas Mackenzie, isn't it?'

Was it significant that Geraint knew Nick's name?

Before Elin could draw breath, Nick launched his attack. 'I've had unfair marking on my dissertation. My supervisor,' Nick nodded in a dismissive way towards Elin and said the word 'supervisor' in a sarcastic tone, 'didnae understand that I've followed everything, like it says in the guidelines. If there's something wrong with my work, I need to know. I need this degree, man.' He spoke directly to Geraint, ignoring Elin, his tone confidential and man-to-man.

'I see,' said Geraint. 'You need to check that your dissertation is up to standard? But the comments your tutor has given you do that. Shows you ways you can work on it to improve.'

Nick snorted.

'That's what I was attempting to explain to Nick, but he responded in a totally disproportionate way. He was obviously upset by my comments but then refused to leave my office. I thought, in the circumstances, it was best if I brought him to talk to you.'

Her face felt hot and flushed and her heart was thumping. The way Geraint spoke to Nick, somehow placed her in the wrong. The little woman who was all upset. She wondered if it had been a female student with problems, whether Geraint would have reacted in this way. But maybe his bluff, man-to man approach was the best one for Nick Mackenzie and might calm him down.

'We do not tolerate aggressive and bullying behaviour to members of staff, especially by male students to female staff.' Geraint's voice was gruff. 'I've had to speak to you before about academic matters, but this behaviour is completely unacceptable. I hope you understand?'

Nick shrugged his shoulders but seemed to back down a little. The fists unravelled and his breathing steadied.

'Right.' Geraint added. 'This is what we're going to do. You, young man, will leave now. There's nothing to be gained when you're in this state, is there now? I will discuss the situation with Dr Fiorelli and get back to you with our advice on the best way forward to support you. But,' Geraint pointed a stubby finger at Nick, 'it's important I make it crystal clear that you, my lad, are on a slippery slope. If you want to get your degree, you need to buckle down and get on with it. This isn't helping anyone.'

Nick seemed to consider what Geraint said. He scowled at them both then capitulated, grunting. 'Alright, I'll go now, nae bother. But I'm no taking any more crap from her.' He pointed a thumb in Elin's direction with a sort of half sneer.

What had she done to make him dislike her so much? Maybe it was women in general? Elin held herself upright, trying to show a calmness she didn't feel. She was not going to get caught up in the drama Nicholas Mackenzie was trying to create by overreacting.

'I mean it. Go now and think about what I've said.' Geraint raised a voice that could carry down a rugby pitch, just a notch, and pointed at the door.

After a moment of facing it out, Nick turned and left with a half-shrug of discontentment.

Elin, legs shaking, sank into the sofa with a sigh of relief.

'Thank you for that. It was getting quite hairy. You can see he's got a big chip on his shoulder. I don't think he'd have attacked me – God, I hope not.' She put a hand to her mouth at the thought of assault. 'But it felt as though he might do something violent, so, spur of the moment thing, I came to you to defuse the situation.'

'Very wise, as always, *blodyn*.' Geraint offered her a bottle of water from the stack he always had to hand for coaching, but she shook her head. 'We know transfer students can be a problem, or, should I say, often bring their issues with them. Mind, we've all got our problems haven't we, now?' Geraint added, with a roll of the eyes. 'You must remember, too, you're in an emotional and vulnerable state with everything going on.'

There it was again. The slight whiff of male complacency, the implication that *he* wouldn't have had the same problem with Nick. Also, he hadn't resolved the situation as far she could see. She answered Geraint in a sharper tone than usual. 'My reaction to this has nothing at all to do with my mother's illness. Nicholas Mackenzie was downright aggressive, completely out of order. If he behaves towards me in that way again, I'll call campus security and the police if necessary.'

Elin stood up. Losing her temper with Geraint was rare but she'd had enough for one day. What now? She just had to hope that her threat of police involvement had shaken him enough to galvanise him into some sort of action. Meanwhile, she had work to do. As she stormed out of his office, she caught Geraint's expression of alarm. Too bad. She closed his office door with a sharp click, and as a reflex action, took her phone out. Three missed calls. She picked up speed and almost ran down the corridor, listening to the first message, from Dr McLeod.

'Dr Fiorelli, your mother collapsed this morning. Please return home as soon as possible.'

Chapter Thirty-One

Elin

By the time Elin reached her mother's house the crisis was over. Mum had slipped and fallen, so the nurse had called for an ambulance. The paramedics had checked her, decided there was little need for hospitalisation, and left again. They had given her some morphine for the pain but otherwise things were normal, or what passed for normal these days. Once she had spoken to the doctor and was satisfied everything was alright Elin drove back to the university, leaving her mother asleep under the nurse's watchful care.

On the way from the university car park to her office she ruminated over the debacle with Nick, thinking through the whole situation. Had she done enough to help Nick Mackenzie? She'd been a bit impatient with him a couple of times, but he'd overstepped the line by a mile, and she couldn't let that sort of behaviour go unnoticed. He had attitude problems, for sure, but it seemed as if Cerys, his girlfriend was helping. He had looked cleaner, more alert at least – and maybe the aggression came from anxiety? Still, that was no excuse. Geraint might have given him a written warning about his behaviour. Or then again...

It was a surprise when she had a call from Jodie almost as soon as she got back in.

'Dr Fiorelli. The Dean wants you here at five o'clock.'

'Any idea what this is about?'

'Sorry, he just said to be here,' Jodie replied, boredom evident in her voice.

Elin put the meeting in her calendar, wondering what could

be so urgent. She arrived just before five, passed Jodie who was in the process of leaving and knocked on the inner office door which Michael had left ajar. He sat at the long conference table and gestured to one of the two empty seats near him, half standing to greet her.

'Ah, Elin, I'm glad you got here first. Geraint told me about the unfortunate incident with your student. I've called him in to discuss his unacceptable behaviour. I won't have my staff harassed.'

Elin was frosty as she sat down at the conference table. 'I've not long come back from Sully. My mother had a fall–'

Just after five Nick strolled in, his dark eyes shadowed, unsure. 'Your PA said it was urgent. What's the matter?'

Michael turned away from Elin towards Nick. So, Geraint had told the Dean. Her outburst had some effect. She noticed Michael's jaw twitching. He indicated for Nick to sit, then put his hands palms down on the polished wood on the table before clasping them together. 'It's been reported to me that your conduct after your tutorial this morning was aggressive. You actually threatened Dr Fiorelli. We do *not* accept that kind of behaviour from our students. What have you got to say for yourself?'

'She dissed me. My dissertation wasn't good enough. I didnae do the referencing "properly".' He challenged Elin with a look. 'Even though I did everything it said in the guidebook.'

Michael appeared to wince but kept his tone measured. 'All that sounds like a fair comment to me.' He stared at Nick. 'Do you think you needed to stand over Dr Fiorelli and rant at her so much that her only course of action was to take you to another, senior member of staff?'

'The fat guy?' Nick retorted, sneering. 'He just gave me a warning. What a joke, her running tae him. I suppose you're going tae tell me I've been a bad boy and slap my hand.'

Elin gasped, hardly believing her eyes and ears. Was Nick drunk or mad? Didn't he know that the Dean had the power to throw him out of the university, even at this late stage of the degree course? Michael jumped up from his chair, flushed with anger. Nick stood, too, with a smirk on his face, not seeming at all cowed by Michael's position.

There was a tense silence for a moment and when Michael

spoke again, he tried to keep his voice low, but Elin could see his anger by the way a nerve twitched in his cheek. His usual suave manner had gone, his hair was less than immaculate, flopping over to one side, and there was a bead of sweat on his forehead.

'Now you listen. Your behaviour was, and is, disrespectful and threatening. It's a privilege to be at this institution and I am sure you do not want to be expelled when you're so close to finishing your degree. So,' Michael glanced over at Elin. 'Dr Fiorelli needs an apology for a start.'

Nick shot a brief look at her and then glared at Michael. 'You academics all stick together. The bloody elite. You wi' your fancy car and personalised number plates.' He sneered at Michael. Then, turning on Elin, he added, 'You wi' your stuck up, know it all ways. Think you're special.' He almost smirked. 'Easy to put the frighteners on you.'

'What do you mean?' Elin asked, her voice little more than a whisper.

'Nae sense o' humour. Didnae like my wee jokes.'

Elin closed her eyes for a second as she thought. When she opened them, her gaze skewered Nick. 'You're the one who put the note on my door, aren't you? You put that image on the intranet, too, I bet. And those phone calls.'

'What phone calls?'

'Ringing my office at night. It wasn't funny.' Elin could see Michael's eyes narrow as Nick denied the charge, shaking his head.

'Hold on now. The note and photo fair enough, but phone calls. That wasnae me. I swear.' He looked from one to the other, eyes wide.

Elin was inclined to believe him, although she could hear Michael's noisy breathing as if he was trying to restrain himself from physically intervening.

'Why all this, Nick? What have I done to upset you so much?' Elin smoothed the leg of her trousers with a clammy palm.

Nick said nothing at first, shifting from one foot to the other and looking down at the floor. Then he muttered. 'You gimme crap marks. I need this degree and you just didnae seem to care. It wasn't fair.' Nick's voice had lost its bravado, a hangdog teenager sort of whining.

Elin jumped as Michael yelled. 'For God's sake, Nick! You're not a child. I should have thought by now you'd have realised you get out what you put in. Dr Fiorelli's one of the most caring and conscientious tutors in this university. If you got poor marks, it was because that's what you deserved.'

He swung around towards Elin. 'Dr Fiorelli, this student has obviously stepped way over the line in his behaviour towards you. In view of today's added threatening behaviour, do you want to press charges? Shall I ring the police?'

Elin regarded both men while debating what to do next. Something was going on here. The familiarity of Nick's behaviour and the Dean's ambivalent attitude towards him indicated something deeper.

Nick appeared startled at the mention of the police and now still stood, shoulders hunched, in contrast to the cocky swagger he'd brought into the office, visibly shaking. Maybe he'd begun to realise what a stupid thing he'd done and the trouble he was in. 'I didnae do those phone calls. I'm not that daft,' his voice came out as an irritating whine.

Elin considered him as he gazed down at the floor. Was he speaking the truth? What was going on in his mind to behave like that? She glanced at Michael who was watching her, shoulders tense. At last, she said, 'I don't want to be the cause of ruining someone's life.' She tried, without success, to catch Nick's eye. 'If Nick is prepared to give me a written apology, outlining what he's done, as a guarantee it won't happen again, then we'll put it behind us. However, I think it's best if another member of staff supervises his dissertation.'

Michael released a breath and turned to Nick. 'You don't deserve it. I hope you know that. You're very lucky that Dr Fiorelli is so fair-minded. I was prepared to make that call.' He pointed his finger at Nick. 'If there is any repeat of the threatening behaviour, if you put as much as a toe out of line then there'll be no further chances. You'll be out of this university and facing police charges for harassment. Do I make myself clear?'

Nick nodded and mumbled, 'Yeah. Sorry. I didnae mean no harm.' He turned towards Elin as he spoke but still couldn't look at her. He bit his lip and sniffed. A sorry case now he had been found out.

'I'll arrange for someone else to undertake your supervision, as Dr Fiorelli has stipulated, so she will be spared any further connection with you.' Michael carried on speaking, as Nick examined the carpet. 'If you meet by chance, in the corridor or the café, you will be totally respectful. Now, I suggest you make haste in drafting that apology. I expect a copy on my desk first thing in the morning.'

With little more than a grunt, Nick bolted out of the office, leaving the door open behind him.

In the silence that followed Michael turned to Elin, running his fingers through his hair, reordering its dishevelment. He seemed reluctant to speak.

Elin felt her shoulders drop with relief. Nick Mackenzie was the source of the negativity that had been directed at her. She didn't need to worry about that any more, wondering who it was and what else was going to happen. She glanced at Michael. 'Thank you. But I don't understand. Why go to such lengths to make my life miserable? I'm always scrupulously fair with my students.' She twisted her signet ring. 'And I haven't seen you so angry since... There's something else going on here.' She looked at him, questioning.

'You should know...' Michael swallowed avoiding her gaze, staring up at the ceiling before he could go on. 'Well, the fact is, Nicolas Mackenzie is my son.'

Elin's head felt as if it was spinning. Yes, of course. She remembered the photograph on Michael's desk when they first met. The dark-haired woman and the smiling boy. Why hadn't she seen the resemblance between Nick and his father? They were the same build, had the same eyes and compelling stare, the same way of standing. She felt disorientated. Nothing made sense and yet everything did. When she spoke, her voice was a whisper. 'Did... did he know about...?'

'No.' Michael shifted on his chair, leaning forward and then back. 'At least, I don't think so. Nick knew about an affair with a student but not her name. He's got serious personal problems. After we moved to Scotland, after...' Michael paused again, 'well, then life seemed to fall apart. His mother's drinking got worse. I suppose I abandoned him when he needed me most. I was a crap father.'

Elin didn't know what to do or say. Nick was the little boy in that photo on Michael's desk when she first knew him. Incredible but true. She had been complicit in wrecking that child's life. Thank God she hadn't insisted on police involvement.

Now Michael had started, it all seemed to pour out as they sat opposite each other. 'I didn't know he was a student here until just after Christmas. He came into the office and created a scene. But he's had a hard time of it. A lot of the blame for his behaviour boils down to an alcoholic mother and not having a father to guide him.'

Michael wrung his clasped hands together. Elin stretched her own towards him in a gesture of empathy. He responded, in a voice cracking with emotion and gratitude. 'Thank you for not pushing the issue. But I would have called the police if you'd wanted. You know that, don't you?'

His eyes told their own story, full of remorse and sincerity. As Elin looked into them, she realised that her feelings for this man had changed so much. First, there had been love, overwhelming love, taking over her life. Then there was trauma, and for a long time, bitterness, making her the person she had become, unable to trust any man enough to form a long-term, loving partnership. Now, she felt sympathy, and with that sympathy came some relief, an easing of the suffering she'd felt for so many years.

'It's alright, Michael. I understand. I played a role in ruining that young man's life once and I don't want to do it a second time. He's had enough misfortune already. I really hope he gets his degree. Let's do all we can to help him.'

Shortly after she left to return to Sully, and as she walked out to her car, she continued to think about Nick. If Michael felt guilty about his son, well, she shared some of that guilt. When they embarked on that tempestuous and ill-fated affair she hadn't thought twice about the child, Nicholas. Michael had told her his marriage was all but over and she'd believed it. She hadn't asked questions because she hadn't wanted answers. Now, childless herself, she felt a rush of shame at how selfish she'd been. The convenient lies she'd told herself. If Nick Mackenzie was a mess, she shared in the blame, even though he didn't know it. And she hoped he'd never find out.

Chapter Thirty-Two

Michael

Early April

Michael looked up for a moment from his papers, as the Eurostar moved smoothly through the Belgium landscape towards Brussels. He felt energised by the prospect of the conference – by life in general. The financial health of the Department was improving, and he had an Easter break with the family in Crete to look forward to.

Okay, it was a while since he'd engaged in the research community, but it was something he wanted to get back into. The TechSWell project was ideal and the empirical data from Elin's notebooks added to the attraction. All the scanned extracts in her italic script and the analyses impressed him with their cogency and insight. She'd been a good research student, but this material showed just how much she'd developed over the last fifteen years.

Plus, he was seriously glad to be out of the office for a while. Three or four of the younger staff had already told him they were looking for jobs elsewhere – not that their departure would make much of a dent in the deficit. A lot to do to get everything on track, but we're getting there, he congratulated himself, sitting up straighter and squaring his shoulders.

At least the incident with Nick and Elin seemed to have been resolved. Elin had accepted Nick's apology. He had kept out of her way, knuckled down to work and generally toed the line. He'd been telling the truth about the telephone calls. Nick hadn't been responsible for the heavy breather calls. A switchboard glitch,

Elin reported a week or so afterwards. Thank God.

Geraint, who'd passed on Nick's dissertation to another colleague, told Michael the lad would scrape through and should get his degree, barring any further upsets. Let's hope to Heaven that's it. Once he was sure Nick was on the straight and narrow and staying clean, he'd see what he could do to introduce him to Anwen and the boys. Too little perhaps but maybe not too late to build bridges. Things could improve if they both wanted to re-establish some sort of father and son relationship. Time alone would tell if that was possible.

For the last half an hour before the train arrived, Michael finished reading through Elin's notes to accompany her Power-Point presentation. He looked forward to presenting the talk. Elin Fiorelli certainly had fulfilled the potential she'd shown as a PhD student – and more. Who'd have thought it? Of the group he'd supervised, although she was talented, she wasn't the obvious choice of rising academic star. Something about her in those days gave out an impression of limitation, indefinable, but evident. Maybe it was the fact that she was a first-generation university student; maybe it was her naivete. Or, and he grimaced to himself, maybe it was because she was so besotted, so in love with him, he didn't see past that to her ability.

He knew she'd never married or had a family and did suspect that, if she'd been happier in her personal life, her academic success might have been less stellar. Can't say that nowadays. Don't be sexist, he reminded himself with a small smile. The woman sitting opposite smiled back and they struck up a conversation about Brussels. She was proud of what the city had to offer a visitor. Michael made a note of a couple of attractions he would visit if he had time. He'd chosen not to attend first day of the conference and the evening dinner, but might squeeze in something that evening.

'Professor Hardwick from Brynderwen University,' he said to the young postgraduate student on the delegates' reception desk the next morning after breakfast, who then handed him a name badge and conference pack. The whole event was, conveniently, being held in the hotel where the delegates were staying; an intensive two days of research papers and then a meeting of the management steering committee. A key purpose was to review and coalesce TechSWell's emerging themes and build on the findings of the different research groups at the end of Phase One.

Michael spent a pleasant morning attending research papers and making notes; and he felt, by lunchtime, that he'd played himself into TechSWell. He went to the reception desk to check on arrangements for his presentation.

'Ah, yes, Professor Hardwick.' Agneta, it said on her name badge, greeted him in perfect English, clipped and without a noticeable accent. 'We are pleased to welcome you to our meeting. You are presenting Dr Fiorelli's paper? Professor Nordin, our project coordinator, asked me to look after you. If you just wait for a few moments, I will ask one of my colleagues to take over from me and then I take you to the room.' She held out a hand. 'First, if you kindly give me your memory stick, I will download the presentation onto the master here.' The girl was very pretty, doe-eyed with long, dark hair, the perfect hostess.

'Professor Hardwick.'

Michael turned to see a tall, thin, young man with a serious expression addressing him. He was handsome, but in a way that was almost coincidental to his other qualities. The main impression he gave was of an intense, cerebral focus.

'Excuse me. I heard you speaking to Agneta. Please allow me to introduce myself. My name is Wolfgang Richter.' He extended his hand. 'I worked with Elin on the project in Finland. We have written a paper together about that experience.'

'Ah, yes. You spent some months together, in the wilds.' Michael managed to convey the impression there might have been something more than just research shared between them.

Either the implication was lost on Wolfgang, or he chose to ignore it. 'Dr Fiorelli is an outstanding researcher. I learnt a lot from her as an older colleague. Although we didn't see eye to eye on some matters, we were both committed to the spirit of the research. I'm looking forward very much to hearing her findings, which you will present at this meeting.'

'Excellent.' Michael was bored already, not with what Wolfgang said, but the way he said it. Little danger of this intense young man having swept Elin off her feet.

Agneta had finished loading Elin's presentation and stood waiting. 'Professor Hardwick. Please come this way.'

Michael followed her to the seminar room, which was a medium-sized space. He estimated there would be about thirty to forty people present, most of whom would be TechSWell representatives from the participating institutions around Europe. When he gave his own talks, on Universities as Sites of Innovation and Collaboration with External Agencies, it was generally to a much larger and more mixed audience of policymakers, civil servants, university administrators and academics. Evaluating the setting, he felt confident he would make a good impression. Quite often, knowing the power and clarity of his speaking voice, he didn't use a microphone. Probably wouldn't today.

The student showed Michael where Elin's presentation was on the desktop and where they kept the wireless gizmo to click through and highlight features on the PowerPoint slides. The room was icy, fanned by the breeze of air conditioning, even though outside it was a warm spring day.

'Could you please turn the air con down?' Michael asked. 'We don't want to freeze our audience.'

'We can adjust it a little, but Professor Nordin likes to keep the temperature cool. I expect you'll get warmer when everybody is in the room. Is there anything else you need? There's water here for each speaker.'

Okay, so Prof Nordin was a hard Scandi man, or the place was full of menopausal women. He smiled at Agneta. 'No, that's all fine, thank you.'

When they returned to the reception area, he saw a couple of Fonetym people he knew. The guys he'd spoken to before. They wouldn't have got the message of Elin's presentation properly without the background context he'd supplied. He strolled over and held out his hand. 'Good afternoon, gentlemen. Delighted to meet you again. TechSWell promises to be an innovative and original project. I am so glad I was able to be here on behalf of our Department and university – and Dr Fiorelli, of course.'

Both men, prosperous, middle-aged, grey-suited and serious

mannered, acknowledged Michael and shook his hand.

'Yes, indeed. Even before we spoke to you, Professor Hardwick, we were impressed by this project. Dr Fiorelli is a fine researcher and excellent communicator.' The more senior of the two men, stout and with a neatly trimmed grey beard gazed up at Michael, a serious expression on his face. 'We're looking forward to hearing more details about her findings at this point in the project.'

There was a general drift out of the reception area and to the seminar room, and shortly after that, the afternoon session began. Michael's paper was scheduled towards the end of the meeting, after which there was a break for refreshments. The project management team had their own meeting over dinner later that evening. If Elin was there, she'd have attended, but Michael was returning home. Far too much happening in the Department to leave for more than one overnight stay. Elin would catch up with the management team later through video link, she had told him. The most important thing today was to present her findings. And he was ready.

As soon as he clicked the first slide on the PowerPoint, he felt how the audience responded, surprised, engaged and largely positive; and, in the light of the other papers, Michael could see Elin's contribution offered a fresh and original angle. Her supporting notes had been immaculate, and she clearly knew the sorts of questions the project team might ask and how to prepare guiding material so that someone else could present her ideas.

The afternoon passed in a flash with other speakers and presentations until it was time for Professor Nordin to summarise the key points. Michael observed he was tall and a distinguished-looking man. His iron-grey shoulder length hair was swept back off his face in a dramatic fashion and he wore bold designer glasses. His English was perfect, American-accented, with a gentle Scandinavian lilt. Michael took notes of his main points to report back to Elin.

'One of the most important aspects to come out of the TechSWell project so far, I think we all agree, is Dr Elin Fiorelli's work, kindly presented today by Professor Hardwick, from Brynderwen University.' Professor Nordin gave an elegant wave in Michael's direction.

'Well-being, as we know, is an area that many smartphones are currently developing. There is a real opportunity now for cutting edge research on practical applications to improve mental health, with the potential to benefit millions of people worldwide. Equally, colleagues have presented today on how technology can increase stress and anger, such as cases where banking or shopping apps fail to respond intuitively; or respond in limited and frustrating ways.'

Several members of the audience inclined their heads in agreement.

'Counteracting the negative effects of technology on well-being will be an important issue into the future. Dr Fiorelli's exploration of isolation from technology, in tandem with Dr Richter's expertise in smartphone technology, offer a novel, indeed unique, contribution.'

Michael felt a rush of adrenaline as he contemplated how this could potentially play out in funding terms for his Department. All good stuff. He'd contact the Fonetym guys again with some ideas when he'd worked something out.

Professor Nordin continued to explain, 'As we see, it is especially exciting to consider ways in which there are practical, real-life applications arising out of our research. So, naturally,' Professor Nordin indicated, with another sweep of his arm, one section of the room, 'we are so very glad that Fonetym are here from the UK. They are ahead of the game.'

There was applause and murmuring as he concluded his overview of the project to date and objectives for the next phase. The buzz continued as the audience dispersed back to the foyer and people chatted over their drinks in the reception area. Michael sought out Wolfgang Richter. He hadn't realised he had expertise in smartphone technology and wanted to quiz him on his part in the TechSWell project.

While Michael was talking to him, from the corner of his eye he saw Professor Nordin approach.

'Professor Hardwick. Thank you again for coming to present today. It was much appreciated that you, as Head of Department, represented your university.'

Close at hand, Michael saw that Professor Nordin was younger than he'd appeared at a distance, probably the effect of the grey hair and designer glasses. Behind the lenses, he had piercing blue eyes. In an instant, Michael recognised a fellow ambitious academic and felt a slight pang of jealousy that he wasn't leading a project such as TechSWell. Despite being successful, to all intents and purposes, to the outside world, he always felt he'd underachieved compared to his two older sisters, one being a Professor of Medicine and the other a Diplomat. He wanted, needed even, to be appointed as Dean and to be engaged again in cutting-edge research.

'How is Dr Fiorelli?' Lars Nordin asked. 'I was so sorry to hear that her mother is terminally ill. Please send her my best wishes and those of all of us here on the TechSWell project. We'll be in touch with her, of course, on administrative matters, but in the meantime, you have given us an important steer on exciting research themes through her PowerPoint slides. We're looking forward eagerly to working with her on the next phase of the research. A valuable member of our team and your university.'

Later that evening Michael sat on the train as it thundered through the tunnel and reflected on events. Not only had the meeting been highly successful, but it confirmed his earlier decision that Elin should be taken off his list of at-risk staff. Her respect in that international field had helped him reach that conclusion. All in all, he was glad he'd gone. A very useful trip in more ways than one. If he played his cards right, Michael reckoned he could solve the Department's problems and secure his job. A very satisfying outcome.

Chapter Thirty-Three

Elin

April – Easter

L ife seemed to be filled with goodbyes. When Jenny rang her
voice was bright with excitement.

'It's a huge step, but... if I don't take the risk then I'd always be
wondering what if.'

'I'm just sorry we couldn't have a farewell weekend,' Elin
gripped the phone tighter, forcing a lightness into her voice, 'but,
hey, what a party we'll have when I can come to Oz and visit you
guys.'

'I'm sorry I won't be there when...'

'Well, nobody knew this was coming. Look, we'll talk again.
When you get there. I want to hear every detail. Okay?'

'You'll let me know...'

'Yes. Got to dash.' Elin closed her eyes. How much she wished
she had Jenny's support now, like all those years ago. Dark times
but she'd survived, adjusted, moved on. Or thought she had.

The Easter break brought Elin relief of a sort. The lecturing was
finished, but the marking period had begun. Undergraduate assignments were mostly online and she had arranged to talk to
her masters and PhD students via video link if they needed face-
to-face consultations. When she explained her home situation to
them; the students, almost as a group, were supportive and that

understanding made things easier for Elin. Her heart was full as she thought again how much she valued and enjoyed her work with these young people.

Mum was failing fast and it was clear that she had little time left. March had drifted into April without either of them registering the change, each day a replica of the last. Then one morning–

'I want to discuss the funeral details again.' Mum's voice was a whisper.

'We don't have to do that today. I know you don't want a fuss. A simple cremation. That's okay.'

Elin swallowed the lump in her throat. Her heart felt heavy with dread. Anticipation of her mother's death and organisation of the funeral were shadowy horrors ahead. She was aware Mum had hated the pomp and ceremony of the Catholic funeral they had arranged for Papa.

Even at death's door her mother remained adamant how things would be done. A ghostly shadow of her old domineering self.

'We... we *do* have to do it. I want my ashes...' she coughed, 'scattered with your father's. His ashes, they're still in... in the bottom of the wardrobe. I didn't know what to do with them. And I wanted him near me.'

Despite her frail condition, a glimmer of a smile appeared. Elin knew her father's ashes hadn't been scattered or interred anywhere, but it was an issue she'd been reluctant to raise. As time passed, they grieved in their separate ways. Mum had made Papa's life difficult at times but there was no doubt she loved him. Elin suppressed a bubble of laughter. The thought of the ashes hidden in the depths of the wardrobe with her mother's clothes and shoes was comical but also touching, a token of her love. Mum caught her eye.

'Yes, he's stuck in there with my high heels... and boots.' Her voice broke on a little sob. 'Poor Papa. I gave him a hard life. Selfish at times. Still, I'll try... try harder if we meet up again.'

'He adored you, Mum. I don't think Papa felt he had a hard life. I remember lots of laughter and lots of love.' As she stroked her mother's hand, Elin reminded her of happier times. 'Papa enjoyed his life right up until he became so ill. Even then he tried to make you laugh with those awful jokes.'

Mum gazed into the distance and nodded. Whatever she was remembering, it was pleasant as she smiled and sighed a little. 'No hymns, Elin. I want the Brahms and... a poem... something uplifting like...'

A coughing fit took over and Mum's frame shook with the effort. Elin held her and rubbed her back. It was like holding a skeleton and Mum was breathless by the time she'd finished. She slumped back onto the pillow, panting as if she had just run a marathon.

Elin stood up. 'I'll go and get you a glass of water with some honey.'

'Too late... time's running... out.' Every word was an effort and Mum's chest heaved as she squeezed out each syllable. 'Some... thing...'

Elin bent and touched her mother's arm. 'Mum, you're exhausted. Rest for a little while and I'll sit with you while you sleep. Tell me after.'

Mum raised a hand as if to protest but the effort was too much, and she dropped it back on to the bed. She closed her eyes.

Elin hurried to bring the drink. She stirred the water and watched as the honey changed from a lump to pale liquid gold, holding the glass close to her mother's mouth and giving her a straw to suck through.

After a couple of sips, Mum pushed the straw away with her tongue and lay back against the pillows. Her voice was weak, 'Love... you.' She gazed at Elin and closed her eyes again.

Mum so rarely expressed any overt affection and Elin could feel her own eyes fill with tears. She brushed them away with a finger. No time for that. There was too much to do and think about.

That was the last time her mother spoke to her. During the night she muttered and groaned a few times. At one point, she called out something that sounded like a name. Then she slipped into a coma. Elin lived in a half-world looking after her mother and waiting to see if she regained consciousness, although she knew in her heart of hearts this was the end. When the doctor came, Elin asked, 'Will it be long?'

Dr McLeod shook her head. 'We're looking at a few days, a week at most. If your mother is in pain, ring the surgery. She seems quiet and peaceful, but that could change.' She placed a hand on Elin's arm, a light touch. 'I'm very sorry. We will do everything we can to make her comfortable.'

Elin felt her throat tighten as a strange calmness took over. She couldn't afford to lose herself in misery now. There'd be time enough to grieve when the nightmare was over, so, lips tightly closed, keeping her emotions in check, she went to the bedroom to watch over her mother, stroking her hand, wetting her lips with a sponge and mopping her brow with a damp flannel. As day passed into night and night into day, Elin lost all sense of time.

When Anne rang sometime later for an update, her aunt's worry was evident in her hushed tone. 'How is she, darling?'

'No change. She opened her eyes once, but they were glazed over. I don't think she could see anything.'

'You sound exhausted, darling. Are you looking after yourself?'

At the words of sympathy Elin's eyes filled. 'It's hard. I feel so useless.'

'Do you want me to come down, darling? To be there. Maybe it would help.' The hesitancy in Anne's voice betrayed her reluctance and Elin knew that, despite her good intentions, Anne would not come until the end. It would be too painful to see her older sister's daily suffering.

'I'll be fine. I'm just worn out. It won't be long. I... I'll ring you when...' Elin's voice broke.

'I'm here for you, darling. When mother died it was sudden. We had no time to prepare ourselves. You're strong. You'll be alright.'

Elin nodded, even though she knew Anne couldn't see her. How could she explain? It was her duty, as an only child, to be with her mother in her final hours and she felt both deep love and the scars of their many battles over the years.

Mum loved her classical music, so Elin moved the CD player into the bedroom and put on some of her favourites. Somewhere she'd read that hearing was the last sense to disappear. The music was soothing, relaxing somehow, she hoped, for both of them.

Now and again, Elin slipped out to have a drink, graze on tasteless food or use the bathroom. At night, she lay on the chaise longue in the corner and covered herself with a duvet. She managed to nap a little, but as time went on, she felt more and more sapped of energy. She knew she looked gaunt, with pale face and dark shadows under her eyes. She was living on her nerves, wound up tight with anticipation and exhaustion. Luckily, her students were supportive, and she'd only had a few email enquiries to deal with. No one had tried to contact her by video; and she was grateful for that.

Sue called one day while the nurses were there. She stared, open-mouthed, when Elin opened the door, putting a hand on her arm. 'Oh, God. You look... you're grey. Have you had any sleep?'

'A bit. I doze on the chaise, but it's not restful.' Elin found it a struggle to speak. 'Every moan or movement and I'm awake. Mum wouldn't want to be alone when she finally goes. The nurses are turning her.'

Sue listened. 'You've put music on for her.'

Elin nodded. 'I've been playing her favourites. It's a bit of comforting background. Coffee?' Elin turned too quickly then, feeling weak and faint, stretching a hand to the wall to steady herself.

'Are you okay?' Sue rushed forward. 'Have you eaten?'

Elin shook her head.

'Well, then, I'll make some scrambled eggs on toast. That's simple, easy to cook. You sit down a minute.'

Elin slumped onto a chair in the kitchen while Sue set about cooking. She asked little, but Elin was glad to talk.

'Even when it's expected, death is so hard, isn't it? I feel as though she's gone already. A body struggling for every breath. Even her eyeballs look an orange colour,' Elin's voice cracked. She bit her lip to stop herself from crying. 'It's like she's not my Mum anymore and there's nothing I can do but watch. It's so awful.'

Sue gave her a pat on the shoulder and put the eggs and toast down in front of her. 'Eat.'

A kind word would have resulted in a deluge of tears and Elin was grateful for Sue's brusque tone. Once she began to eat, she was hungry, shovelling the food into her mouth. When did she last have anything more than a drink and a biscuit? Two days? Three?

Before leaving, the nurses came to speak to Elin. The older one, short, scrawny and with dyed hair pulled back into an untidy bun, said, 'Her breathing has changed. It won't be long now. I'll be back to spend the night here.'

Elin opened her mouth. The agency nurses were paid by the hour. They didn't come at night.

The nurse raised a hand to stop Elin from speaking. 'It'll be a privilege, love. Mrs Fiorelli was kind to me when my Gwyn passed on. I'm not working for the next three days. What I do in my time's none of the agency's business, is it now?'

Elin had no memory of the woman, even when she said her name, Myfanwy Pritchard. What kindness had her mother performed? Everything was a blur. Still, Elin was grateful that she wouldn't be alone when it happened.

The night stretched on. Sue left and Elin sat and watched her mother's body rise and fall as if it was being pumped up. Every breath was an effort. It was heartbreaking to watch and difficult to know what to do to ease the suffering. When the nurse returned around ten o'clock, the rattling in Mum's chest was obvious. Elin expected each breath to be the last. She couldn't take her eyes from her mother's face. Willing the suffering to be over and yet dreading it. She sat holding her mother's hand, stroking the wrinkled skin. It was already cold.

A sudden gasp. Then nothing. Elin felt a pain in the centre of her own chest. Time seemed to stop. She tried to speak but her throat was dry. At last, she managed a strangled whisper.

'Is... I think she's gone.' Elin turned to the nurse who felt for a pulse, then put her hand on Mum's chest. Elin held her breath.

'You can go now,' the nurse said, her voice a whisper. The body heaved a final time, expelling one last breath.

Catherine Fiorelli's life had ended. Elin was alone in the world.

Chapter Thirty-Four

Elin

April

Elin woke up from one of those heavy, almost drugged sleeps brought on by exhaustion. It was the morning of her mother's funeral. From across the corridor, she could hear the loud, rasping snores of her aunt. After all the anxiety and listening out for breathing of the last weeks, it was strangely reassuring. Had they got everything sorted? Flowers for the church; music; caterers; printout of tribute. Elin went through the last of the many lists made over the week-and-a-half since her mother's death. The undertaker had been helpful, but Elin wanted to double-check everything. That bit, at least, was the same as when her father had died: a sort of suspended animation of normal life, full of hectic, practical activity in preparation for the funeral.

'Good to keep busy at a time like this, Elin,' Aunt Anne had said, as they had been ringing round to find caterers for the funeral tea a few days before. 'Your Mum would never settle for second best when it comes to organising an event, and this is her goddamned funeral of all things.'

They had both laughed in shared understanding of her foibles. In the end, they had found an expensive, top-end catering company and were pleased with the selection of quality products they offered.

Elin remembered that her mother had done all the catering for her father's funeral. It'd been a culinary masterclass, an outpouring of her love and grief. Elin knew she was a very mediocre cook herself, another way she was different from her mother, and she was glad Aunt

Anne was there to help. Every now and again, in the midst of all the busy organisation, she had a desperate feeling of grief and loss. She knew of friends whose parents were both alive, who even had grand-parents hale and hearty into their eighties and nineties, and siblings so they could support each other. She had never felt so solitary.

At twelve o'clock, Elin and her aunt were picked up by the funeral director and driven to the new crematorium. The gardens and wild-flower section at the front looked beautiful in the spring sunshine, as if it had been there for years, a peaceful setting to say goodbye.

'Ready, darling?' Her aunt squeezed her hand and they got out of the limousine.

The bright sunshine made Elin blink as she looked around at the small group of people standing outside the chapel. She saw Uncle Julio and Aunt Maria first. They were not actually related to her family, but Uncle Julio had given her father good contacts in the Italian Welsh community when he arrived. They'd worked together as Angelo had built up the business. She hadn't seen him for a few years, and he looked older and more wizened than she remembered, especially next to the substantial figure of his wife.

'Uncle Julio and Aunt Maria. Thank you so much for coming. Good to see you.'

They kissed each other on both cheeks. Looking around, she saw some of Mum's friends from the village; the couple from next door and the nurse who had been so good to her mother over the last few weeks. Seeing Myfanwy evoked an image of her mother in bed those last few days. Elin felt a lump in her throat and tears rising to her eyes.

Elin nodded to them, struggling for composure. It was a relief to see a small group of staff from the Department, including Geraint and Sue, but no sign of Michael. Sue came up to Elin and gave her a hug. Geraint shook her hand and spoke on behalf of the group.

'We wanted to pay our respects. Thank you for the invitation to the tea as well, but we won't come back to the house afterwards. Take care, *blodyn*.'

Elin and her aunt went towards the smaller of the two chapels. Mum had wanted a humanist service and a piece by Brahms at the exact moment of the cremation. As the coffin was rolled in, smooth on its brass wheels, they followed behind. Elin focused on the pink and blue flowers she had ordered for her mother, placed on top of the coffin, trying to draw enough strength to be able to give the eulogy she'd written. Both Aunt Anne and Sue had offered to read for her if she found it was too difficult. In the end, when the time came, she managed; and read her tribute well, as people told her later.

As she left her seat and went to the front to speak, Elin saw a tall figure slip in quietly and sit at the back of the chapel. Oh, good God. Michael.

He caught her eye, nodded and she inclined her head slightly. Yes, it seemed right he was there. Following her eulogy, other friends and relatives came forward to speak about her mother or to read poems: Aunt Anne and another of Papa's colleagues, Marcello Conti, greying but still charismatic, the owner of several Italian restaurants in and around Cardiff.

Then Elin heard a familiar voice, with its distinctive London accent. Sue.

> *When I am dead, my dearest,*
> *Sing no sad songs for me;*
> *Plant thou no roses at my head,*
> *Nor shady cypress tree:*
> *Be the green grass above me*
> *With showers and dewdrops wet;*
> *And if thou wilt, remember,*
> *And if thou wilt, forget.*
> *I shall not see the shadows,*
> *I shall not feel the rain;*
> *I shall not hear the nightingale*
> *Sing on, as if in pain;*
> *And dreaming through the twilight*
> *That doth not rise nor set,*
> *Haply I may remember*
> *And haply may forget.*

Sue read the Christina Rossetti poem beautifully, and as she got to the line, 'I shall not hear the nightingale,' Elin could not prevent her sobs. Her aunt passed her a clutch of tissues. The conclusion of the service was peaceful and fitting with the music her mother had chosen, Brahms *Morning Mood* drifting in the air.

Afterwards, outside in the spring sunshine, people stood

talking. The group from Brynderwen stood slightly apart from the rest and Elin left her aunt to go over and speak to them.

'Thank you so much for coming. It means the world to me that my friends and colleagues are here. If any of you are able to, please do come back to the house.'

Michael took Elin's hand in his and said, 'It was a beautiful service, Elin. I'm so sorry that I arrived a little late. We just returned this morning from our holiday; our flight was delayed.'

'It's fine. I hope you can join us back at the house.' Elin was speaking on autopilot, the only way to get through the day.

'Thanks, but unfortunately I can't accept. I have meetings this afternoon.'

His words seem to come to her from a long distance, but they registered, even at this moment when she had the least interest in work than she had ever had in her life. Behind Michael, Elin could see her aunt approaching.

Anne held out her hand and gave Michael one of her bold and captivating smiles. 'It's good to see Elin supported by her colleagues. I'm Anne, Catherine's sister and Elin's aunt.'

Elin cringed as Anne held Michael's hand for a moment too long. It might work with most men, but this wasn't the right time, or place. Still, Michael seemed amused rather than offended and perhaps he was flattered. Aunt Anne was very charming in her own, overpowering way. 'Delighted to have met you, Michael. I hope we might meet again in the future.'

'Excellent.' Michael smiled down at her and gently released his hand. Then he made his excuses and went over to his car. Aunt Anne, of course, noticed its personalised number plates. She rolled her eyes and pursed her lips at Elin, who wouldn't be drawn on any more details about the Dean.

Not long after, everyone left the crematorium and went back to the house for the funeral tea. The caterers had done a good job. An appetising smell of fresh-brewed coffee and baking greeted everyone as they went in. This was well timed, the distraction needed after the sadness of the service.

'Smells divine,' said Aunt Anne, and went into the dining room to see what was being set out.

Sue came up to Elin and said, 'Is there anything I can do?'

'No thanks, Sue. The caterers have it all under control.'

'The house is ideal for the funeral tea, isn't it?' Sue said. 'Plenty of room for everyone and you can go out from the conservatory into the garden.'

'Yes, I remember very well some of the parties we used to have here in the old days. Your mother was a wonderful cook and hostess,' a voice interrupted. It sounded so like Papa that Elin nearly jumped.

Uncle Julio and Aunt Maria had come up to where Elin and Sue were standing in the front room. Aunt Maria had a plate of sandwiches and canapés, which she put down on a nearby side table in order to hug Elin. Elin felt claustrophobic in the tight, fleshly embrace, but there was nothing she could do to escape. Sue made her excuses and left them to their conversation.

'Now is not the time, I know, but I wonder will you stay in the house, or are you thinking of selling?' Uncle Julio asked.

He always had an eye for business; and close contacts with one of the local estate agents. That was how, in fact, Elin's father had found the house in the first place.

'Julio, Julio,' Aunt Maria said, 'you're terrible. Not now. Take no notice of him, *cara*.'

'Yes, it's too soon to make any decision,' Elin replied, looking towards Sue for help.

Sue obliged and swept across the room, linking her arm through Elin's and pulling her away. 'Elin. You're to come with me now to get some food. You've been on the go since early this morning. You're looking quite pale.'

'Yes, yes, you go, Elin, and eat. You are much too thin,' Aunt Maria said. 'We'll speak another time.'

As they went into the dining room, Elin said, 'Thanks. And you're right. I'm very hungry. I was beginning to feel quite faint.'

'Not surprising. I don't expect you've eaten anything, have you? They're quite a pair.' She gestured towards Uncle Julio and Aunt Maria. 'Remind me of some of my aunts and uncles.'

'They're not actually relatives. But you know the Italian Welsh community is a close one and they helped Papa a lot when he first came to Cardiff.'

Elin was loading a plate with delicious food and congratulating herself on their choice of caterers. Her mother would be pleased. At that thought, the tears came. 'Oh dear, Sue, I'm sorry.

I'm off again.'

'Don't be daft. Now, have you got enough food? Do you want a drink?' Sue was holding a glass of white wine.

Elin shook her head. 'Coffee would be great. And thank you for everything today. You read the poem beautifully.'

'I'm glad I could help. I was very fond of your Mum. She made me feel welcome.' Sue pointed to a nearby sofa. 'You sit down. I'll be back in a min.'

Elin was glad to rest for a moment. She leant against the soft cushions on the sofa nibbling at a couple of sandwiches and some of the tapas on her plate and began to feel less heady and faint. Out of the window she could see white clouds dancing across a big blue sky. The garden looked better than it had done for a long time, every blade of grass standing to attention, flower beds weed-free and colourful, and Elin thought about what Uncle Julio had said. Selling the house was something that had been at the back of her mind as she considered the future but there would be time enough to think about that after today. She closed her eyes for a moment.

'Are you alright?' Aunt Anne stood looking down at her.

Elin nodded and gestured to the space next to her. Anne put her wine glass on the side table and flopped down into its soft depths.

'About the same. I'll be glad when today is over. But it seems to be going well.' Anne turned to Elin with sudden interest. 'By the way who was that drop-dead gorgeous fellow at the crem? You know, the guy you were speaking to at the end? The Dean, someone said.'

'For goodness sake, Aunt Anne, give it a rest.'

'I see,' Anne said, raising her eyebrows. 'You've got a thing for him, have you?'

Sue came up with two cups. Elin thought Sue's presence would put a halt to the topic, but Aunt Anne was not to be distracted.

'Sue,' Aunt Anne said, 'back me up here. Is your new Dean a dreamboat or what?'

Sue put the cups down and said, 'Michael Hardwick. Oh, yes. He is rather.' She avoided meeting Elin's eyes.

'Michael Hardwick? Isn't he...?' Aunt Anne's eyes had widened.

'The same. Still a man who attracts the ladies – and now happily married,' Elin added, with a look that cut off any further comment.

Chapter Thirty-Five

Elin

May – Term Three

The summer term was underway with students in a frenzy to complete any outstanding work and tutors knee-deep in marking. An email offering voluntary severance had sent everyone into a flap. Speculation was rife in the Department. Who would leave and who would be pushed? Already a couple of the younger staff had new jobs elsewhere, but was it enough? The threat that had hung over them all year was no longer something that might happen in the future. It had become a reality.

Her mother's death had taken its toll on Elin. She wasn't eating or sleeping enough. Work had provided a distraction in the past, but at this time of grieving that no longer helped and she seemed to have lost all her vitality. The huge strains of the previous months had sapped her health and well-being. Her movements were sluggish and dreamlike, and she found herself unable to concentrate on anything, flitting from room to room in the Sully house, indecisive and distracted. She knew that it would pass, but there was something deeper, something still festering away.

Seeing Michael again had triggered it, all the pain and the horror of fifteen years ago resurfaced fresh and agonising; that terrible time when Michael had abandoned her, had wrecked her life. Another time. Another grief. And he didn't even know. Now, with Michael in charge there was no respite. Elin would have to continue to face that memory of trauma every day. It was impossible.

Redundancy had, at one point, felt like the end of her world. With her mother's death, came a sort of freedom. She had a generous inheritance as the house alone was worth nearly half a million. The solicitor had given her the headlines, a few bequests but most of the wealth was left to Elin.

Mum had indicated as much one evening before she became so desperately ill. 'Papa was a good businessman. You'll be alright, when I've gone.'

It was true. When Elin realised the extent of her inheritance, she knew she was financially independent. She didn't need to work at such a furious pace. She'd have to work, of course. She couldn't imagine being idle. But she could afford to take a year or two off, travel, maybe find a different way of living, somewhere far away from Brynderwen.

The three months in Finland had taught her something about herself, allowing her space to think and write. Ironic that her knowledge of the healing power of communing with nature had come at exactly the time that she faced a personal crisis. But she also had the draft of her book on well-being, a publisher's interest and other possibilities, including the offer of another post. Elin saw that the incubation time for the book was going to be a further nine months, like a pregnancy. And, above all, she needed time to recover her equilibrium after everything that had happened.

Jodie raised one over-plucked eyebrow when Elin popped her head around the door to the Dean's office. 'Is Michael in?'

'Yeah. Did you have an appointment?' She glanced at the on-line diary. 'There's nothing in his calendar.'

'No. I called in on the off chance he might have a minute. It won't take long.'

Jodie picked up the phone, pressing the button with a puffing sound. 'Dr Fiorelli's here. She'd like a word, if you've got time? Oh, and I'll be leaving in five minutes.' Jodie put the phone down and nodded to Elin. 'You can go in. I'm off to my dress fitting.' Her wedding was in June, as everyone knew.

Elin knocked once and pushed the door to the inner office. Michael peered up from behind the computer screen and smiled, welcoming and friendly. Once, a long time ago, Elin's stomach would have flipped, but that was before. Now his spicy aftershave evoked memories she'd rather forget. He had taken off his jacket, his blue striped shirt rolled to the elbow, reminding her of the younger, more casual, Michael she once knew so well.

'You wanted to see me? Take a seat.' He inclined his head towards a chair but stayed behind his desk, his glance flitting back to his screen.

Elin sat examining the criss-cross pattern on the carpet. It was going to be harder than she thought. He'd been kind, understanding, more than she expected but... She wasn't sure where to start. She lifted her head, not able to meet his eyes yet, observing a butterfly fluttering on the windowpane outside. 'I wanted to talk to you about something. Things have, well, things have been very difficult...' Her voice trailed away.

'Yes, your mother's death must have been an awful blow. It's not easy watching something like that. Plus, that unfortunate business with Nick. I'm endlessly grateful you didn't take that any further.' Michael tapped the desk before he continued. 'He deserved to be punished but–'

'He's had enough bad things in his life.'

'–I believe he's turned the corner.'

Elin looked him in the eye now. There was no easy way to say what she needed to tell him. The words blurted out. 'I came to say I want to apply for voluntary severance.' Michael's eyebrows shot up in shock and he opened his mouth to reply but Elin silenced him with an upraised hand. 'No, please let me continue. I came back to the Department in December after that research trip looking forward, believing that my future was secure. I'd been more, or less, promised a professorship.'

'Huw?'

'Your cuts dealt with that. Oh, I know you had to do it,' she said, rushing her words, 'but I felt betrayed. Then, everything with Mum and Nick just left me feeling vulnerable. Everything I wanted in life was gone.'

Michael leant forward in his seat as if to intervene, but Elin shook her head, stopping him again. 'I... I need to reflect on what I want in the future, my direction. I've been offered a job. It's a sideways move but the opportunity to continue with my research. I'm thinking about it.'

Michael's face registered disbelief, the smile faded, and with it, his usual confidence. 'What?' He put both hands on the desk as if to steady himself.

'Plus, I need to get away from this university.' And you. The grief from that time was buried but not resolved.

He stood up and came around to the other side of the desk, close to where Elin sat, dragging a chair out from the conference table and dropping into it. When he spoke, his voice was almost hoarse, as he scrutinized her face, 'You can't really mean that. I haven't had time to tell you in detail about TechSWell in Brussels.'

'You told me that my work had been well received. That's good. I'm glad you didn't have any awkward questions.' Elin played with her signet ring, turning it around and around her finger.

'It was more than well received. I had Wolfgang, your colleague, extolling your virtues and your professionalism. Lars Nordin himself, cornered me, glowing in his praise. You've made a conquest there. The project will be continuing, and they definitely want you to be a part of it. You don't want to miss that opportunity, do you?' Michael had become more enthusiastic and excited as he spoke, leaning forward, his face lit up with anticipation.

Elin just regarded him as though what he was saying held little interest for her, impassive. 'I'd have to stay here to do that. Much as I'm tempted, I... I can't. I've heard the rumours about Huw. I take it he isn't coming back?'

'It's not certain, yet, but it looks that way. He's close to retirement, anyway.'

'And if Huw doesn't come back, then they'll offer you the job?'

'I hope so, despite all the difficulties of this year.' He stretched his hands out wide to encompass the problems he had had to deal with. 'I'd like that – for the family as well. Cardiff's proved to be the right place for us.'

Elin sat still, listening but his words came to her muffled as though through fog. A pulse throbbed at the side of her head where she had clenched her teeth. She just wanted to get out of this office and go home.

'Elin, this university needs you. You've proven to be one of its greatest assets. Without you, Fonetym will be unwilling to give us the money for further research. You'd be letting your colleagues down.' He hesitated a moment and lowered his voice as he bent towards her. 'You'd be letting *me* down.'

Elin puzzled at these words. What was Michael doing, trying to dissuade her from leaving? Using that charm of his again. Did he think she'd fall for that?

'Look, I know you wanted the professorship. I can set things in motion for you. See if we can accelerate the process. Fonetym are willing to put in twice as much money as last time.'

'It doesn't matter.'

If she had slapped him in the face, he couldn't have reacted more strongly, straightening up and leaning back again, his mouth agape. 'What? But it's what you wanted, isn't it? A chair. The kudos. More time for research and writing. It's your dream.'

Elin looked him in the eyes, challenging. How would he know what her dream was? Had once been? 'As I said, I need to get away from here.'

'I don't understand. I thought it's what you've worked so hard for... Look. Don't make hasty decisions. Why not take the summer off and see how you feel come September?' He paused, an edge to his voice. 'We *need* that funding.' Michael was almost begging. 'We've been using those figures to get us out of the mess.'

Elin could feel a storm of emotions building inside her. Her head was throbbing, her heart pumping too fast and all the pent-up feelings rising to the surface. 'So, it's *all* about the money, is it? It's always been about what *you* want. How could I ever trust you? I thought you'd changed but you're selfish as ever.'

'I thought I'd explained. Once the finances are stable again, we can look towards your professorship.'

'I'm not talking about promotion. You ruined my life once. I'm not sticking around to let you do it again.' Her voice was taut, strained. The muscles in her neck ached and traitorous tears were threatening to surface.

Michael frowned, confused, thoughtful. Then his eyes opened wider as comprehension dawned. 'I'm sorry. I let you down badly all those years ago. Is that what this is about?'

Elin shook her head and swallowed. She couldn't speak. She mustn't cry.

'I've regrets too. I thought I owed it to my marriage to try again but it was a mistake.' Michael's voice was sincere. 'You don't know the times I wished I'd stayed with you. Things were pretty awful for me too.'

How could he? 'What? Awful for you?' She spoke in a gasp, then let fly, 'Your arrogance is unbelievable, just unbelievable.'

'You can't still be angry with me, for God's sake? That was a lifetime ago. Is this some sort of revenge? That's not the Elin Fiorelli I knew. She wouldn't be so bitter and twisted.' He seemed to be getting riled, fingers of one hand tapping a rhythm on the table as he spoke.

'You've no bloody idea... no idea.' All the anger and anguish she had buried for so long rose to the surface and exploded, the words gushing out, tumbling over one another, 'You left me, you left me and... and I was pregnant.' Elin was crying now, painful sobs racking her, arms wrapped around her body.

The colour drained from Michael's face, as the words registered. 'You had a baby?'

Elin gulped back the tears, stuttering over the words. 'I had... had a... termination. Then I... I was ill. Work was all I had left.'

The silence was thick between them, broken by the sound of Elin's sobs.

Michael ran a hand through his hair, stood and paced over to the conference table and back again before returning to sit near where Elin sat hunched in her chair. 'I don't know what to say. I'm sorry for you and for us, too.' His voice was heavy with emotion. 'We might have had a future together, once. But we can't live in the past, Elin. And it's not too late for you. You can still have a child.'

'No. No I can't. There were complications. The doctors told me that I... I can never have a baby. When I got better again, then... I just couldn't depend on any man. So, so my work was... it was my life. Then... then you came back and tried to take that life away, too.' Her voice was shaking as she looked over to him, tears and mucus coursing down her face but she didn't care.

Another silence as the implication of her words filtered through. When Michael spoke again his voice was low, even, calm. Not a tone she'd heard before. For a second, she imagined this was how he would speak to his children when they were hurt or upset.

'Why didn't you tell me? If only I'd known. Things would have been so different. For God's sake, Elin. Didn't you think I had a right to know? It was my child, too.'

'You'd already gone when I found out. I didn't know what to do. I couldn't tell my parents.'

'You could have sent a message.'

'Really? I don't think so. What would I have said?' Elin raised red-rimmed eyes to meet Michael's gaze. A sadness hung in the air between them, shattered dreams. They had both changed, and yet somehow there was still a shared bond.

At last Michael exhaled. His voice was gentle and full of sympathy. 'You've carried that hurt inside all this time? I'm so sorry. You must hate me.'

Elin had begun to calm, her sobs racking her body from time to time. She knew her face was blotchy from crying and her shoulders sagged but inside she experienced a lightness, soothing, like when Papa used to brush her hair as a child. 'I don't hate you anymore. Really, I never hated you. I hated what had happened to me after you left, and I grieved for the future I could never have. Children. A family life. I buried myself in my work.' She glanced around the office, the neat files on the shelves, the empty mug on the desk and piles of paper on the conference table; order in a messy emotional world.

'I channelled all my energy into it. This pain has been festering inside me for so long. But now, well, now I feel better. I'm glad you know.'

Taking a tissue from the box on the desk, she blew her nose and dabbed her eyes before continuing. 'I'm sorry. Now you understand why I have to leave.' Her mascara had run down her face, a trail of black tear stains captured in the tissue.

Michael leant over and cradled her hands in his, warm fingers enclosing her fists, which clenched the sodden tissue. 'You're right. We both need time. Please, just give me a couple of days to sort something. I might have an idea to help us both out.'

Chapter Thirty-Six

Michael

When Elin had left, Michael sank back with a thud into his computer chair. He leant his elbows on the hard edge of the desk and put his face in his hands. What a mess, what a bloody, awful mess. She'd unleashed a timebomb. He took this job for the potential it offered to get back into the UK university scene, and for Anwen and the boys. He groaned as the memories returned. All those years ago. Elin had been carrying his child. What a total, unfeeling bastard he'd been back then. A baby. His chest felt tight at the thought of it and a whole future he'd thrown away. But he hadn't known... He sighed and lifted his head from his hands.

'Elin, Elin, Elin.' Michael spoke her name aloud as his thoughts raced. Why hadn't she told him? It could have changed everything. He imagined a daughter. She'd be fourteen now and look like Elin. But he kept asking that question: Why? Fathers have rights, too, and it would have been his child, as well as Elin's. Then a painful thought which made him squeeze his brows together. She didn't trust him to be the father of her child – else she'd have got in touch, wouldn't she?

And the damn thing is, she was right. In those days he wasn't interested in being a father, too busy with his job – and the rest. A blessing that Nick didn't know about Elin, not then, not now. The boy always had a foul temper. Those tantrums. God. He'd let him down, too, all those years ago.

But regrets were pointless. Get a grip. Move on. Do what you are great at. Fix stuff. He thumped the table hard with his fist. The side of his hand hurt but it felt good. Elin's career hadn't suffered anyway. Still, Michael had hated seeing the look of desolation that morning in her eyes. She had really endured some tough emotional stuff. He stared glumly at the photograph on his desk. Anwen and the boys stared back. He knew he was a lucky sod to have them. Shit. He'd made some awful mistakes in his life, but he'd had a chance to become a different person, settle down, concentrate on his family.

If Elin Fiorelli left, so did that funding, and most likely his job. He had to do something to avoid that happening.

Michael's mind was whirling. Thinking back to the meeting in Brussels and conversations with Professor Nordin and the Fonetym people had given him an idea. He still had contacts in the United States and useful links with the international academic community. There were a few favours he could call on to get what he wanted. He understood Elin's need to put some distance between them, to grieve, to heal and to come to terms with the shadows of the past; and maybe, just maybe, he could sort out a solution. He straightened his shoulders and brushed back his hair.

The ping of a reminder popped up on screen. Damn. He'd set a couple of hours aside to work with Sue, but the meeting with Elin had blown everything out of the water. Have to wing it and rely on Sue's professionalism and hard work to fill in the gaps. A firm knock followed this thought and Sue popped her head round the door.

'Hi, there,' Michael said, half turning from his desk, as she paused in the doorway. 'Listen, come back in three quarters of an hour, will you? Have to make a few calls.'

'Sure, no probs. Gives me time to double-check some stuff.'

Michael noticed Sue sounded cheerful. She was looking good, too, her blonde hair glossy and with an energy about the way she held herself. One happy Finance Officer. Happier anyway.

Michael stood up and stretched to his full height. He went over to the water fountain and poured himself an ice-cold cup. He needed to keep a clear head and sort out this Elin situation. Time to make those phone calls.

Chapter Thirty-Seven

Elin

July

The summer evening was perfect. Good weather, herringbone clouds were high in a blue sky. At eight o'clock the dry and dusty pavements radiated heat in the way they do after a hot spell. Cardiff Bay was busy, milling with visitors and locals – chatting, strolling along the boardwalks, sightseeing, taking pictures in front of the bronze statues of 'People Like Us', deciding where they would go for a drink or a meal. Seagulls soared on the air currents as a faint breeze rippled across the sparkling waves, bringing a welcome relief from the heat as it drifted through the open wind ruffling the linen tablecloth.

Music, a romantic ballad, floated in the air and the odd burst of laughter from passing groups punctuated the general hum of voices. It seemed that everyone was enjoying the warmth and the opportunity to relax at the end of the week. Elin had booked a window table in the Italian restaurant on the upper level so they could look out over the water and watch the sunset. The restaurant was still quiet, with just a faint tinkle of crockery and cutlery from other early diners, although people were beginning to drift in. A delicious aroma of garlic and herbs hung in the air and Elin's stomach rumbled, reminding her that she hadn't eaten for hours.

'Cheers.' She held up a glass of Prosecco, condensation clouding the outside of the flute making it wet and slippery. She clinked glasses with Sue. 'Here's to the end of term, survival and becoming Professor Fiorelli.'

'Congrats on the chair,' Sue said. 'Is that what you academics call it?'

Elin laughed. It did sound weird the way Sue said it, but she felt a thrill of pleasure every time it was mentioned. She'd achieved her dream and it was the start of the next part of her career.

'Survival, yeah.' Sue was carrying on. 'It's been a helluva year of it, hasn't it?' She looked at Elin, pursed her lips and whistled. 'Couple of times I thought of jacking it in. Work in an office or a shop. Nine-to-five, you know.' She broke off a piece of bread stick and nibbled it. 'Talk about stress. How you've managed to hold it all together with your Mum and all...'

'It's been tough.' Elin stared at the menu trying to decide. 'I was ready to leave after Easter.'

'Never.'

'Funny how it can all change, though.' Having made her decision, she closed the menu.

'Know what you mean,' Sue said, shuddering. 'That thing I had for Michael. God, what an idiot.' She sipped her drink, shaking her head. 'Could've done for me.'

'All water under the bridge.' Elin took a sip of the cool wine, savouring its crispness. 'So, this is my treat tonight before I become too tied up with arrangements for the trip. Still need to sort out some of Mum's things and the financial stuff to hand over to the solicitor too before I head to New York, but whatever–'

'Ah, New York, New York,' Sue sang, out of tune and a bit too loud for Elin's liking. 'You're so lucky. I wish I had the opportunity to work abroad. I know Michael sorted some of it for you. Come on. I want the juicy details. Was it payoff for not bringing charges against that student?'

'Maybe. In a way.' Elin gazed out over the water and her eyes had a faraway look. 'But it was more to do with the money. When I told him that I wanted to apply for voluntary severance, he hit the roof. TechSWell is carrying on to the next phase and Fonetym would only give Brynderwen increased funding if I continued in post.'

'Wow. You were headhunted!' Sue's eyes were round. 'Where does the three months in New York come in?'

Elin laughed. 'It's the next phase.' She glowed with excitement.

'Three months in the frenzy of New York, which is as far away from the last research trip as possible. Expected, this time, to live as much as possible using technology. I'm hoping Wolfgang will be there too – I'll be glad of his geeky knowledge.'

Sue winked. 'The prude. But he might be tempted this time.'

'Sue. This is work.' Elin giggled in mock horror at the suggestion. She was at ease with herself, more so than for a long time.

'Yeah, yeah. Tough but someone has to do it.' Sue wagged her finger.

'You're shocking.' A bubble of laughter escaped. 'It'll be full-on, including keeping an online diary and engaging in social media.' Elin sipped from her glass, soaking in the beauty of the evening. 'They'll monitor my health using technology similar to the techie stuff they use with astronauts. I really don't know. I'll have a further briefing when I get there.' Her head was light and she was unsure if it was the wine or the thought of the new life ahead.

Sue chewed a thumbnail, subdued, serious. 'I'll miss you, though. So, what happens after December?'

'Well, that's where Michael's influence comes in. After I told him I wanted to leave, he got into a bit of a panic, rang around his contacts in the States, and sorted guest lectures for me at various places. I haven't got the full itinerary, yet, but somehow, he also managed to get Fonetym to part-fund that. God knows how.'

'That's our Dean for you,' Sue said, tapping her nose. 'He knows all the right people.'

'Ok, yes, that was pretty impressive.' Elin's lips curled as she thought of how hard Michael had worked to persuade her not to leave. 'And there's the book. The publisher wants me to do some publicity stuff while I'm in the States. It's going to be busy, frantic I think, but I don't leave until September, plenty of time for a few more fun times. God knows we deserve it.'

Around them the restaurant was filling up. A family party came in, reminding Elin that her only family left was Aunt Anne. She shook the thought away. Now was not the time to be sad, gazing over Cardiff Bay while sipping a glass of bubbly. She raised her glass. 'I have a big favour to ask you. I wondered if you'd house-sit for me while I'm away. I'd rather have someone I can trust in there than rent it out to strangers.' Sue's eyes widened in disbelief as Elin continued, 'You'd only have to pay for the council tax and utilities. It should work out less and there's loads more space.'

As she watched Sue's mouth drop open in surprise, Elin laughed. 'No wild parties though.'

Sue seemed to stutter. 'Elin, that's really generous of you. I... I don't know what to say.'

'Just say yes. Please. It would be a huge weight off my mind knowing that the house is safe. Honestly.' Sue nodded and Elin raised her glass again. 'Good, let's toast to that as well. Win-win for both of us I'd say. Now, I think I'm having the Boeuf Bourguignon. What do you fancy? Apart from that waiter you're eyeing up.'

Sue glanced away from the man in question to the menu. 'Hmm, so many delicious options.' As the waiter approached, she winked. 'I don't know. Maybe the Coq au Vin.'

As they ate, talked and laughed Elin relaxed, knowing her life was getting back on track after this terrible year. Despite her mother's death and the emptiness that left behind she was lighter in spirit. After they left the restaurant, they wandered out along the waterfront past the Senedd to the Norwegian church, watching the lights begin to flicker and dance on the water and darkness descend turning the sky from cyan to sapphire and navy. Elin mimicked their waiter's fake French accent, complete with gestures, making Sue laugh so much she was crying. They joked together as they watched the boats bobbing on their moorings and the whole other life going on aboard. Someone was playing a guitar, singing a Dylan song, *The Times They are a Changing*, and the sound, a haunting refrain, drifted over the water.

Back in her flat that night Elin reflected on the things she hadn't told Sue. Michael had been very solicitous after her confession in his office. Sharing her secret had breached the gap between them, banished the lies she'd told herself. The go-getting young man she'd known had gone, and with maturity had come greater empathy. Perhaps having young children of his own had given him greater insight into her situation. Seeing his reaction of shock had dissipated some of her pain. Maybe she'd been wrong to deny herself the pleasure of a relationship. But there was still time. A different life stretched ahead. Who knew what opportunities would arise while she was away?

The end of the summer term was a relief for everyone. With graduation over and only the post graduate students to work with, things slowed down a little. Elin had completed her report for Phase One of the TechSWell project, with recommendations for the next phase and further research questions. When she saw an email from Lars Nordin, the project co-ordinator, in her inbox it was no surprise. She'd found him insightful, challenging at times, but with a good sense of humour and he'd dropped hints occasionally that there could be job opportunities if she were interested in moving away from Brynderwen.

> *Elin,*
> *May I congratulate you on your professorship, a fine achievement and well deserved. I'm going to be in New York for a few days before you officially start your research. I should be very pleased if we could meet up.*
> *By the way, you should be very comfortable in Professor Jackson's apartment. I've been a guest there myself.*
> *I am very much looking forward to seeing you again.*
>
> Yours,
> Lars

Elin read through the email a few times. Puzzling. There was little mention of the report, or the expectations for the next phase of the research project. Then again, she hadn't been to the conference, so he probably wanted to discuss those things with her in person. If he'd been to New York before, his knowledge of the city could be useful. A new and exciting phase of her life beckoned.

Chapter Thirty-Eight

Elin

End of July

There was a good turnout for the last research meeting of the year. Geraint stood up and beamed over his glasses at the group of twenty or so academics crowded around several tables in Seminar Room One. Occasionally, as the door opened and closed, sounds of laughter and excited English language learning could be heard from adjoining classrooms. The summer school season was underway; a reminder to the Department staff that they were itching to get off for their long-anticipated summer holidays.

'Michael has asked me to welcome you and start the meeting off, as he's going to be a bit delayed. He'll join us in about quarter of an hour.'

Geraint gestured to a small buffet laid out at the back of the room, covered in cling film. His voice boomed in the small space, 'Please help yourselves. There's tea, coffee, juice – nothing stronger, unfortunately, but I may see some of you in the Cricketers' Arms later.'

A gentle buzz of conversation followed this announcement, as people turned to their neighbours to chat, and some stood up to go to the buffet. It was a hot July day, but on this side of the building, north facing, the ambience in the room was comfortable, in terms of temperature as well as conviviality. There was an almost discernible air of optimism. News had got around that Michael Hardwick was going to be confirmed in post and that the necessary reductions to staff had been met. A few old hands had taken the generous voluntary severance package and some of the newbies had decided to make a break for it, to jobs elsewhere, or to travel.

'You're off as well then, Elin?' Geraint asked, his plate piled high with crisps, pizza slices and various other tapas items. He took a large bite from a chicken sandwich and Elin was distracted for a moment by a wet crumb at the corner of his mouth. She resisted the temptation to tell him about it and moved a couple of crisps round on her plate.

'Yes, a new phase. You know I'm going to the United States? I'll be coming back, though. You won't get rid of me so easily.' Elin felt a surge of excitement as she said this.

'Well, *blodyn*, you deserve it after the year you've had. And now the professorship, eh?'

Geraint winked at her, and Elin thought, whatever else, he was a good team player. Other staff might have been jealous, but not Geraint.

'Ah, here's the boss.' He put his plate and glass down and went to greet Michael. Looking at the two men and the unselfconscious way Geraint had called Michael 'the boss', reinforced Elin's feeling she was doing the right thing: leaving, but not leaving for good. She was part of Brynderwen and would have more to offer in the future.

The trip to the States was something Elin had thought long and hard about. She knew Michael had acted because he wanted her on the Fonetym project, to maximise its funding for the Department. She also realised he'd gone the extra mile to facilitate the exchange. It was a great opportunity for her to consolidate the research done in Finland and consider where she was taking her work in the future.

Other good things were in the pipeline. The publishers were enthusiastic about her book, setting up some promotion events in the States. But for Elin, the deal breaker was that the USA trip would give her a breathing space to adjust to her new life. A life without family, apart from Aunt Anne, and with Michael as an ally rather than a painful reminder of her traumatic past. All positives. She watched now as he stood in front of them and waited for a lull in the conversation.

'Can I ask everyone to sit down, please? I won't keep you long.

Don't worry, I know the sun's shining and the summer holidays are calling, but I do want a few words. I thought I'd update you on progress and reassure you about the future.'

As Elin sat next to Sue, she thought, I'm beginning to turn the corner. That was one of Papa's favourite English phrases. He was a fighter and so was she. Sue gave Elin a thumbs-up sign.

Michael confirmed pretty much everything that the grapevine had already established. It was good to hear that Huw had made a full recovery and decided to retire. The names of those who had accepted a voluntary severance package were announced, together with words of thanks for their contribution over the years. Bouquets and tokens of appreciation were handed over amid much clapping and smiling. The two or three young members of staff who were also leaving were given honourable mentions and good wishes for the future. Michael paused, straightened his shoulders and adjusted his cufflinks in a gesture that Elin recognised very well. It meant he was nervous, even though to the casual eye he appeared confident.

'I'm delighted to be able to tell you that I have been confirmed as your new Dean. It's been a tough year with a focus on balancing the books after our large initial financial deficit, but with good luck and the help of skilled staff,' Michael gestured to Sue, who beamed back, 'we're making an excellent recovery. And I'm particularly pleased to announce the substantial new funding we are going to receive during the next academic year from Fonetym. This will transform our research capabilities and put us back in the game.'

Michael looked at Elin then. 'You won't be surprised to know that Professor Elin Fiorelli has been instrumental in our success at acquiring this new funding.'

There was a spontaneous ripple of applause, a few cheers and Elin glowed in the warmth of her colleagues.

'You may also know that Elin will be visiting professor at two American universities during the next academic year. She'll be carrying on her work with Fonetym, and also publicising her book on the topic of well-being and technology. It's aimed at a wider commercial market and will undoubtedly enhance the university's reputation, as well as being of real value to the general reader.'

Michael bent down and took a spray of pink and white carnations from a large carrier bag that he had brought with him into the room, courtesy of Jodie.

'And so, Elin, on behalf of myself and your colleagues in the Department, I'd like to wish you *arrivederci*, not goodbye, and we look forward to working with you in the future. All good wishes for your time in the States and – don't forget to come back.'

Elin went up to collect the flowers from Michael. He bent down and kissed her on the cheek. In that very public place, it felt like a final reconciliation. As she gazed up at him, he said, sotto voce, 'Thank you, Elin.'

Later, with heels clicking, she made her way down the corridor. She took the stairs at speed and was soon out of the building. As she walked across the baking hot asphalt of the staff car park towards her red mini, the ghosts of the past started to fade away. She was lighter, energetic again as she headed towards this new phase in her life. Who knew what the future would hold?